W9-BNN-111

A TUCKER ASHLEY WESTERN
ADVENTURE

Backed to the Wall

C. M. Wendelboe

THORNDIKE PRESS
A part of Gale, a Cengage Company

Farmington Hills, Mich • San Francisco • New York • Waterville, Maine
Meriden, Conn • Mason, Ohio • Chicago

Copyright © 2017 by C. M. Wendelboe.
Thorndike Press, a part of Gale, a Cengage Company.

Thorndike Press® Large Print Western.
The text of this Large Print edition is unabridged.
Other aspects of the book may vary from the original edition.
Set in 16 pt. Plantin.

LIBRARY OF CONGRESS CIP DATA ON FILE.
CATALOGUING IN PUBLICATION FOR THIS BOOK
IS AVAILABLE FROM THE LIBRARY OF CONGRESS

ISBN-13: 978-1-4328-5643-4 (hardcover)

Published in 2018 by arrangement with C. M. Wendelboe

Printed in Mexico
3 4 5 6 7 8 23 22 21 20 19

ACKNOWLEDGEMENTS

I would like to thank Craig and Judy Johnson for their frequent help in this writing business; to my editor, Alice Duncan, for pushing me to make this project as good as it can be; for my wife, Heather, for always having faith in me and encouraging me to continue telling tales I think folks will enjoy.

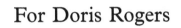

For Doris Rogers

CHAPTER 1

Tucker Ashley awakened as if in a fog, his head thick, pounding. He rubbed his blood-caked eyes and tried to sit. But the room swirled around him as if he'd been caught in a rushing river eddy, and he dropped back down on the bunk. Feet shuffled in the next room. Metal-on-metal scraping echoed inside his pounding head, and he used the side of the bunk to sit once more.

The odor of coffee brewing reached him then, just ahead of the smell of cooked hog fat. He sucked in a quick breath; the odor of the fat assaulted the whisky lying in his gullet like a stranded stray in a buffalo wallow.

He forced an eye open and squinted against the morning light, only slightly brighter than the white-washed adobe walls his bunk was bolted to. Flat slat metal bars positioned equidistant from one another surrounded the tiny cell, all leading to the locked door. He was in a jail then; nothing new to Tucker. Except he remembered little about two nights ago, or how he got here.

Footsteps approached. He lay back down and winced in pain as he closed his eyes.

The outer door opened, and jingle bobs tinkled against large Spanish rowels that announced a man's entry. "Too late to be wary now," the voice said. "Time for caution was a couple nights ago before I put the grab on you."

Tucker turned over and cracked an eye. He gazed through shaggy black hair hanging over his forehead and ran his fingers through his mop. A large gash on top of his head caught his chipped fingernails, and he gently pulled hair stuck to the wound. Sunshine filtered through greased-paper window coverings, and he shielded his eyes as he wiped blood on his shirtfront.

"You awake now?" The jingle bobs clinked as Aurand Forester turned on his heels. He left the door open while he walked into the outer room and sat at his desk. He picked up a fork and speared a piece of meat. He daintily chewed the bacon while he looked over his fork at Tucker. Aurand grinned and laid his fork on his plate while he dabbed at the corners of his mouth with a checked napkin. He sipped coffee and cocked his head while he spoke. "I thought you'd never wake up."

"What day is this?"

"Tuesday," Aurand chuckled. "You been on a bender since day before yesterday."

Tucker swung his legs over the feather ticking bunk. A grayback louse the size of his thumbnail scurried from beneath him. He swatted at it and nearly lost his balance before he dropped back onto the edge of the bunk. He felt his head again and came away with a bloody palm.

"That wasn't my doing," Aurand said. He folded his napkin and laid it atop his empty plate. "I didn't have to lay a hand on you. You were passed out when Philo and I grabbed you and carted you in here."

Tucker's eyes began clearing as he watched Aurand walk to the Franklin stove in the middle of his marshal's office. He refilled his cup from a warming pot and strolled through the door separating his office from the single cell that housed Tucker. Aurand stopped in front of the cell and tugged at his wispy, blond mustache. As if tugging at it would help it grow. For as long as Tucker had known Aurand, he had tried growing a 'stache. And failed. "Don't seem likely that I'd arrest Tucker Ashley without winding up in the cemetery." Aurand held

11

up his coffee cup as if to offer a toast. "But I got nary a scratch."

"Why am I in here?"

"Next you'll say you don't remember a thing."

"I don't."

Aurand laughed. "They all say that."

"Enough!" Tucker lunged for the cell door, and Aurand stepped back. His hand went instinctively to the gun on his hip, his grin momentarily gone. When it returned, he nodded to Tucker's arms groping through the bars inches from Aurand's head. "Might as well relax, Tuck. You're here for the duration."

"Duration of what?"

Aurand slowly sipped his coffee, dragging his answer out. When he spoke, his smile was gone, and his gray eyes seemed to bore holes through Tucker. "Until the territorial judge rides in here next week and tells the hangman when to set the date."

"What are you rambling about?" Tucker's dizziness returned, and he sat back down on the edge of the bunk. "What trumped-up charge you got me on now?"

Aurand grabbed a chair and placed it in front of Tucker's cell just out of reach of his long arms. Aurand sat backwards and rested his arm over the chair back. He studied his coffee like he were studying tea leaves. "You're telling me you don't recall killing that roustabout?"

"What roustabout?"

"The one you knifed after you robbed him night 'fore last."

Tucker held his head in his hands. "I didn't rob or kill anyone."

"You just don't remember it." Aurand tossed the rest of his coffee onto the dirt floor and twirled the cup around his finger. "You killed a roustabout off the *Belle of the Ball.*"

Tucker shook his head to clear his memory. Two nights ago he recalled passing the stern wheeler docked at the levee on the way to meeting Lorna Moore. Indian annuities sat unloaded on the paddleboat, but Tucker had paid no mind to it as he walked past the boat on his way to the mercantile. He vaguely remembered Lorna stocking shelves behind the counter as he entered the trading store. And how pained he'd been when she told him they would have to cancel their dinner date just as Maynard Miles appeared from the back room. He'd stood close to her, and his ear-to-ear grin seemed to challenge Tucker for her affection.

"We have work tonight, Lorna and me."

The shopkeeper moved closer to her. "I'm afraid it will take most of the night." He winked. "Maybe most every night."

" 'Member now?" Aurand asked.

Tucker shook his head, and it felt as if marbles rattled inside his skull. He had stomped out of Moore's Mercantile and directly to the Bucket of Blood. He bought the cheapest bottle of forty-rod whisky a half-broke army scout could afford and sat on the walkway outside the tent saloon. Roustabouts started off-loading the *Belle of the Ball,* but he'd ignored them. Men clomped along the wooden walkway, but he paid them no mind either as he drew on the bottle of whisky. And some time well past darkness — while he finished the second bottle he'd bought — he lost all memory of anything.

" 'Member now?" Aurand taunted.

"Suppose you tell me."

Aurand stood and walked to the coffee pot warming on the Franklin.

"How about a cup of that over here," Tucker called after him.

Aurand ignored him as he came back and sat in the chair in front of Tucker's cell. "I'll tell you how it happened, just 'cause we're old pards." He stroked his mustache. "Way me and Philo figured it, you waited outside

14

the Bucket of Blood for a roustabout . . ."

"For what reason?"

"That's the best part," Aurand said. "And I'm coming to it." He sipped his coffee. "You knew those roustabouts from that steamer had just finished off-loading those annuities. Knew they just got their pay, and that gold ladies would be jingling in their pockets. And the first roustabout that was drunker than you, you waylaid him. Drug him behind the saloon, and stole all the money he had." Aurand leaned closer. "Only thing I don't know is if you knifed him before or after you robbed him."

Tucker stood and gripped the bars, his bleeding head forgotten for the moment. "You're a damn liar. I never stole —"

"We found three double eagles in your pocket. Now how do you suppose an army scout making twenty a month would get himself three gold ladies? And who do you know besides roustabouts would be carting that much money around? This is Dakota Territory, not Chicago or St. Louis."

"You ever known me to steal?" Tucker asked. "We've known each other since . . ."

"Ft. Laramie," Aurand said. "Don't remind me. And how the hell should I know if you've ever stole before? What I do know for certain is that you stole that roustabout's pay. And that you're a killer."

"As are you."

"This isn't about me." Aurand stood abruptly. His leg caught the chair, and it fell against the wall. "That roustabout's throat was slit just like the Sioux are fond of doing to a man. Who do you know besides the Sioux would slit a man's throat like that?"

Tucker looked away. He knew where Aurand was going.

"No answer, big man? Then I'll answer for you — just like I'll do in front of the circuit judge when he shows. I'll testify that a man who's friendly with those death-thirsty bastards would kill the same way they do."

"I'm not friends with the Dakota," Tucker said, doubts creeping into his lost memory from that night. "I just respect them."

"And respect their ways of killing, no doubt."

Tucker bent over and held his head in his hands. The darkness of that night's drunkenness was his only answer, and still he could not recall. "Get Major Reynolds. He'll vouch for me. He'll figure out what happened . . ." Tucker looked at Aurand's grinning face. "You're not going to get the major, are you?"

"Ride to Ft. Sully?" Aurand said. "Not

16

hardly. Nor will I get any of my deputies to get you out of this pickle. I've waited five long years to see you dangle from a stout piece of hemp."

Had it been five years since Tucker met him? Aurand had been a Confederate soldier, captured toward the war's end, bushwhacking with Bill Anderson in Missouri. Faced with prison or becoming a galvanized Yankee, Aurand chose the Union army and was sent to Ft. Laramie. He'd worked himself up to captain, and his path crossed with the post's chief scout, Tucker Ashley. When Aurand's company rode into the Powder River country, Tucker scouted well ahead. He was miles away when G Troop stumbled across a Lakota family emaciated from starvation. Aurand had felt it his duty to interrogate them much as he interrogated Missourians or Kansans loyal to the Union during the war — by force. He spoke no Sioux, and they spoke no English, so when Aurand got no answers, he killed them. When Tucker rejoined the column, the other soldiers in the company told him what Captain Forester had done.

Tucker lost his head that day, and it took a half-dozen troopers to pull Tucker off the captain. He later learned from soldiers at the Ft. Laramie guardhouse that Aurand had spent two months in the post hospital from that beating.

These five years had been kind to Aurand. He'd somehow managed to get himself appointed as deputy marshal for the Dakota Territory, prancing around in his office wearing fancy stitched boots and a new felt hat that Lorna sold in her store.

Five years hadn't been so kind to Tucker, sitting on a lice-infested jail bunk, dressed in trail-worn dusty dungarees with more holes than cheesecloth. The only thing Tucker had to show for those five years was twelve dollars of army pay in his pocket, and more scrapes and scars from barroom brawls and Indian fights than he could count. At least he had Lorna, or so he thought until he went to pick her up for dinner two nights ago. He massaged his head. But he certainly wouldn't have her today after she learned he was under arrest for a murder he himself did not remember committing.

"When's breakfast?" Tucker asked, suddenly famished.

Aurand hitched his gun belt up. Twin Smith and Wesson .44s rode on each hip, reminding Tucker the man was truly ambidextrous, proficient with either. He sauntered over to the cell door, and his annoying grin reappeared. "You get no chow this morning. You woke up too late, pard. Maybe lunch. We'll see how good of a boy you are."

Tucker sprang to his feet and lunged through the cell bars. Again, Aurand adeptly stepped back out of the reach of Tucker's flailing arms. "If you had any guts you'd let me out of here. If only for a minute."

Aurand polished his five-star badge with his shirtsleeve. "I'm no fool. I wouldn't let you out of there for all the money in Ft. Sully." He rubbed his jaw, still misshapen from when it healed improperly after their last fight. "Unless you wanted to face me with your gun." He jerked his thumb at Tucker's gun belt hanging on a deer horn coatrack in the outer office.

Tucker looked through the bars at the genuine hatred lining Aurand's face, and it chilled him. Tucker knew that — given the chance — Aurand would gladly face him in the street. And although Tucker was fast, Aurand was faster. Faster, many said, than Bill Longley down in Texas, or Bill Hickok in Abilene. And most people seeing Aurand in action would later say he got more pleasure from killing than rumors claim the James boys did. The irony of Aurand wearing a badge sickened Tucker.

Aurand finally broke the stare, and his

grin returned. "A damn shame," he said as he walked into the outer office. He grabbed his white Montana Peak from the coat rack and set it at a steep angle on his head. "I doubt you'll live past that long drop at the end of the rope to find out who's fastest. A damn shame is what it is." And Aurand's laughter grew fainter as he closed the door separating the office from the cell. "I got to go find some missing woman," he called to Tucker. "Now don't go away, hear?"

CHAPTER 2

Someone in the outer office tipped over a chair and cursed. Tucker called as loud as his parched throat would allow to whoever stood guard on the other side of the door. But no one came, and he eyed the water bucket hanging on the far wall. Condensation dripped off the clay pot and onto the ladle hanging over the side, but it did Tucker no good. It hung just out of his reach.

He dropped back onto his bunk. Perhaps it was the fact that if he didn't get water soon, the hangman would be cheated. Perhaps it was not knowing if he had killed that roustabout or not. Either way, his throbbing head was forgotten among all his other worries. They made him wish his bloody head was his only problem right now.

He took his bandana from his neck and wiped drops of sweat forming — and as quickly drying — on his face, running into his head wound, itching mightily. The stifling noonday heat inside the windless confines of the tiny cell made it hard to breathe if he moved, so he lay still on the bunk.

But sleep evaded him, and only his own hoarse, labored breathing talked back. His mind would not allow himself to sleep, wondering if Aurand was right. If he were, then Tucker had no argument to give the circuit judge. The worst for him, though, was the look on Aurand's face when he left the jailhouse this morning. He knew that confining a man like Tucker — so used to the open trail, so comfortable under the stars — might kill him just locked up in this stagnant jail cell. Either way, Aurand Forester would win. And *that* grated on Tucker.

Sometime in the afternoon, exhaustion from lack of food and water and thinking too much got the better of him, and he drifted off. In his fitful sleep, a snake hissed at him. And hissed again. And called his name. But snakes didn't talk, and Tucker sat upright on the bunk.

"Tuck," a voice whispered again. "Come to the winda'."

Tucker stood on the bunk and grabbed onto the window bars facing the alley in back of the jailhouse. Jack Worman balanced atop his paint pony, a leg hooked over the pommel. He clung to the bars while he looked nervously around the empty alley. "Got yourself in a fix this time," Jack said. His horse snorted, and he stroked the gelding's muzzle to quiet him. "What's with that roustabout?"

"You tell me," Tucker said, " 'cause I don't remember a thing about it. What'd you hear?"

"Just what they're saying around town," Jack whispered. "About how you killed that feller right off the steamer. The other roustabouts are madder'n hell." A cup dropped in the next room, and Jack ducked. After long moments, his face was once again framed in the window. "Those other roustabouts and teamsters are getting liquored-up down at the Bucket. Talking lynching they are."

"Great." Tucker kicked the pillow, and more lice scrambled away. "Don't look like my chances are getting any better."

"Got other problems around town, too." Jack looked down the alley. "Lorna's gone."

"Gone where? If she went south to Yankton with that Maynard Miles . . ."

"She didn't go with him. He's the one who sounded the alarm." Loud voices rose and fell in a dangerous crescendo from the Bucket of Blood a hundred yards down along the river front. "He said Lorna left the general store late last night after doing inventory. Maynard escorted her upstairs to her room and went back downstairs. While his nose was buried in bookwork, he heard some commotion about midnight but just thought it was drunks stumbling back to the steamer. Until this morning when he went to take Lorna to breakfast. She was gone, and he come running to get Aurand."

"Maybe she just had to get away for a while. That Maynard can be an annoying SOB . . ."

"Aurand figured she was embarrassed because of your arrest and left town."

"Me?" Tucker asked hoarsely. "And hand me your canteen."

Jack took the cork off his canteen and passed it through the bars. "Aurand figures she might not be able to live with you murdering that roustabout and took off by her lonesome. He thinks she went back home to Sioux City."

"That's not smart, a woman alone in this country."

"Especially with the Lakota close by. They've been known to steal white women."

"What Lakota?" Tucker forced himself to talk in a whisper as he kept an eye on the door. "The only Indians around here are

Santee Sioux down at Crow Creek, and some Dakota farming up north. How d'you know Lakota took her?"

"Aurand," Jack explained. "When Lorna came up missing, he come and got me to work through any sign around the mercantile. Unshod ponies had been hobbled out back of the store, all right. By their droppings, they've just come up from the Badlands."

"Has Aurand formed a posse?"

"Not on my information," Jack said. "He ain't taking it too seriously."

The man in the outer room cursed loudly, and Jack ducked down again. When he was sure the guard wouldn't come busting into the cell and spot him at the window, he stood and pressed his face against the bars again. "Soon's I saw it was Lakota and that Lorna was gone, I figured they took her. But if I told Aurand what I found, his bunch would muck things up. They'd trample over any sign the Indians might have left, and we'd never get her back. Hunting down deserters and petty rustlers is one thing. But that bunch Aurand's got with him couldn't find buffalo tracks in the snow."

Tucker nodded. If Jack said pony droppings indicated Lakota waited behind the mercantile last night, it was gospel. He read trail sign as well as — sometimes better than — Tucker.

He felt his headache returning in spades, and he rubbed his temples. "And she didn't hop a steamer south?"

"None's went out for three days." Jack accepted the empty canteen and hung it off his pommel. "Remember those pony tracks we ran into northwest of Ft. Pierre last year, the ones we swore were made by two Dakota riding double?"

" 'Cause they were so much deeper than the rest." Tucker felt the blood drain from his face. "Blue Boy," he breathed.

"That's him," Jack whispered. "I'd bet a month's pay that was Blue Boy's sign I cut in back of the store. Got him six Miniconjou riding with him now, if I read their trail right."

Tucker slumped against the wall of his cell. Blue Boy got his blue eyes and pale skin from his white mother, and all the other looks and size from his Lakota father. After Blue Boy's father had been killed by an English trapper in the Shining Mountains, Blue Boy's mother took her young son to relatives in Minnesota to live. How Blue Boy came to be in the Dakota Territory, Tucker had no idea. But by the man's reputation, Tucker didn't care to get close

26

enough to ask. For every enemy Blue Boy came in contact with — the rumor among Indians went — he killed. "Maybe Lorna's just visiting a friend . . ."

Jack reached inside his shirt. He thrust a patch of cloth through the bars, and Tucker snatched it. He could almost smell Lorna on the gingham, the identical pattern as the weave of the dress she wore that night in the store. "I found this two miles south of town," Jack said, "along the river bluffs. Looks like they stopped to water their horses sometime last night and dismounted. This was hung in sagebrush beside a woman's tracks. A little too coincidental, Lorna gone the same day as Lakota tracks out back of her store."

"So she's alive?"

"At least she was when she left that," Jack said. "Can't guarantee her luck won't play out."

"How much jump they got on us?"

"Half-day by now," Jack answered "And how you figure 'us'?"

"Who's standing guard outside the door?" Tucker asked.

"Philo Brown. And he looks plumb ready and willing to use that Greener lying across his fat lap."

"Give me a gun," Tucker said, watching

the door.

Jack reached into his saddlebags and handed Tucker a well-worn .41 Remington. He passed the derringer through the bars, and Tucker stuffed it into his pants pocket.

"Not very smart, going against a shotgun with that thing," Jack said.

"Let me worry about that. Where's Aurand?"

"Seen him disappear into a crib above the Bucket with that new dancer."

"Good." Tucker felt better already. At least he was forming an escape plan, even if it was harebrained. He patted his trouser pocket. The twelve dollars he had left after buying the whisky two nights ago was still there. He handed Jack a ten-dollar gold piece. "Take this eagle and go buy the best whisky you can. Come back here, and give it to Philo."

"Let me get this straight," Jack said. "You want me to buy good whisky for a man that'd as soon kill you as look at you?"

"Something like that. Except tell 'ol Philo you bought it for me. Ask him to pass it into my cell."

"He won't. The damn fool will drink it himself."

"Exactly." Tucker grinned, thinking of the fat man guzzling booze until he couldn't waddle straight. "Philo won't risk drinking outside where Aurand might see him, no matter how hot it is in this office. No, he'll do his drinking inside where no one can see him. And when he comes in here nine sheets to the wind, I'll put this little gun on him."

Jack grinned, and his off-color gold tooth gleamed in the bright afternoon light. "It just might work."

"It better," Tucker said, "for Lorna's sake. Now go get that bottle, and pass it to Philo. Then saddle my mule, and bring it out back."

Jack looked both ways along the alley before dropping into the saddle and riding off.

Tucker turned and sat on the edge of his bunk as he took the derringer from his pocket. He covered it with his hat and waited until Jack made the purchase.

CHAPTER 3

The jailhouse door opened and just as hurriedly slammed shut. "That you, Philo?" Tucker shouted.

Philo Brown threw open the door leading to the cell. He hitched his gun belt up over the double roll surrounding his hips. But it drooped back down when he raised a bottle of whisky high so Tucker could see it. "A gift to you from your friend Jack Worman."

"Let me have it," Tucker said, judging the distance from the cell door to Philo. If he shot the deputy now and Philo dropped where he stood, he would be too far away for Tucker to reach the keys on his belt. He needed Philo closer. "Let me have a pull."

Philo backed up into the office but left the door open as if to taunt Tucker. Philo grabbed the cork in his teeth and spat it on the floor while he held the bottle up, toasting Tucker. "Can't let my prisoner be poisoned," Philo said as he brushed dried food from his beard. "It's happened before, I heard." He took a long pull from the bottle and wiped his mouth with his shirtsleeve. "I'll taste just enough to make sure it's safe. Wouldn't want to cheat the hangman now, would we." He grinned. "Man's got to make an honest living like the rest of us." He exaggerated a bow. "Present locked-up company excepted."

Philo dropped into Aurand's padded captain's chair. He propped his feet on an open drawer and grabbed a tin cup. He tossed the cold coffee onto the dirt floor and filled the cup to the rim with whisky. He gulped the liquor, and some spilled into his beard. Within moments, the cup was empty, awaiting a refill. "Ah." He drew out a long sigh. "That's drinkin' whisky."

"You always did like your hooch." Tucker recalled the story of Philo Brown and four other buffalo hunters. Fresh from a heavy kill day, they were on the prod to celebrate. They'd got liquored-up on the whisky in their saddle bags and found a small village of Brule' Sioux camped along the Bad River. Other Indians who knew the story claimed it took only minutes for the four hunters to kill the six warriors from long distance, leaving the women to a much more horrible fate that lasted for days until they, too, succumbed. Tucker was certain it was Philo's natural brutality that had caught Aurand's eye when he needed deputies. He was Aurand's left-hand man. But just this moment, the left hand was more interested in what it held to his lips.

"Seems like I should have a sip of that." Tucker gripped the derringer concealed in his hat. "After all, it was my friend who dropped it off."

Philo's words began to slur. "I'm still not sure it's safe to drink," he sputtered between gulps.

"Well, it won't be safe to drink once Aurand finds out you got liquored up when you were supposed to be watching a prisoner."

Philo's smile faded, and he stopped with the cup midway to his lips. "How's Aurand gonna' find out? He's with his woman." He forced a laugh. "Tied up, so to speak."

"I'll tell him." Tucker stood upright with his hat toward the cell door. "If you don't give me a pull of that bottle, I'll tell Aurand."

Philo remained silent for a long moment as if weighing his options. Aurand hated Tucker, but he might hate drink even more. If he learned Philo had got drunk in the jailhouse, Philo might not make it out of the building alive. And he knew it as well. "And if I give you a drink, you'll keep your mouth shut?"

"On the Good Book, I swear." Tucker cocked the derringer under his hat.

Philo looked to the cup, then to Tucker, then back to the cup. He poured three fingers into it and set the bottle on the desk. As he walked toward the cell, Tucker shifted the gun in his hand.

Philo handed Tucker the cup through the bars. "Here's your damned drink."

"You keep it." Tucker dropped his hat and jammed the derringer through the bars into Philo's belly. "This little gun's only got the one barrel, and it might not kill you outright. But if I gut-shot you this close, you'd eventually die. Only sawbones in these parts is the fort surgeon. And I doubt he'd help you, the way you treat soldiers."

The older man slumped as if he'd already been shot. "What do you want?"

Tucker nodded to the keys dangling on the fat man's suspenders. "First, skin that Colt. Careful like."

Philo slowly plucked his gun from his holster and handed it to Tucker.

"Now open the door."

"You're not gonna' get away with this. We'll hunt you down and —"

"Lock me up on some other trumped-up charge?" Tucker opened the loading gate of the Colt so it wouldn't fall through his pants. "You peckerwoods would never frame me, right? Now get in here." Tucker moved aside.

Philo had to turn sideways to stagger through the narrow door, and he leaned against one wall. "You gonna' kill me?"

"I should," Tucker said. "For all the soldiers you killed lately."

"They're deserters. Snowbirds."

Tucker had witnessed more than a few deserters returned to Ft. Sully draped over the back of an army mount led by Philo or another of Aurand's deputies. The army offered twenty-five dollars for the return of deserters on the frontier, dead or alive. It wasn't enough to entice bounty hunters, but it was just enough to put Aurand and his men on the trail. And Philo usually took the dead-or-alive clause to heart.

Tucker grabbed Philo's snotty bandana from around his neck and gagged his mouth. "Lie face down there." He motioned to the bed.

While Philo dropped onto the bunk, Tucker backed out of the cell. He grabbed shackles from a peg on the wall, probably the same shackles Philo used on unlucky deserters. Tucker clamped one on each wrist and secured Philo to the bed before shutting the cell door.

Loud footsteps sounded on the wooden walkway outside the office, and Tucker drew Philo's gun from his waistband. He crouched to one side of the door leading to the outer office. When the footsteps clomped on by, he walked to Aurand's desk and opened the drawers until he found his Remington .44 conversion. He snatched his belt from the coat rack and fed it through the loops on his trousers. Jack had made fun of him for wearing a belt instead of suspenders. Tonight it would prove an asset as he strapped on his belt and holstered his gun. He snatched his Bowie from Aurand's desk drawer and kept an eye on the door while he positioned the knife sheath in front of his holster.

He turned back to the cell. Philo thrashed around like a beached catfish. "If you get thirsty," Tucker said, nodding to the water jug out of reach of anyone in the cell, "take a cool sip. Just like I did." He dropped Philo's gun into the water pot. Philo's struggle became muted as Tucker shut the door.

He cracked the door leading out of the marshal's office and peeked out. *The Belle of the Ball* sat at dock, her Indian annuities

35

off-loaded and guarded by a squad of soldiers from Ft. Sully. Their Springfield rifles hung loosely from their shoulders, freeing their hands to wipe the sweat from their faces and necks. Dirt had caked around their collars and armpits from the wind coming off the river kicking up fine Dakota dust.

On the other side of the street toward where the mercantile sat, two boys played mumblety-peg in the dirt. One threw his knife and narrowly missed the other's bare feet. They tilted their heads back and laughed heartily while one retrieved the knife for another round.

Beyond the mercantile a dozen horses stood three-legged, tied to the hitching rail. And beyond that lay the Bucket of Blood, where a crowd spilled onto the street. Drunken, angry cries rose and fell with the mob's undulations as they staggered toward the jail.

Tucker craned his neck to look in the direction of the dock. Along with the soldiers guarding the annuities, teamsters had backed their freight wagons to await loading by the roustabouts. Another wagon sat with buffalo hides piled high, the teamster impervious to the swarm of blowflies attacking the hides. And, next to him, a wagon sat parked loaded with bags of manganese, all waiting loading and off-loading by the growing crowd of roustabouts approaching the jail with bad intent.

Satisfied no one guarded the jail, Tucker pulled his shirt collar up and his hat low and stepped lightly onto the wooden walkway in front of the jail. He fought the urge to look over his shoulder at the approaching crowd and walked as calmly as he was able toward the alley.

"Over here," Jack whispered.

He sat his pony, all but hidden behind a stack of empty pickle barrels. He held the reins of a sixteen-hand mule. The critter's ears perked up when he saw Tucker running toward him.

"The roustabouts got themselves a damn fine-looking noose," Jack said, glancing about the alley.

"You sound happy. It was my neck gonna' be stretched by that rope."

Jack shrugged. "I just like to see people take pride in their work."

"If we don't get the hell out of here" — Tucker swung into the saddle and patted the mule's withers — "that mob's going to need two nooses — one for each of us."

They started out of the alley, riding slow, like they had no cares. When they ran out of alley two blocks down, the crowd had reached the jail. Two men staggered inside and ran back out. Gunfire sounded like a mini battle outside the jail when they discovered Tucker had escaped.

He and Jack rode slowly until reaching the outskirts of town, where they picked up the pace. Tucker kept an eye on their back trail, but Aurand had not mounted any posse, and Tucker imagined he was still tied up with that dancer from the Bucket.

A mile outside of town they turned west until they reached the river bluffs. They rode down the steep embankment and let their animals drink from the Missouri, safe in the secluded hills.

Tucker drank from the slow-moving river and filled his canteen, still dehydrated from his time in the jail cell. He wet his bandana and carefully washed the blood from his head. What Aurand or Philo had hit him with, he had no idea, but it had made a wicked gash.

"Think we can catch up with those Lakota?" Jack sliced off a chunk of jerky and handed Tucker the rest. "They've made no attempt to hide their tracks up to now. Like they don't care if they're followed."

"Or they want to be followed," Tucker said, looking about the high river bluffs.

"Keep on your toes, Jackson."

"We might have another problem." Jack unfolded a paper and handed it to Tucker. Lorna's image had been sketched on a paper offering a thousand dollars for her return.

"What's this?"

"Maynard Miles got hold of old man Moore in Sioux City by telegraph." Jack draped his canteen over his saddle. "Lorna's father put up the reward money. Now every amateur in the area will be mucking up their tracks trying to find her. I heard that the first person who grabbed one of these fliers was Simon Cady."

"Great." Tucker swung up into the saddle. "All we need is a professional bounty hunter getting in our way."

Tucker washed jerky down with tepid river water and handed the chunk back to Jack. "Lakota usually kill women outright if they got a mind to. Not take 'em. If they still got Lorna, there's a reason they want her alive. And you can bet the farm she's doing whatever she can to be a burr under their saddle and slow them down." Tucker grabbed the reins and started following the Indians' trail.

CHAPTER 4

Blue Boy sat his horse overlooking the river below. The dun gelding — as the *wasicu* called it for the yellowish coat and dark stripe down the back — stood with muscles twitching, eager to take Blue Boy as far and as fast away from here as it could. The horse, stolen in a raid last year of four wagons crossing into the land of the Cheyenne, had caught Blue Boy's eye. Larger by far than other horses he had ridden, the gelding suited him well. It was perhaps the only horse he had owned that did not make him look too big to sit its back, and he was still able to keep pace with his band.

He shielded his eyes against the bright setting sun until he spotted his warriors far below as they skirted the banks of the *wakpa' sica*. The Bad River. His warriors picked their way carefully amidst the sharp rocks and fields of prickly pear cactus with their wildly blooming yellow flowers, around boulders the size of tipis, and through sage as tall as a horse's withers.

His gaze fell upon the white woman. Blue Boy's first reaction upon taking her last night was of a headlong rush to the Great Wall of the Badlands. But Black Dog, his trusted friend and cooler head, objected. "Soldiers will hunt us," he told Blue Boy after they had taken the yellow-haired woman from the river store. "Maybe those who enforce the white man's law will follow as well. They will come after us, and they will come with blood on their lips. If we race through the prairie like wild buffalo, even the soldiers will spot our trail."

Black Dog had been right, of course. Blue Boy knew that. He watched the line of single-file riders led by Black Dog, as they avoided clumps of porcupine grass. A fast rider would tramp the grass down in the direction they headed and point out to the soldiers the direction they went. Still, the strong urge to scoop up the woman and race to safety gnawed at him.

By thinking and taking their time, they would make it to the Badlands without interference. This was country that would confuse even the best trackers the soldiers could send after them. Black Dog was right: they would be hunted relentlessly. Taking a white woman was a serious matter and not to be done without counsel. But seeing the woman for the first time last night, something inside him had snapped, and he knew — even over objections of the others — that he had to have her. The woman would slow them down, but that bothered Blue Boy little. He would elude the scouts as he always had, and they would enter the *Oski-ski,* the Badlands, without incident. And in the end, she would be his and provide the basis for a new generation of Miniconjou Lakota.

He studied intently the horse in the middle of the line of riders. Blue Boy had stolen the large paint mare from the Shoshoni, and he would often ride her to give his gelding a rest. But on this journey, Blue Boy had set the woman on the tireless pony in front of Jimmy Swallow. Even at this distance, he marveled at her long locks blown across her face by the stiff wind; at her chin-up attitude that showed defiance even as captive. And whenever she glared at Blue Boy, it was out of eyes as blue as any lake in the *He Sapa* — the sacred Black Hills.

Blue Boy checked their back trail before riding down to join the others, pleased by their progress. Guessing by the sun, they were a half-day's ride from the river town. They had trussed the woman up last night and followed the big river south without covering their trail. When he was certain soldiers could track them to the river bluffs, Blue Boy had led his people north to pick up the Bad River, now cautious with their tracks. By the time the soldier-scouts had worked out their ruse and discovered their direction, they would have gained another half day.

The column stopped abruptly, and Blue Boy nudged the dun down the steep hill. He reached the warriors just as the woman dropped to the ground beside Swallow. She looked back over her shoulder at Blue Boy as he rode down the embankment. The woman's chin jutted upwards in that haughty posture Blue Boy had come to expect from white women, and she disappeared over the bank toward the water. Blue Boy stopped and dismounted beside Swallow. "What is happening?"

Swallow threw up his hands. "She wanted — no, she demanded — to go to the river."

"And you let her?"

The young man shrugged. "She is stubborn. She needed to . . . rid herself of water. What could I do?"

"You could keep her close, like I told you."

Black Dog dismounted beside them. He leaned over and plucked a clump of buffalo grass growing on the hillside. He began rubbing his horse's shoulders and withers, smoothing the sweat from the its lathered hide. "If you wish her to reach the Badlands" — he chin-pointed to the woman's form, barely visible as she squatted by the muddy water — "we need to slow. She is frail. I am afraid she cannot ride like a Miniconjou woman."

"If she were a Lakota woman I would not have taken her," Blue Boy blurted out and instantly regretted it. He had been with Black Dog since he was wounded and scalped and left for dead by soldiers at the Washita two years before. Even though he was several years Blue Boy's junior, he possessed wisdom well beyond those years. Blue Boy knew he should listen to him. "All right. We rest. But just until the woman catches her wind."

Blue Boy pulled a clump of the grass and began rubbing the dun's flanks, when he caught Hawk staring at him. "You wish to say something?"

Hawk jerked his thumb at the woman's back. "She slows us."

Blue Boy smiled. Hawk had that little man-attitude Blue Boy had come to recognize in many men his size. But Hawk's attitude was even worse than most. The young man went through life bragging about his accomplishments, from the Spencer rifle he carried that he claimed he'd taken off a dead trooper at the Fetterman fight, to the scalp locks tied to the mane of his war pony Blue Boy knew he'd found. Even the army mount he rode hadn't been stolen from soldiers but traded for two fine ponies, just so he could brag he stole the soldier-horse in battle. "Something else bothering you, little one?"

Hawk stiffened at the name. "The store last night held many rifles, and yet we came away with *her.*"

Blue Boy continued brushing his horse. "And you think we should have forgotten about her. Broken into the store and stolen the rifles?"

"He is right." Wild Wind dropped from his pony and stood beside Hawk. They could have been twins, if one discounted Wild Wind's missing ear. "We will have nothing to show for our long journey to the river town."

Blue Boy looked at them and nodded. "You both are right."

Their stiffness left them. Blue Boy knew they expected to be slapped to the ground

45

for their insolence. Instead, he talked to them as equals.

"It is my fault that we did not gather up rifles and what else the store had to offer." He waved his hand in the direction of the river town. "So I will allow you two to ride back to the white man's town. Wait until this night and break into the store. Take whatever you desire."

Hawk and Wild Wind exchanged looks.

Blue Boy tossed his handful of grass aside and stepped toward them. He glared down at them. Gone was Blue Boy's friendly demeanor, replaced by the look of a man about to kill another. "You know I lead this band of warriors."

They nodded.

"And I lead at the whim of those who follow me. So" — he waved his arm to the others — "if you wish someone else to lead you, then now is the time to speak."

Hawk took a step back and tripped over sagebrush, while Wild Wind began trembling. "That is what I thought. If no one else has a problem with being led by me . . ." He let his words trail off. No one spoke. No one came forward. After long moments, Blue Boy smiled and clamped his hand hard on their shoulders. "Go. Attend to your ponies. We leave soon."

Paints His Horses grinned as he watched the two young men walk their horses toward the river. He had walked his mare toward Black Dog and stood leaning on her, much as old men do when they are exhausted. And Paints His Horses was — in the way of the warrior — an old man. "In time they will learn humility."

A sad look overcame Blue Boy. "I wonder if they ever will."

"You were like them once."

As the eldest member of Blue Boy's band, Paints His Horses was old enough to be the father of anyone there. This was the old man's last raiding party, Blue Boy was certain, and he wished to make the most of it. He wanted the old man to ride into his lodge with something to show for his last effort. But when Blue Boy saw the woman last night . . . "Do you have a problem with my decision to take the woman?"

Paints His Horses took out a pipe and tamped it with tobacco from a pouch made from a Crow's penis. "It was . . . spur of the moment, is how I believe the *wasicu* calls it. We could have ridden to the Badlands fat with trade goods: rifles and powder and knives to barter with the Cheyenne and Arapaho. But to answer your question, I have no problem with whatever decision you

47

make. I am just here to count coup once more."

Blue Boy looked over at Pawnee Killer. As always, he was the thinker among the young braves following him. He stood beside his horse and talked quietly to the animal, as if gaining insight into what he should do.

"You have not spoken about last night," Blue Boy said.

Pawnee Killer adjusted the hackamore rubbing the top of his pony's nose. "What is there to say? I know so little about such things. If you say it was necessary to take the woman rather than guns and powder, then you are right."

Blue Boy wished the other youngsters were like him. Pawnee Killer had been stolen from the Pawnee during a raid in the Sand Hill country when he was an infant. Raised a Lakota, the other boys taunted him, for they knew he was not one of them. And he worked every day to prove he was more Lakota than they ever were.

Blue Boy handed Pawnee Killer the reins to the dun and walked to the edge of the bank overlooking the river. The woman bent to the water with her back to him, and her lithe form produced an elongated shadow on the muddy bank of the Bad as she knelt. She dipped her dress into the brown water and wiped the dust from her face and neck. She became aware that he watched her and spun around as if seeing him for the first time. "So you cannot ride for long," he called down to her. "Not like a Lakota woman, who rides all day — walking beside her horse to let it rest."

"You speak —"

"Your English?" He walked the last few feet down the embankment and handed her a deerskin water bladder. "I was raised around whites. But that is a story for a long winter night."

The woman drank of the lukewarm water before handing the bladder back. She craned her neck up to look him in the eyes. "I am not used to travelling. Not like this. It hurts. Very much it hurts. Please let us rest a moment longer."

Blue Boy looked into eyes that were as deep blue as his, and he saw no lie lurking there, yet he remained cautious. He had not lived a violent life so long not to be wary of this woman who could cloud his mind if he allowed her to. "We will rest. For a moment. But I will lose my patience if you lie to me."

"Thank you."

As she scrambled up the bank, she lost her footing and slid down the embankment. Blue Boy thrust out his hand and caught hers. For a moment they stood in awkward silence until he pushed her in front of him up the hillside. "What do they call you," he asked, "back in the river town?"

Lorna smoothed her dress. "Lorna Moore."

She walked past him towards where the others waited, placing her hands at the small of her back and stretching. Once again he wondered at her beauty, at the way she stretched like the coyote stretches, graceful underneath her bustling white woman's dress. She reminded him of his own mother, and he dismissed the thought from his mind. Instead, he imagined his hands on this woman's small waist as he admired her free flowing golden hair cascading down her back as she looked skyward. In beaded buckskins, she would be a wonderment for all. In buckskins, all would envy his possession. This one, he thought, would be his alone. No other man would have her, as was their custom. He might even divest himself of his other wives to be with her alone. Except for one, perhaps two others, to pitch the lodge, skin the *tatanka,* and render the buffalo fat to make pemmican for long hunting journeys and raiding forays. For he could not see this one soiling her hands doing such work.

Blue Boy mounted his horse, a signal for the others their rest was over.

Jimmy Swallow swung his leg atop the mare and held out his hand for the woman to grab. He hoisted her in front of him, and Blue Boy watched as she flattened her dress over her legs. She turned her head and caught him staring at her.

He looked away, blushing, he was certain, thinking of the last time he had taken a woman in a raid. It was before White Swan had walked the *Wanagi Tacanku,* the Ghost Road. Blue Boy had been called by the ailing chief to attend his deathbed. His *sicun,* his guardian spirit, he told Blue Boy, wanted him at the old man's side. White Swan had passed to Blue Boy his wish that Miniconjou kill all *wasicu.* And until last night, his singular purpose was to carry out White Swan's wishes. The last thing on his mind as they crept into the town to steal rifles had been taking a woman captive.

They had lain hidden in the shadows in back of the river store listening to the uproarious drunken crowd a block away and the sound of riverboats testing their steam machines. They had planned to break into the store and steal rifles and powder, knives and trades axes, and leave before anyone saw them.

Then Lorna Moore walked past the window, silhouetted by flickering kerosene lamplight, and Blue Boy had rubbed his eyes. A woman like he had never seen before passed the window for the briefest moment, and he was certain he had just beheld a vision. Then the lamplight dimmed, and the woman emerged, walking beside a tall man in the garb of the shopkeeper. Blue Boy had drawn a sharp breath, as had Black Dog beside him. "We will take her," Blue Boy said at once.

No one said anything against the altered plan until Hawk spoke up. "We must get those guns. They will make us as many. They will make others in the lands of our fathers as many, as well." That had been the only discussion as they waited while the shopkeeper walked Lorna outside the mercantile and upstairs to a room. They spoke words Blue Boy could not hear a moment before the shopkeeper bent to her, his lips brushed hers lightly, and she drew back. Blue Boy nearly bolted to her defense as she spoke a single word of anger to the man and quickly disappeared into her room.

"We must get those rifles," Hawk repeated.

"I think he is right," Black Dog whispered so the others did not hear him. "If we take the woman, we cannot take what is in the store. We will be seen. We need those rifles."

"I cannot allow such a woman to remain here in a white-man world," Blue Boy said. "Such beauty was meant for the Lakota."

And so they had waited outside the trade store, hidden by the deep shadows until the light in her room went out. He positioned two of his braves to watch the storekeeper in case he heard something, and Blue Boy took Pawnee Killer with him. They had crept up the steps, the creaking under Blue Boy's weight loud in the humid night air. Yet there were other sounds of the town that drowned them out, and they reached the upper floor unseen and unheard.

Blue Boy rubbed his cheek where Lorna's long fingernails had gouged him when he burst into her room. Pawnee Killer had clamped a hand over her mouth, and she had bit him. She'd drawn in a deep breath to scream when Blue Boy hit her on the chin. Not hard enough to damage someone as lovely as she but sufficient to silence her for a short while. As Blue Boy looked at her sitting tall on the horse in front of Jimmy Swallow, he knew that, in time, she would forgive him.

"Hawk," Blue Boy called.

The young brave stopped his pony beside Blue Boy.

"We get hungry."

Hawk started to speak when Blue Boy held up his hand to stop him. "I know: if we would had broken into the mercantile, we could have stolen oysters. Maybe peaches in those cans you like. But we didn't." Blue Boy motioned ahead. "Go and find us game. And build a fire so that we may cook."

"Put the woman to cooking."

Blue Boy shook his head. In his younger life, he would have run Hawk through with his blade for his insolence. But now he needed to keep his warriors together and alive. Nothing was more important than getting Lorna safely to his lodge. "And when you are done cooking," he said, ignoring the protest, "you will bury the campfire and the bones of whatever you bring us. Do not leave any sign for those who may follow us."

Hawk's jaw clenched, but he said nothing as he rode ahead of the others. He unsheathed his Spencer carbine as he disappeared over the next rise.

The column rode up the steep embankment, and Blue Boy rode ahead to take the lead. It would be better for their survival if he rode in front where the sight of the woman would not affect his judgment.

There would be time enough later to gaze in awe upon her. After the Great Wall.

CHAPTER 5

Tucker stopped just below a hill above the Bad River that overlooked a deep, parched valley. He stood in his stirrups and shielded his eyes with his hand. Somewhere on the other side of the heat-shimmering waves Lorna rode with the Indians who'd taken her. "They're close. I can smell them, and Ben can, too." The mule's ears laid back, his eyes drawn to the west as his nose tested the hot, dry wind.

"Might be their campfire he smells." Jack dismounted and stretched his legs. "They must have ate supper by now." The sun had begun its nightly descent, and Tucker continued looking into it. They had been lucky today. When Jack led him along the Missouri to the tracks of the raiding party, Tucker thought it strange that Lakota stealing a woman from a white man's town would do nothing to mask their escape.

Yet after two miles, their tracks disappeared. The Indians had begun hiding their trail.

Jack and Tucker had worked first west, then north until they cut the sign of the raiding party a mile away. They finally located the switchback where the raiders had turned north to parallel the Bad River.

Tucker climbed off Ben and led him to the water's edge. The mule drank the brackish water while Tucker sipped from his canteen as he tried reading the countryside. They had lost the Indians' tracks again.

"There," Jack pointed. He broke a vine off a dead thistle and bent to circle the track he found.

Tucker squatted beside him. The low-lying sun cast perfect shadows and filled impressions for anyone looking into the brightness. "They dismounted here," Jack said.

Tucker put his hand on the faint scuff mark on the red rock. The hard ground would yield her secrets grudgingly, and Tucker was grateful for this one mistake their enemy had made. He looked farther to the west. A broken sagebrush lay askew. The raiders were following the Bad.

While their mounts drank, Tucker and Jack leaned against a cottonwood tree. Jack bit off a chew of plug tobacco and offered it to Tucker. He waved it away and unbuttoned his shirt to cool off before he grabbed a chunk of jerky. He bit off a piece and stared at the scuff mark.

"You figure they took Lorna to sell her?" Jack asked, his cheek puffed out. How he could sip from his canteen and not wash the plug down his throat, Tucker never understood. "It wouldn't be the first time Indians sold women captives."

"But not the Sioux," Tucker said. "They're not about money. They're about honor and ego. It would give a brave powerful bragging rights to parade a looker like Lorna through his village."

"Especially a woman taken in the middle of a white man's town," Jack added.

Ben snorted, and his head jerked upward, testing the wind. Tucker rose and tipped his own nose into the stiff breeze. He caught a faint odor of something decayed carried through the air.

He led the mule from the water's edge, and handed Jack the reins. He'd scouted with Tucker long enough to know the drill. Jack grabbed Ben's reins and kept his own horse well away from disturbing any sign while Tucker walked hunched over the ground in the direction the odor came. Forty yards from the broken sagebrush he spotted dirt darker than the sun-bleached prairie earth.

As if the Indians had buried something.

Off to one side, a dead cottonwood switch with dirt caked on the end had been absently tossed on the ground. "They're getting confidant nobody's following them." Tucker took out his knife. He prodded the soft earth. His knife hit something hard, and he moved the dirt away.

"Looks like they had a campfire." Tucker scooped sand off a blackened tree branch, and he uncovered more burnt firewood. "A bigger campfire than I would have made if I stole some white woman." He dug until he hit something hard and grabbed it. He shook dirt from a bone of a prairie chicken and tossed it aside. "At least they're eating good, even if they are becoming careless."

"Careless is an understatement." Jack pointed. He led his paint to a thicket of scrub chokecherry bush and plucked a piece of white gingham from the middle of the barbs. It had been impaled on the thorns like a miniature distress flag.

Tucker held it to the light. "This has been torn straight." He held the piece of dress to his nose before carefully folding it and stuffing it inside his shirt. "At least we know Lorna's alive."

"But in what condition?" Jack asked.

That worried Tucker. He had no way of knowing if she had been hurt when the Indians took her. Or what they might have done to her on the trail. "She's in good enough condition to keep her wits about her."

"But for how long?"

"I wish I knew." Tucker swung atop Ben. "I just hope she can slow them enough to allow us to catch up before they reach the Wall."

CHAPTER 6

Lorna dipped the edge of her dress into the muddy waters of the Bad River. Stinking and brackish, it was nonetheless water, and she was grateful for it. By the diminishing depth and width of the river as they made their way southwest, she feared this might be the last time she'd have the luxury of washing the dust off.

A mudpuppy flopped against the silt-covered bank, and she jumped back, startled. Her father's creek had no such creatures, and she forced herself to close her eyes. She let her mind drift to another place besides here. Another time besides now, when there was nothing in her future but pleasant tidings. She imagined that the Bad River she washed herself in was the cool, clear creek meandering past her father's house just off the Mississippi on the Sioux City side of the river. Horses romped in the vast green pasture, fitting for a man who made his fortune in dry goods and mercantiles across the West.

On her school breaks from Rhode Island, she would return home and ride any thoroughbred in her father's stable. She would sleep late in the mornings and stay up as late into the night as she wished. She had few cares then. Even with the war raging between the Union and Confederates, she was insulated from it at the college.

A stone rolled down the bank and landed in the water beside her. Jimmy Swallow guarded her from the hill above. The young brave had treated her well thus far, and even now he kept his back turned while she bathed. She kept Swallow in her peripheral vision as she tore a piece of material from her dress and stuck it on a thistle beside the water.

She dipped her dress in the river once more and winced as the fabric touched the blisters on her neck. Always, the blazing sun that beat down on her and blistered pale skin left unexposed. Swallow said the Badlands to which they rode had a different kind of sun — an angry sun that seemed to beat hotter and brighter than any other. It was the kind of sun that protected the Lakota against the pale *wasicu*.

The leader of these criminals — the very

large man riding a horse that looked altogether too small for him — had freely spoken of Lakota women, and of his many wives, on the trail. They could travel endlessly, he said. They never complained, he added. She was no Indian, yet something inside her wanted to show this man she was the equal of any Lakota in his . . . stable. Was it pride she inherited from her father? Or was there something else that forced her to want to show she was equal to any woman this Indian knew? She had met many Lakota who came into the mercantile for goods. They were sedate, even polite, as they bartered corn or meat for dry goods. But this one was different. This one was as wild as any bronc that escaped its rider at branding time. So why did she care what he thought of her?

She felt as if someone watched her, and she looked about. Swallow remained atop the bank with his back turned to her. There was no one else, yet she knew — just knew — other eyes watched her every move. Then she caught the flutter of black hair behind clumps of sage twenty yards upriver. She strained and watched as a small form rose from his crouch behind the bush. Wild Wind grinned at her and slowly walked up the bank to the camp. Had he seen her tear a piece of her dress off and leave it as a sign?

She gathered her dress and stepped into her shoes. She laced them before stumbling up the bank. Swallow heard her and turned around. He offered his hand, but she hesitated. There was nothing in Jimmy Swallow's gesture that led her to believe that he was anything but honorable. As honorable as raiders stealing a woman can be. She accepted his help and scrambled the rest of the way up the bank.

She looked around the Indian camp. When the band had stopped earlier by the big cottonwood, the ones called Pawnee Killer and Hawk had ridden out in opposite directions. She had been around soldiers long enough to know they were flankers, lookouts. But looking out for whom? The only man she knew who was skillful enough to follow them in this country was sitting in jail for murdering a roustabout.

She closed her eyes and recalled the terrible news Maynard had given her — with as much glee as he could muster — the morning Aurand arrested Tucker. "The marshal's got Tucker dead to rights," Maynard said. "Hanging's certain. They're giving odds down at the Bucket of Blood that he'll swing before the week's up," he added. Maynard went on to relate in grisly detail

64

how Tucker had robbed a roustabout and slit his throat. "At least that's what the marshal said at breakfast this morning." He laughed. "He'll get a confession, he said. Whenever Tucker comes to, that is."

She told Maynard she felt a little nauseous then — something she ate hadn't agreed with her — and excused herself that morning. She walked to the jail to see Tucker and find out about the charges against him. But that heavy man Aurand had working as a deputy — the one she smelled long before she actually saw him, Philo Brown — told her with a grin, "Only one who's gonna' see Ashley is the hangman."

She returned to her room and lay in the bed mulling her options for helping Tucker. She could wire Yankton or Bismarck, and the finest lawyer would be on the next paddle wheeler here. But would there be time? She knew Aurand Forester's trials were historically swift for those who even made it to a trial.

She had concluded she had no idea how to help Tucker but decided to wire her father the next morning. He'd know what she should do, and so she went downstairs to the store and blindly went about the job of running it with her father's partner, Maynard Miles. And when Maynard asked her to stay late to work on inventory again, she could think of no logical objection why she should not.

They had wrapped up inventory late, and Maynard took advantage of Tucker being in jail. He had escorted Lorna to her room above the mercantile and haughtily proposed they merge their efforts in marriage. He had even bent to kiss her, when she shoved him away. Maynard was her father's selection of a mate for her, but he wasn't hers, and she managed to escape to the safety of her room.

She unbraided her hair that night and sat in front of the vanity mirror, brushing the hundred strokes as her mother had done up until the day she died. How could Lorna make her father realize she came out West for adventure? To meet someone just as . . . wild as she, she thought, when she heard faint scratching outside her door. She turned on the vanity stool, prepared to yell at Maynard, when the largest man she'd ever seen burst through ahead of a much smaller Indian. The sight of them caused her to take a deep breath, and, in that moment of hesitation, before she could scream, the smaller Indian clamped his hand over her mouth. She rubbed her lips thinking she could still taste his blood when she bit

66

down, a moment before her lights went out. She still felt the numbing of her chin where one of them had hit her.

Blue Boy squatted by the fire talking with Black Dog and the old man Paints His Horses. No one paid any attention to her, and she thought for the briefest time that she could leap atop one of their ponies and be out of camp before they realized it. But as good a horsewoman as she was, she knew these men were born to horses and would catch her in little time. Then there were the two braves riding somewhere out in the brush as lookouts; they would quickly seize her and return her to camp.

And then what? She had heard so many frightening tales of the Sioux that she knew they would beat her, and she'd never again try to escape. But nothing she had heard or read about them fit with what she'd experienced these last two days. She had been fed and accommodated when she needed to visit a bush pile alone. And except for Wild Wind watching her bathe in the river, she believed none of the warriors would violate her. She bit her chapped lips to remind herself these were enemies of the United States government, not gentlemen of the plains just out for a camping trip.

Wild Wind hunkered down apart from the

others. He had positioned himself so that he could watch her and Blue Boy at the same time. She was certain there had been words between them over her, and she thought she might be able to exploit that somehow in the days ahead.

She turned her thoughts back to her rescue, if there were such a thing under way now. Surely the town would have been alerted that she had been taken. Men would literally fall out of the Bucket of Blood stumbling toward their mounts, eager to be the one who located her and received the reward money Maynard was sure to post.

And she was just as certain they'd have little more luck finding her than Marshal Forester would. He was no tracker and confined himself to arresting drunken soldiers and rowdies at the faro table he owned at the Bucket of Blood.

Philo Brown? She knew Philo and the Crow Indian Red Sun often tracked deserters for the marshal. Would they track her? If the reward Maynard posted was sufficiently high, they would. But that was assuming Maynard had recovered from the sting of her rejection and offered one.

Blue Boy caught her attention as he plucked a piece of rabbit roasting over the fire and glanced at her. She saw that same dreamy look in his eyes that she'd seen earlier. It wasn't a frightening look like the first impression he'd made that night in her room. This was a look of tenderness, and something more. Desire? Perhaps this was something she could use to her advantage as well.

He motioned for her to approach the fire, and she neared cautiously. Blue Boy handed her the piece of meat skewered on a stick. "Eat as much as you can," he told her. "Sometimes it is days between meals."

She tested the meat: charred a bit, but tasty. "You do speak very good English. Tell me more. And tell me of this." She pointed to scars running over both sides of his massive chest that looked as if he had been in a knife fight.

He looked down and closed his eyes as if he were thinking of something painful. "The *Wiwanyag Wac'ipi,*" he said reverently. "The Sun Dance," he said, and no more. None was necessary, for Lorna understood. Tucker had told her about the ritual of the Sun Dance, and how the bravest of warriors underwent the grueling ritual of piercing their chest muscles, offering flesh to their god. They would endure the ordeal of seeking a vision for four days that would guide them through life. But Blue Boy explained

69

none of this, and Lorna concluded he was a very private and humble man not used to talking about himself. "We will talk another time of me," he said. "And of you. Eat now."

She sat atop a large rock and ate the rabbit. When she caught Blue Boy looking at her, he quickly turned away. She thought that his face reddened, easier to tell by his complexion, which was as light as hers. She thought as she ate that Tucker living out of doors was darker than Blue Boy. And he did not possess the high cheekbones of the Sioux she'd seen come into the store from Crow Creek, nor did he have the angular nose many Dakota did. In another time, another area of the country — dressed differently — Blue Boy could pass for a white man.

"Tell me," she called to him, "is it true we ride to the Badlands?"

The old man asked something of Blue Boy, and he translated what Lorna had asked. "Paints His Horses thinks I should not tell you," Blue Boy said. "He does not trust you. But it matters little what you know." He chin-pointed to the west. "We go to the Great Wall. To the Badlands of my people."

She casually looked around the camp, weighing the options for escape. The band had turned south and west yesterday. And to the southwest lay the Badlands, a foreboding place if you believed travelers fresh in from the frontier. A place where one could go for days without water except what you carried over your saddle. A place where the seemingly solid ground gave way to popcorn shale that sucked horse and rider down into hundred-foot drop-offs and crevices. Travelers wanted nothing more to do with the Badlands, and neither did Lorna. Before they reached the Wall — that place of two-hundred-foot cliffs and secret trails — she knew she must escape.

And, oddly, she knew that she would be protected until they reached the Wall, and she berated herself. If she ever wanted to flee these heathens, she needed to throw aside any emotion of empathy for them and plan her escape.

CHAPTER 7

Blue Boy studied Lorna out of the corner of his eye, careful not to appear to watch her lest she catch him staring again. She squatted by the river bank and picked at barbs of porcupine grass that had embedded themselves in the hem of her dress. Beneath the ruffles he imagined her lithe form. She dipped her dress once again into the river, and her dress rode up, exposing her pale calf.

He quickly turned his head away as he thought of times he'd seen other white women exposed. Blue Boy often dressed in white man's garb to enter a town looking for horses or guns to steal. On more than one occasion in saloons he had walked past, women exposed themselves to entice men to enter. He would be drawn to look at them as the white men looked, only to feel shame in doing so. If Lorna were an Indian woman, dipping her dress in the water — or even fully naked — it would be normal, expected if a woman were to keep herself clean. But she was not Indian, and looking at her in that condition brought that inner shame back.

"Did you hear me?" Paints His Horses asked.

Blue Boy turned his back on Lorna and on temptation. "Tell me again."

The old man sighed while he stroked the shaft of his buffalo bone war club. The old man — the only Oglala Lakota in his band — had made a lifetime out of counting coup on the enemy and was once a living legend among that band. He had killed soldiers at the Battle of the Hundred Slain and at the Wagon Box fight outside Ft. Phil Kearney. And had more scalp locks dangling from his war shaft in front of his tipi than any other warrior. If he made an observation, Blue Boy had better listen to him. "Two men follow. At first I thought they came our way by chance. But they follow us by design."

"Are you sure?" Blue Boy asked.

Paints His Horses nodded. "The larger of the two discovered our campfire. I do not know how, but he dug around and found the bones from our meal."

"How is this so? We made certain we buried deep . . ." Blue Boy looked over at

Black Dog. "Who did I tell to bury the campfire when we were finished?"

Black Dog ran dirt through his fingers to clean them of rabbit fat. "Hawk," he answered.

Blue Boy felt his anger rise. He snapped a large twig between his fingers. "Hawk needs a lesson . . ."

Paints His Horses laid his hand on Blue Boy's arm. "Hawk is young. He made a mistake. Have you never made a mistake in life?"

Sounds of the woman approaching the fire caused Blue Boy to pause. He motioned her closer and gave her a piece of roasted meat. She wanted to talk about him. Wanted to know more. Any other time he would be flattered. Any other time he would welcome the attention. But right now, two men might be on their trail, and he needed to think.

When the woman sat on a cottonwood log Blue Boy turned back to Paints His Horses and whispered. As if the woman understood Lakota. "Why would white men want to follow us? As far as those two men are concerned, we are but a hunting party passing through."

"Perhaps there is a reason." Paints His Horses reached inside his shirt and held out a piece of cloth. Black Dog took it and waited until Lorna turned her head away before he passed it to Blue Boy.

"Perhaps Hawk was right," Black Dog said and held up his hand when Blue Boy started to speak. "He might be right in that this woman slows us down. On purpose. She leaves pieces of her cloth so that others can follow easily."

Paints His Horses grabbed a wild onion and bit into it. Juice dribbled down his stubble of gray whiskers. "We could have been at the safety of the Wall by now if not for her."

Blue Boy thought that over. They might not have been able to make the Badlands by now, but they would have been far closer riding alone. What he knew for certain was these men who follow needed to be stopped. "Where are the white men now?"

Paints His Horses waved his hand around the prairie. "They hide their tracks like we should. They are trail wise those two. But they are out there."

"Bring in Hawk and Wild Wind," Blue Boy told Paints his Horses. "Take Hawk and ride our back trail. I want those men dead by the time the sun sets."

Paints His Horses grinned. "We will have two fresh scalps when we ride back in tonight."

Blue Boy watched as the old warrior rode into the shimmering mirage in search of Hawk, and Blue Boy wondered if he were up to the task. Black Dog laid his hand on Blue Boy's arm as if he could read his friend's mind. "Paints His Horses will be all right."

"I was not worried about him."

"Of course you were." Black Dog grinned. "You think because he is old that he is not up to the task of killing two white men."

Blue Boy hesitated.

"Paints His Horses was fighting the *wasicu* before any of us were born. He will do good."

Black Dog left for the bushes, and Blue Boy sat on a rock watching Lorna heap more driftwood onto their roaring fire. He looked at her differently now after learning what Paints His Horses showed him. She was clever, that one, even if she wasn't as strong as a Lakota woman. The tearing of her dress to leave as a sign was brilliant. And as for her over-feeding the fire so men following might see it, Blue Boy would soon extinguish it. He would remember her cleverness, and he would watch her closely in the days to follow.

CHAPTER 8

Aurand Forester stuffed a pepperbox .36 into his saddle bags. He was tossing in an extra box of .44 Henry cartridges for his rifle and .44 Russian rounds for his pistols when the door to the marshal's office opened.

"I would like a word, Marshal . . ."

"Don't have time," Aurand said, not looking up from his packing chore. "Got a man to hunt."

"Precisely why I am here."

Aurand closed the bags with the "Confederate States of America" stamp branded on the outside. He headed for the door that was blocked by a man taller than he and forty pounds heavier. The deep crow's-feet under his eyes and his leathered face put him in his late fifties, perhaps early sixties. His gray hair peppered with white flowed down in a neat cascade over the collar of his deerskin shirt, which was sweat stained to the color of yellow phlegm. "I wish to speak with you about the man you hunt."

Aurand eyed the stranger warily. "What's Tucker Ashley to you? Unless you're the man who helped him escape."

The man waved the air in dismissal as he sat on the edge of Aurand's desk. He shook out a package of rolled cigarettes and offered Aurand one.

"Been a long time since I had a factory smoke," Aurand said.

The man lit it with a lucifer he'd grabbed from a pocket inside his buckskins.

"Like I asked, what's Tucker to you?"

"Nothing. Find and kill the rascal. And good hunting. Who I *am* concerned with is the missing woman."

The man unfolded a "Wanted" flier and laid it on Aurand's desk. A thousand dollars had been offered for Lorna Moore's return by her father.

Aurand handed the flier back. "Still don't see the connection to the man I'm hunting."

The stranger blew interlacing smoke rings upward. "I understand the man you're after and this Miss Moore were friendly. Perhaps close acquaintances even."

"I don't get your drift."

"My drift, Marshal Forester, is that it was

mighty coincidental that she disappeared about the same time your man escaped. Perhaps this young lady helped in his brazen jailbreak."

"And you think she might be with Tucker?"

The man shrugged and dropped his cigarette butt on the dirt floor. He snubbed it out with the toe of his moccasin. "We may be able to help one another."

"Look, Mister . . ."

The man remained silent.

"Tucker went one way by the tracks we cut, but nothing indicated Lorna went with him. I understand her father and she have had somewhat of a falling-out recently, if you believe the partner, Maynard Miles."

"What I do not believe in, Marshal, are coincidences."

The door burst open, and Philo Brown stumbled into the office. He half-ran across the room to the rack of rifles locked beside the desk when he froze. His jaw dropped, and he backed up. When he hit the wall, he stood, shaking, as he pointed at the stranger. "Simon Cady," he breathed.

Cady tipped his hat. "I am at a disadvantage. You are?"

"Philo Brown."

"Ah, yes. I thought I recognized you. The

very bad cheating gambler."

"You're Simon Cady?" Aurand's hand inched under his vest toward his gun.

"No need for that, Marshal." Cady nodded to Aurand's gun hand. "I am quite harmless."

"Harmless until we turn our backs." Philo had gathered courage enough to talk, though his eyes never left Cady as he moved beside Aurand. "You're looking at the bounty hunter who brings all his wanted men in over their saddles. He's a damned back-shooter."

"Mr. Brown," — Cady picked his words carefully — "I have killed no one who did not wish to kill me. And every man I bring in has 'dead or alive' pasted across his poster. You are a testament to the fact I don't kill everyone who harms me." He turned to Aurand and smiled. "Mr. Brown sought to cheat me in a game of poker in Hays City some years ago. I caught him." He looked at Philo. "But all I did was . . . educate Mr. Brown on the merits of playing honestly."

"If by educate you mean that beating you gave me."

"Mr. Brown," Cady said, shaking his head, "that might have been the only education you ever got in your miserable life."

Aurand edged closer to the door. If there was to be gun play in his office, he wanted space to maneuver. "Let me get this straight: you're working on the bounty of Lorna Moore?"

"I am."

"And are you going to shoot her in the back as well?"

Cady tilted his head back and laughed. His curly hair bounced on his thick shoulders. "Heavens, no. When I bring her back, she will be as safe as when she was tending store."

"So you are proposing we combine our resources?" Aurand asked.

"That is just what I propose."

"I don't deal with back-shooters."

Cady's smile left him. "If my sources are correct, Marshal Forester, *you* are the back-shooter among us. But then, wasn't everyone who raided with Bloody Bill Anderson during the war a back-shooter?"

"I think I have heard enough from you for one day." Aurand pulled his vest back, exposing his hand that rested on a pistol riding high on his belt.

Cady held up his hands as if to surrender. "You've got the best of me, Marshal. But remember my words: wherever Tucker Ashley fled to is where Lorna Moore will be."

As Cady headed for the door, he kept his eyes on Aurand and Philo. He stopped in front of a wall with "Wanted" posters tacked to it and snatched the top poster. He took out spectacles and held the poster at arm's length. "White male wanted in a series of stage holdups," he read aloud, "between Billings and Miles City last month." He looked over the "Wanted" poster at Aurand. "Says here the man is early- to mid-thirties. Six foot two or three, and weighs between two-forty and two-fifty. Murdered a stage guard in one instance. A passenger in another." He folded the poster and stuffed it down his buckskin shirt. "You won't mind me taking this poster and making an honest living, Marshal?"

"If you call bounty hunting an honest living," Aurand said. "Take it and find that man if you want. Or Lorna Moore. Anyone. But just stay out of my way."

Cady smiled. "Why, Marshal, I always stay out of the way of the law."

The door shut, and Philo slumped against the desk. He leaned on it to steady himself as he worked his way around to the chair. "You do know who you just talked to?"

Aurand shrugged. "Damned bounty hunter."

"Damned murderer."

"I got no time to worry about Simon Cady. Where's Jess?"

Philo looked at the empty spot where the "Wanted" poster had hung a moment ago. "Somewhere between Billings and Miles City, as of last month. I wired his room in Pierre to meet us on the way."

CHAPTER 9

Blue Boy cut a piece of charred rear-quarter meat and handed it across the fire to Lorna. The flames flared up now and again in time with the wind that seemed to always blow from the west on the prairie, bringing a mini-blizzard of dried cottonwood pods mixed with fine dust. Some white fluff fell on Lorna, and she brushed it from her hair. "I cannot eat this. It would be like eating my . . . pet Schnauzer."

"It is coyote," Blue Boy said. "And it gave its life so we may live. Eat. It may be the last meal for some time."

"I saw pronghorns this morning," Lorna argued. "What is wrong with eating them?"

"They must be shot," Blue Boy explained slowly, as if educating a child. "It takes a long stalk to get within arrow range, and we have no time . . ."

"You have rifles."

"We have rifles for fighting. And we have

no desire to have anyone hear our shots." He tore off a piece and ate it. "And coyotes can be called easily within range of our arrows."

"How is it you speak such good English?"

"The meat." He motioned. "Eat and I will answer your questions."

Lorna took the skewer and began eating while Blue Boy turned to Black Dog and asked in Lakota, "Have you heard anything from Paints his Horses or Hawk?"

Black Dog continued staring at their back trail. "Nothing. They should have been here hours ago. Do you wish for me to drop back and find them?"

Blue Boy considered that. Black Dog's suggestion was good tactics: following their back trail until he learned about the others was wise. But he must reach the Wall with Lorna at all costs. "No. We will leave soon. I have to believe they can kill the two white men who follow us."

Blue Boy turned his attention back to Lorna. Where yesterday she had nibbled tiny pieces of meat when she ate, she now tore at the chunk of coyote with a vengeance. She ate noisily, chewing the sinewy meat and swallowing hard. She became aware that Blue Boy watched her, and she stopped, her grace returning as she took tiny bites once again. "What do you intend doing with me, sell me?"

Blue Boy laughed. "We do not sell our mothers. Or our fathers. Or any other loved ones."

"So I am a loved one now?"

Blue Boy felt his face flush, and he turned away. "Do not talk of such things."

"All right," she said. "But I deserve an explanation of just what your intentions are for me."

He nodded and sat cross-legged in front of her. "You are correct in deserving an explanation." He gathered his courage; it *was* time to tell her. "You will belong to me as soon as we reach the safety of my lodge." He nodded to the west. "On the other side of the Great Wall you will be mine."

"What if I do not want to be yours?"

He had never considered that she would not accept her new life. "With the Lakota, all is beauty: the air and sky, and everything else *Wakan Tanka* has given us. We do not abuse such things. We do not destroy them for the sake of gold-colored rock imbedded in Mother Earth. We live within ourselves and take only what we need. This is beauty. You will grow to accept the Lakota way."

She finished the meat and dabbed at her mouth with the sleeve of her blouse. She stuck the bone in the dirt, and it protruded from the ground several inches. So that anyone passing by could see it. Before they broke camp, Blue Boy would retrieve it and bury it properly. In case those who followed made it past his warriors. He glanced at their back trail, hoping to see Hawk and Paints His Horses ride in with fresh scalp locks.

"How is it that you speak good English?" Lorna pressed.

Blue Boy sighed. She would have to know this in time. "My father was Lakota. He took my mother, who was white, in a raid outside Omaha. When a trapper after the beaver murdered my father, my mother was released to go where she wished, and she wished to live with her relatives in Minnesota." He nibbled at the meat — not because he was hungry, but because it helped him gather his thoughts. "I was a child when we moved there, and I attended a white man's school."

"You must have fit in."

He waited for an explanation.

"You look white, with your fair complexion. Blue eyes."

Blue Boy nodded. "Even with that I did not fit in. The other boys knew I was *ieska*. A half-breed. They teased me ruthlessly."

"Somehow, I cannot imagine you being teased."

Blue Boy frowned. "Until I was twelve or thirteen. Then my growth took off, and the others wanted nothing to do with taunting me then." He tossed the wooden skewer in the fire. The fat left on the stick crackled with the heat. "I stayed around Minnesota. Hiring out to farms. Never wanting to be a part of my father's side until . . ." He looked away, thoughts still painful even after all these years. "During your war between your states, some of the Santee Sioux took up arms against the whites. The Indian traders were corrupt. They withheld annuities owed the Santee. Many whites were killed." He looked away. "And Mother with them. None of the Santee knew she had a Lakota son, or they might have spared her."

Lorna laid her hand gently on his arm. "Must have been painful for you."

He nodded. "Up to a point. Then rage overcame my grief, and I took up arms with the others. When the soldiers caught us, I was locked up along with the Santee who started the killing." He shrugged her hand off. "And the day after Christmas that year, they hanged thirty-eight warriors. The largest mass hanging in the history of your country."

"I heard of that in college," Lorna said. "But you survived."

Blue Boy looked at their back trail. Still nothing of Hawk and Paints his Horses. "The soldiers sent me and many others away to prison. But they released us two years later. I guess they didn't want the expense of feeding us while your war was still going on."

"Why come back here? It sounds as if you could have hired out to farms anywhere."

Blue Boy stared at the woman. Had she not understood anything he had told her? "Because I do not choose to live in your world, where there is so much senseless killing. Misery."

Her face reddened. "You Sioux kill your share —"

"Not over a card game or over a drunk woman or a mere slip of an angry tongue. We kill when it is necessary. That is why I *chose* to live Lakota. And, in time, you will, too."

He stood and walked to where Black Dog sat talking with Jimmy Swallow and motioned to him. "I have need of your spare breech pants and your shirt. For the woman."

Swallow looked past Blue Boy at Lorna staring into the fire. "I have only my fringed set with me. They are the finest I have. My mother herself softened the deer. They fit me so well, so fine. If I should be called to the council fire . . ."

"And they will look good on the woman, too." He laid his hand on Swallow's shoulder. "I would not ask if it was not necessary."

Swallow nodded and walked to his pony tethered to a clump of cactus. He opened his saddlebags, took out his folded set of deerskin clothes, and walked back to Blue Boy.

Blue Boy thanked Swallow and handed the clothes to Lorna. "There is that bunch of dead cottonwood." He chin-pointed toward the river. "Go over there. Put these on, and give me your dress."

"I will not," Lorna answered hastily.

"Do you wish that Swallow help you change your clothes? Or Black Dog?" He nodded to Wild Wind. "How about him . . . ?"

"No!" Lorna said. "But why?"

"You have been leaving pieces of cloth torn from your dress for those who follow us —"

"So someone *is* on our trail," Lorna blurted out. "Who? What do they look like? Have you seen them?"

"That is of little concern to you," Blue Boy answered. "By the time the sun sleeps this night, those fools who follow will be no more." He motioned to Swallow's deerskin clothes. "And I challenge you to try to tear pieces of deerskin to leave behind."

He watched as Lorna disappeared to the sanctuary of the cottonwoods to change into Jimmy Swallow's clothes. "Do not worry, little one," he whispered. "With Paints His Horses and Hawk on the trail, those who follow us will be no more."

CHAPTER 10

Tucker reined his mule beside the trickling stagnant stream that was the Bad River. In wet years, the Bad would overflow its banks on the way to joining the Missouri. In wet years, the Bad could become a deadly torrent of water overrunning anything in its path. But this was a dry year, much like the last several years in the West.

Ben plowed the damp banks with his sharp hooves for the milky water underneath the ground, while Jack's horse sniffed the air, unsure where to get its next drink. "This is why I ride a mule," Tucker said.

Jack dismounted and led his horse to the edge of the dry river bank beside Tucker's mule. His horse bent its head and drank the water that had sprung from the hole Ben made. "Not hardly enough to fill a man's canteen."

"More here than where we're going," Tucker said.

"Think so?"

"Never been to the Badlands before, have you?" Tucker took off his hat. He brushed the hair out of his eyes and let the stiff breeze cool his head.

"Came close," Jack said. "We started after that bunch of renegade Brules last year, but the major turned us around soon's we crossed the White River. He said he didn't feel like losing men to that God-forsaken ground." He handed Tucker his canteen. "What's it like there?"

Tucker dropped the reins and tugged at a clump of buffalo grass. He looked to the west, trying to talk himself into going in there. If it had been anyone besides Lorna . . . "The Badlands is beautiful in its own way. The rocks — if you could call the shale and limestone rocks — seem to give off their own kind of glow when the sun sets and makes it kind of pretty. Until they start losing their heat, and then they can be as cold and barren as that dancer you've been seeing down at the Bucket of Blood."

"How'd you know — Never mind," Jack said and took his canteen back.

"And the wind. This time of year is the worst." Tucker began rubbing Ben's legs and withers with the grass. "It comes whipping off the Shining Mountains and picks up steam through the Black Hills. By the time it reaches the Badlands, the wind's lost all its moisture. So don't count on any rain from that wind. It gets so dry it'll suck moisture right off your tongue."

Jack corked the canteen. "But it looks like we got no choice. Blue Boy's headed there, and we got to make do. Or die. It's the horses I fear for."

"Well, between your paint pony and my mule, we can go anywhere Blue Boy's Lakota can." He patted his mule's rump. "And Ben will help us find water in his own kind of way."

They stood beside their mounts and waited for them to drink the last from the mud bog. "Figure she's alive?" Jack asked.

Tucker had been thinking of nothing else since he broke out of Aurand's jail. "She's alive. If Blue Boy wanted her dead, he would have killed her right off, and we'd have found her body as a warning. Lord knows she's been slowing them down. Be better for them if she wasn't with them. But no, she's alive. That's the one thing I am sure of."

"But why take Lorna?"

"If you had a choice between Lorna and that dancer . . ."

"Don't say it."

Tucker grinned. "My guess is he'd take most any white woman. Let her live, too. Call it a soft spot for *wasicu* women. Might have something to do with his mother being white."

"Some soft spot that one has, with the killing he's been doing these last years."

"You remember Bill Hickok being credited with killing a man in every gunfight you heard about?"

"Who hasn't?" Jack reached down and grabbed the reins of his pony. "Man's been in so many shootouts, it's hard to keep track of them."

"By my calculations — now I got no formal education like you do — Hickok's killed upwards of sixty men."

"And your point?" Jack asked.

"If you believe everything you hear about him — and halve it or quarter it — then that might be closer to the truth."

"So you're sticking up for the man who stole your woman?"

"I am not sticking up for him. I'm just getting a feeling of who Blue Boy is so I can hunt him. And Lorna's not my woman."

"Yet." Jack winked.

Ben's head jerked up from the ground. Mud dripped from his muzzle, and his ears twitched. Tucker followed where Ben looked up the hill. Tucker slowly walked around to get the mule between him and the hillside.

"I smell them, too," Jack said. He slipped the strap off his gun and untied the leather thong securing his rifle to his saddle. He squatted in the dirt and looked up at the high hills overlooking the river. "White or Indian?"

"Could be either, if Lorna's got a reward out for her." Tucker strained to see through the heat shimmering off the hot rocks, which created distracting waves of air. He casually thumbed the strap off his own gun and began to ease the Sharps out of the scabbard when he slipped it back in. Whoever watched them watched them from close, and the buffalo gun would be a disadvantage. Besides, it rested in the scabbard on the far side of his saddle. If he went for it now, whoever waited above would spring the trap on his own terms.

"What do you think, Tuck?"

"My guess is they're some of Blue Boy's Lakota." Tucker scanned the hillside as casually as he could, as if he merely stood drinking in the afternoon sun. They had let their guard down and allowed the Indians to gain the high ground. The last thing Tucker envisioned was for Blue Boy to send men back to hunt them. Tucker had been certain the raiding party would make a run for the Wall with Lorna in tow. Unless — as Jack said — white men followed Blue Boy's Lakota looking to cash in on Lorna's reward. Either way, it was a mistake Tucker would not make again. If he and Jack lived through this.

CHAPTER 11

Aurand Forester stood on the promenade deck of the *Belle of the Ball* listening to the slow dips of her paddles into the water as the stern wheeler backed out of the dock. When the bow cleared the levee, the paddle wheel stopped abruptly and gave one great shudder as if dreading the journey ahead. The wheel began to dip slowly again, gaining momentum until it frothed the waters of the Missouri heading south to the next port at Crow Creek.

The churning paddles had started lulling Aurand into complacency when he caught himself. Any other time he would welcome a river trip south, perhaps as far away as the capitol in Yankton. Or Sioux City. But this was business, and a deadly business at that.

He lit a smoke and leaned over the railing, thankful the ship left so soon after Tucker escaped. The trip to Crow Creek would be ninety miles and would place him and his men on ground far more hospitable than the way Tucker had escaped. By Aurand's calculations, he and his deputies would be able to get ahead of Tucker by a full day. Unless something happened on the river — raiding Indians or a submerged tree ripping a hole in the boat.

He needed Red Sun. The old man tracked for Aurand whenever there was a trail Philo Brown could not work out. Son of a Crow mother and French trapper who breezed through Crow country one winter, Red had run away as a youngster to scout for the army against the Crows' traditional enemy, the Lakota. And even though he acted more white than Crow, there was no mistaking his Indian parentage.

Aurand would need Red. Tucker was savvy enough he could confuse his trail, and only the best tracker — like Red — could decipher it. Aurand had paid two Indian hangers-around-the-fort a jar of whisky each to find Red and give him a note. Philo had found Tucker's tracks when he turned away from the Missouri toward the Bad River. "Meet us at the first stop the *Belle* makes," the note said. "We'll need you."

As the speed of the riverboat picked up, the two great chimneys rising thirty feet in the air belched huge puffs of smoke. The twin engines connected to the pitman, which connected to the wheel, coughed again, and Aurand lurched forward. He caught himself on the railing before he tumbled over. Below, on the lower decks, the boat was loaded with furs and grain to be off-loaded at Yankton, a full crew, and more passengers than the pilot wanted. The *Belle* owned a shallow draft that allowed it to navigate the Missouri, with unexpected sandbars and half-buried trees jutting upward as if beckoning to passing ships it wished to ensnare. Already, the river appeared menacing to Aurand.

He flipped his smoke into the water and turned to the walkway. He clung to the rails as he climbed the precarious ladder leading to the pilothouse. He reached the narrow walkway surrounding the wheelhouse and felt his lunch begin to come up for an encore. Captain Merriman opened the sliding window of the boxy structure. "You sure you want to be up here, Sonny?" Merriman grinned and whipped the wheel as if to punctuate his point. "Gets mighty rough up here."

"Wouldn't be here if I didn't want to," Aurand answered as he opened the door and stepped into the pilothouse.

A sudden jarring tossed him against the

hand railing next to the large wheel Merriman's hands grasped. When Aurand regained his footing, he looked down at the river. The boat had skidded over a partially-exposed sandbar.

"Get used to it, Sonny," Merriman said, more cheerful than Aurand thought he should be. "We'll be hitting many of those before reaching Crow Creek."

Aurand tried concentrating on the windows surrounding the pilothouse. The evasive pattern of the *Belle* matched the flow of the river, and Aurand felt himself getting sick again. Yet he dared not say a thing, for this was the flagship of the Coulson Line, with the right honorable Henry Merriman as captain. A former Ohio River captain who commanded the utmost respect for his knowledge and skill as a ship's pilot, Merriman was known to take a particular disdain for landlubbers. Especially when they became sick on his ship.

"How long's it going to take us to get to Crow Creek?" Aurand asked to get his mind off his queasiness.

Merriman jerked the wheel hard to avoid an old oak lurking just under the water's surface. "You know how I knew that tree was there?" he asked, ignoring Aurand's question.

"All I want to know is how long —"

"Do you — Mister Marshal — know how I knew?"

Aurand sighed. "No. Just how *did* you?"

Merriman picked dried tobacco juice out of his beard, which reached to his upper chest. "I read the river, that's how. You've got to read the river when you spend as much time with the ol' bitch as I do. You got to read the eddies swirling around old trunks like that last one. You learn to gauge the current by the feel of the water passing under the bow."

Aurand closed his eyes and rubbed a headache away. "Just what is your point, Captain?"

Merriman took his gaze off the river and looked at Aurand through eyes as hardened as any he'd seen. Then the captain turned back to his wheel as he continued talking. "It's my business to read these waters. That's why I get paid seven hundred dollars a month. Marshal, you get paid to know men. That's your business — men and the hunting of men."

Aurand began to speak, but Merriman held up his hand to silence him. "That Ashley feller didn't murder my roustabout."

"Were you there, Captain?"

Merriman shook his head. "Hell, no. I was

just as drunk as the rest of my crew. It's just that I've seen my share of men in my lifetime that I'd as soon not see again. Thieves. Cutthroats. Killers of every persuasion who would slit your throat for the price of a bottle of rotgut. I've seen that Ashley feller around. Talked to him a time or two. He's no murderer of my roustabout, that I can tell you. And I'll testify to that if a judge will allow me."

"Like you said, Captain, that's my business."

The boat jerked as it skidded over another sand bar, and Aurand grabbed for the railing. "When are we going to reach Crow Creek?"

Merriman tamped tobacco into his white clay pipe and patted his pocket for a match. Aurand took a lucifer from his watch pocket and struck it for the pilot. Merriman sucked hard until the tobacco caught, then he blew perfect smoke rings to the ceiling of the wheelhouse. "It depends," he said at last.

"On what?"

"On what those woodhawkers charge us for firewood along the way. They scalped us for eight dollars a cord on the trip up to Ft. Pierre last week."

"So pay it."

"Pay it!" Merriman bellowed over the

noise of the engine and paddles and people milling about on the below decks. "This old girl uses thirty cords of fuel in a day's ride. That's —"

"Two-hundred-forty dollars."

Merriman jerked the wheel, and the bow of the *Belle* dipped to avoid a snag. "If they charge us that, we'll have to slow down to conserve wood. Maybe cut our own, and that'll slow us even more."

"When?" Aurand felt his patience fading, and he smoothed his pigskin vest to calm himself. "When?"

"Three days, the way this trip's starting out."

"That's unacceptable."

Merriman shrugged. "It is what it is, Sonny. The river is shallow this time of year. More so with the drought. And that's three days if we don't hit any major sandbars or snags."

The boat lurched to the lee, and Aurand felt his breakfast rise dangerously close to his throat. His plan to take the paddle wheeler as far as Crow Creek and off-load there was looking dimmer with every passing sandbar. Still, even if they disembarked at Crow Creek a day later and headed straight west — over terrain far friendlier than the way Tucker rode — they would be able to get in front of him.

Aurand descended the stairs, and his stomach felt better when he reached the boiler deck. "See my deputy?" Aurand asked a deckhand.

The kid jerked his thumb over his shoulder. "He's in there."

Aurand entered through the door the deckhand had indicated into a smoke-filled room every bit as nasty as the Bucket of Blood on a payday night. Philo Brown straddled a peach crate opposite a drummer squatting on the other side of the signboard they had placed atop a pickle barrel as a table. A third man, a skinny *vaquero* sporting a *sombrero* nearly as big around as the barrel, teetered precariously on a three-legged milking stool. He looked at Philo and tossed two bits into the center of the makeshift table.

Aurand watched the game progress. Philo lost every hand, as he always did at first when the inevitable bait came. "Let's up the ante," Philo said. He fished into his pocket and came away with a half-eagle and tossed it in the kitty.

The drummer loosened his tie that matched his gray herringbone suit and hesitated. "Oh, what the hell," he said and dug in his pocket for a five-dollar gold piece.

The *vaquero* followed suit. "Why not?" He tipped his *sombrero* back on his head. "It is a long trip, no?"

Philo smiled as he shuffled the cards, the same deck he'd had when Aurand first met him in Ft. Laramie, Aurand was sure. Philo had just taken money from two cowboys and a rancher in from calving in a field adjacent to the army post. Aurand had stopped on the way to the fort to pick up a man wanted for killing a family at Ft. Thompson and stood watching the game from across the room. Aurand had seen a lot of cheats, but Philo was in a class all by himself. He commenced to win every pot until the other players went bust. When the two cowboys accused Philo of cheating, he feigned being hurt. Which lasted just long enough for him to unload his shotgun into their chests. When the rancher dropped his objections and backed out of the tent, Marshal Forester drew a bead on Philo's noggin. Aurand demanded that Philo take off his jacket, and cards tumbled out of the false sleeve. "Since when does a deck of cards have six aces?" Aurand asked.

Philo shrugged, ignoring the bleeding corpses on the other side of the card table. "A man's got to make a livin' somehow."

"Maybe there's a better way for you to

earn a living," Aurand said. "Say a steady seventy-five a month."

"Who do I have to kill?"

"Any fugitive or deserter who doesn't come with you peaceably."

The boat lurched, but Philo smiled at the drummer and the *vaquero* while he dealt cards, that same taunting grin Aurand recognized as Philo's dead smile.

"Game's over," Aurand said abruptly. He stepped to the table and divided Philo's winnings between the two men.

"But we got a lot of playing left —"

"You're a deputy marshal, and, as such, we got official business." Aurand tipped his hat to the other two players. "Enjoy your winnings." He turned to Philo. "Let's go." When Philo didn't budge, Aurand hoisted him erect by his shirtfront and shoved him out the door. He bounced along the railing as Aurand steered him toward his cabin. Philo stumbled and hit his head on the top of the door jamb.

"Why'd you break up the game?" Philo rubbed the side of his head. "I was gonna' win the next hands."

"You're drunk."

"Of course I'm drunk." Philo caromed off the wall of the cabin and staggered to the edge of his bunk. "But not too drunk to win some extra money."

Aurand glared down at Philo. "You're a fool. We're hunting Tucker Ashley. Not some kid deserter fresh from the farm, or some old drunk Indian. The man is dangerous. And unpredictable. I need you, but I need you clear headed. Getting drunk and caught cheating won't help us any."

"I didn't get caught." Philo grinned. Tobacco juice trickled down his chin, and he wiped it away with the back of his hand. "You ever knowed me to get caught righteous?"

"Simon Cady says otherwise."

"So one time I slipped up. Wouldn't have happened with this bunch of yahoos . . ."

"You would have, and then you would have had to kill those peckerwoods. I don't have time to smooth things out after another one of your boners. Just stay here and sleep it off. We need to keep a low profile until we can get off this thing."

Aurand walked out the door and headed for the main deck. He took the stairs and nearly fell over when the shuddering boat hit a snag.

"Fancy seeing you here, Marshal." The man, appearing even broader from the back in his buckskins, turned and smiled. Simon Cady brushed long, gray hair out of his face as he stepped away from the railing. "What's the odds of you and me being on the same boat together?"

"None." The bounty hunter caused hairs to ripple along Aurand's neck, and he rested his hand on his pepperbox hidden inside his vest. "What *are* you doing here?"

"Same's you," Cady said. His hand went inside his buckskins, and Aurand drew his gun.

Cady came away with a lady's paisley hairbrush and began to brush his hair. "Even you wouldn't shoot a man for brushing his hair."

"Why are you here?" Aurand holstered his gun.

"Like I said, same reason as you — hunting people. Except with me it's that little lady who came up missing. You still after that Tucker Ashley feller?"

Aurand nodded. "Why do you think Lorna Moore's to be found on this boat?"

"I don't." Cady pocketed his hairbrush and stepped closer to Aurand. "But the only way for a lady to leave that river town is on one of these contraptions. Surely you don't object to me hitching a ride to the end of the line, maybe as far as Sioux City. I understand she's from there."

"Thought you were convinced she was

travelling with Tucker Ashley."

Cady winked. "I've had what's called an epiphany. I figure she went back home. That Maynard feller at the mercantile said she probably had a belly full of her western adventure."

"Good. Then stay away from me and my deputies."

Cady put his hands up as if he were surrendering. "Don't worry about me, Marshal. I make my living finding people wanted by the law." He bent closer. "Unless there's been a reward posted for your escapee."

"By the time I could get the poster printed, Tucker Ashley will be leaking blood all over his mule's saddle."

Aurand turned on his heels, keeping Cady in his peripheral vision. He walked the row of cheaply built, thin cabins, their wicker doors flapping in time with the wind created by the paddle dipping into the water. He looked a final time down the narrow walkway. Simon Cady still leaned over the railing, and he looked upstream as he smoked his pipe.

Aurand walked into his room and froze. Jess Hammond lay on his back on the bunk. His floppy, felt hat was pulled over his eyes, and his long duster — with the Wells Fargo logo on the front showing where Jess had stolen it — brushed the floor.

"Jesus, Jess." Aurand cracked the door and peeked out. Cady still admired the view from the railing.

Aurand shut the door and propped a chair against it. "What the hell you doing here?"

"Nice to see you, too." Jess stood and stretched. He had Aurand by several inches and forty pounds. "I got your wire. What's the problem?"

"Ever hear of Simon Cady?"

Jess's face blanched. "Of course I have. Why?"

"He's on board. Not thirty yards down that walkway."

Jess slipped the thong from the hammer of his gun. "He here for me?"

"Why? You done something you shouldn't have?"

Jess remained silent.

"Wanted poster says a man fitting your description killed a couple folks and robbed a stage up Montana way."

"That your jurisdiction?"

"You know it's not."

"Then do like you always do and don't worry about it." He looked past Aurand as if expecting the door to burst open when Cady entered. "What's he here for if not for me?"

"Lorna Moore went missing."

"Never heard of her."

"Runs the mercantile with her father's partner. There's a reward out for her. And he smells blood in the water."

"How much blood?"

"Thousand dollars."

Jess whistled. "Now that pisses me off."

"How so?"

"Do you know how much the reward was for that . . . stage robber in Montana?"

"Wells Fargo put it at five hundred dollars."

"Like I said, that's embarrassing."

"Not as embarrassing as riding into town dead over the saddle of your horse. To be safe, stay in here while Cady's on board."

"What — stay cooped in this stuffy room?"

"Remember your corpse-over-the-horse thing?"

"I'll stay," Jess said. "Just find me some food. I'm hungry."

"The purser says we're to take on wood in an hour," Aurand said. "Figure that'll give us time to scare up a campfire. I packed some side pork and eggs from the mercantile. I'll bring you something then."

"Good, 'cause I'm starved enough I could eat a horse."

Aurand snapped his fingers. "That's what

I need to check on."

By the time Aurand left the room, Simon Cady was gone from the railing. Aurand started aft of the boiler when the loud bell on the wheelhouse clanged. A deckhand ran to a long pole along the railing and thrust it into the water. When it hit bottom he yelled to the captain, "Three fathoms stern" and replaced the pole in its holder.

"I'm looking for my deputy, Con Leigh."

The deckhand, a young man in his teens with a pockmarked face and one eye cocked to the side like he'd been slapped once too often, shook his head. "Don't know him, Mister. Ask the first mate."

Aurand walked to the stout, balding man clutching a pair of hog chains. "Looking for a deputy of mine — Con Leigh. Twenty, I think. Brown hair. Wiry."

"He was tending those horses of yourn," the first mate said. "But that was an hour ago."

Aurand walked down to the cargo hatch, where their horses were tied to rings in the ceiling. "You down there, Con?"

"I'm over here."

Aurand descended the narrow stairs to the cargo hold, the odor of wet feed and fresh horse dung pungent. It took several minutes for his eyes to adjust to the dark.

When they did, he spotted Con lying atop bales of straw in a horse stall. His sweat-stained hat ringed the end of a pitchfork handle stuck in a bale beside him. Their horses had been loaded by a roustabout, and Aurand didn't like the arrangement. Each stall contained two horses packed tighter than he liked. But at least he and his deputies weren't alone, as the roustabout had stuffed a donkey in with a large chestnut gelding in a stall next to theirs. A horse hung its head over the stall to sniff Aurand, the white blaze looking like it winked at him. "Any sign of Red?"

"Not yet." Con reached inside his shirt and came away with a small pouch. He opened the drawstring and began building a smoke. "We won't see him, either, unless he wants us to. But you can bet he has Tucker's direction pretty well worked out by now."

"I don't think I'd do that."

"Do what?" Con asked.

"Light that smoke while you're sitting on bales of straw."

"Good point," Con said and stowed his tobacco pouch away. He stood and put his hat on. "You always been scared of him?"

"Who?"

"Tucker Ashley," Con answered.

"I'm not afraid of him."

"Oh?" Con cocked his head as he looked at Aurand. "If I was a betting man, I'd say you're frightened to death of the prospect of facing Tucker Ashley out here. In the open, where he's got the advantage."

Aurand felt rage rise within him. Connie, or, as he demanded to be called, Con, worked on and off for Aurand as a deputy when Aurand needed an extra gun hand. The young man had made it his mission to get into as many gun fights as he could in his short twenty years. And he'd always come out the winner. "I have half a notion —"

"Make sure it's just half a notion." Con grinned.

Aurand looked coldly at the smaller man and breathed deeply to still his anger. Aurand was a match for anyone in the territory, either with six-guns or rifles at long range. But even he was no match for Con Leigh. And the latter was the only man who derived more pleasure in killing than even Philo Brown or Jess Hammond. As eighteen men could attest to, if they weren't dead and buried by Con's gun.

At last Con's wide smile broke the tension. "Relax. I was just breaking the monotony. I got no beef with you, as long as I collect my pay. I just want you to know that I

115

know — everyone gets scared now and again." He walked to Aurand and laid his hand on his shoulder. "And when the time comes, I'll go against Ashley for you."

Aurand slapped his hand away. "The hell you will! I've waited five years for a chance at Tucker Ashley, and I damned sure ain't going to have anyone take that from me."

Con backed away. "All right, Boss. He's yours. But" — a dreamy look came over his ruddy face — "it would look good for the man who killed someone like Tucker Ashley."

Aurand became aware that his hands shook. Just thinking and talking of fighting Tucker, he had become scared. For the first time, he even admitted it to himself. But his hatred would overcome his fear when the time came, and the memories of Tucker beating him nearly to death at Ft. Laramie five years ago would make up for his fear. It didn't even matter that, in killing Tucker, Aurand's reputation would grow into legend. He just wanted Tucker in his sights.

Aurand started out of the cargo hold for fresh air when he paused. That he wanted Tucker in front of him was a certainty. His death would make Aurand's life complete. But what — just what — would happen if Tucker's ride into Lakota country brought about his death at the hands of the Sioux? For Aurand that was the worst scenario, and he prayed the Indians would not find Tucker before he did.

CHAPTER 12

"Kick me in the butt if I ever let my guard down like this again." Tucker studied the hill just above where they stood beside their mounts. "You able to move real fast-like if you got a need?"

"Just give the word," Jack answered, "and I'll move quick, shaking knees and all."

"You got your Henry ready?"

"It's on this side of the saddle. Your rifle?"

Tucker looked at the Sharps in the scabbard hanging off the far side of the mule, thinking it might as well be in the next territory. "If I reach for it, the shooting will be over before I can get to it. We'll have to make do."

"Making do is when you substitute an ingredient for another in your corn bread recipe." Jack's voice broke. "I hope your plan is more than just make do."

"Me, too." Tucker gauged how far he thought the men were up the hill. "I can just make out some black hair blowing through that main clump of junipers. I figure at least one of them's there." Tucker eased his pistol out of the holster. "When I yell, you dive for cover and start slinging lead up there."

"When?"

"Now!" Tucker slapped Ben's rump and dove for the cover of a shallow impression in the ground. A split second later Jack slapped his pony as a bullet hit the saddle and glanced off. Tucker frantically searched the ground above them and saw the puff of smoke halfway up the hillside behind the junipers. "Sixty yards'd be my guess," he shouted at Jack, who had fired four quick shots before ducking back behind a dead cottonwood. Another shot kicked up dirt in front of Tucker, sending grass and dirt into his eyes. "Behind that big juniper."

"I see it," Jack yelled back. "But I can't see the shooters."

"They're there. Just shoot into the bushes as quick as you can."

Jack fired three rounds uphill, giving Tucker barely enough time to study the terrain. Thirty yards to one side of the attackers ran a shallow arroyo, dried hard in the hot season, making a trench deep enough to conceal a crawling man. "Give me some cover on three . . . two . . . one . . ." Tucker sprang for the arroyo as Jack fired three more quick shots. Tucker hit the ground and landed onto a cactus. He stifled a scream of pain as he lay on his back breathing hard. He expected shots to come his way, but none did.

By Tucker's calculation, Jack had four rounds left before he needed to reload, and he waited until Jack fired again before sticking his head up out of the gully. If he made it to the top undetected, he would be within thirty yards of the shooters. Thirty yards was on the long side for a horse pistol. But Tucker carried a Remington, with its stiff top strap, for the accuracy it provided. And he was different from the fast-draw artists he'd met, like Aurand, who seemed to beg to get their names etched on a boot-hill marker. He had taken running game farther than this. Still, he did not know how many men waited for him topside.

The steady rhythm of firing from the shooters on the hill intensified. Slugs bore deep furrows in the ground in front of Jack, quick shots, from what sounded like a Henry, and a Spencer rifle.

Tucker suddenly became aware that Jack's rifle was silent: he was out of ammunition, and the only other rifle rounds Jack had were in his saddlebags on his pony somewhere over the next hill.

Tucker chanced a quick peek over the depression. Two Indians, one on each side of the junipers, fired from the safety of the thick bushes. Jack was pinned down, with only his Colt to wing rounds their way. Soon they would realize Jack was under-gunned, and they would start moving laterally to get a bead on him. Jack moved some yards from the cottonwood trunk and fired wildly at the attackers. His bullets hit the dirt harmlessly ten yards in front of the Indians.

Tucker took another calming breath before crawling up the arroyo. The cactus spines drove deep into his legs, and he forced himself to concentrate on stealth. He kept his head down, instead trusting his ears to tell him how far he'd crawled and where the Indians were in relation to his position.

Silence.

Tucker chanced another peek over the gully. They had stopped firing. So had Jack, and Tucker knew he was out of ammunition for his pistol as well.

The Indians stood. They shouldered their rifles as they started down the hillside. Tucker imagined the thoughts going through Jack's mind as he drew his knife. Somehow, Tucker didn't believe the Indians would get close enough to let Jack use it.

The two — one older warrior and another who could be his son — advanced down the hill with bad intentions and smiles on their faces. Jack gathered his legs beneath him as they approached. Tucker leaned out of the arroyo and braced his hand against the ground. At twenty yards from Jack, they stopped and talked amongst themselves. As if they'd forgotten about Tucker.

He estimated they were thirty yards from where he lay, and he lined his Remington's crude sights on the chest of the farther Indian. Tucker let out his breath and took up slack on the trigger as both attackers raised their rifles toward where Jack crouched.

Tucker's first shot caught the young brave high chest, the .44 slug drilling through him. He looked down at the bloody hole a moment before he dropped to his knees, dead before he hit the ground.

The old Indian jerked his head around, trying to find his attacker, when his gaze locked onto Tucker. The Indian swung his rifle in a wide arc toward the gully.

Tucker snapped a shot. His round grazed the warrior's shoulder. The old man's legs buckled, and, by the time he'd recovered, Tucker had ducked back into the safety of the arroyo.

The old man shot four quick times, each shot kicking up dirt where Tucker had been a moment before. When he popped up ten yards farther along the gully, Tucker took just enough time to find his sights. He fired two quick shots, the bullets appearing as twin bloody holes in the old man's chest. The Indian tried feebly to operate the lever of his Henry as he dropped onto his back. Tucker stood and hobbled toward the old man. He kicked the rifle away as Jack ran up the hill. When he saw the Indian was helpless, he sheathed his Bowie.

Tucker knelt beside the dying man. "*Ta'ku en'icyapi he?* What is your name?"

The old man tried to focus on Tucker through eyes glazing over.

"What is this warrior's name so all will know he died a brave Lakota?" Jack asked again.

"Paints His Horses," the old man sputtered between gasps.

"I know this name," Tucker said.

Frothy blood smeared the Indian's lips.

"The woman?" Tucker asked. "Has Blue Boy hurt her?"

Paints His Horses began to speak when his death gurgles intensified. He coughed blood over Tucker's hand and forearm before going limp. Tucker closed the old man's eyes. For whatever reason he had attacked them, the man had died like a warrior. "The Sioux believe that, when a man dies, his *sicun,* his guardian spirit, escorts him along the *Wanagi Takanku.*"

Jack nodded. "The Spirit Road. I hope I die as bravely as this man."

"I hope I don't find out any time soon," Tucker said. "Get the other one's gun."

Tucker grabbed the old man's Henry and rooted through his pockets. He found five more shells and stuffed them in his trousers.

"You knew this Indian?" Jack asked. He smashed the young warrior's rifle against a rock.

"I know the name." Tucker sat on a rock and grabbed his knife. "He scouted for General Welch up in Ft. McKeen years back 'fore he went renegade with Blue Boy."

"Good warrior?"

Tucker winced as he pulled the first cactus spine from his leg. "Blue Boy picks only the best."

"Just not good enough today," Jack said.

Tucker walked uphill past the young warrior, whose blood soaked up the prairie, to the Indians' ponies hobbled just on the other side of the rise. Tucker approached the first horse, a paint not thirteen hands high. He spoke softly as he approached the animal, running his hand along its lathered neck. He felt the horse's stunted but powerful hind legs as he squatted beside it. He picked up a piece of dung from the ground and crushed it between his thumb and finger. He handed it to Jack.

"Bindweed."

Tucker nodded. The horse's dropping showed the undigested white petals from the twining plant. "Eagle's Nest Creek?"

" 'Bout the only place this time of year with enough moisture to grow it," Jack said. "The Indian ponies live off the stuff. If most horses eat this, it'd drive them crazy."

"Not ours," Tucker said, untying the hobble and swinging a leg over the pony. "Your paint and my mule can eat damned near everything. Speaking of which, unless you throw a leg over that government mount and help me catch my mule and your horse, we're sentenced to ride these two critters for God knows how long."

"Don't you want to bury them?"

Tucker looked at the dead men. He did want to bury them. But he wanted to find Lorna alive and well even more. They hadn't the time to give their enemies a burial. Still, the two men took a moment to lay them in the arroyo Tucker had hidden in and covered them with rocks.

Before he swung a leg over the paint, Tucker debated whether or not to take the old man's Henry and thought not. Tucker had a scabbard for his Sharps, and lugging another rifle around would slow them down even more. He flung the rifle hard, and it landed in the mud of the Bad River. He handed Jack the rifle rounds he'd taken off the old man.

They rode in the direction their horses had run when the shooting started. They would capture them and turn the Indians' mounts loose. They would find their way back to Blue Boy, and he would know his warriors were dead. Tucker counted on Blue Boy's hatred of white men to stop their ride to the Wall long enough to avenge their deaths.

If he and Jack didn't rescue Lorna by the time Blue Boy reached the Badlands, they'd never rescue her.

CHAPTER 13

That night as the sun set over the rough river bluffs, the boat ran aground onto an enormous sandbar. Merriman shouted frantic orders to the first mate, who ran around yelling orders at roustabouts and deckhands. Aurand watched all this with detached interest. In this little trip downriver, it was the closest thing to entertainment they had to break the monotony.

The first mate bolted past passengers watching the spectacle from the main deck. The rooster Aurand talked with yesterday worked furiously on the derrick connecting the capstan engine to the cables. The first mate ran behind the rooster. He slapped him hard on the head and dragged him along to the engine room. Philo rubbed his bloodshot eyes and joined Aurand on deck. "What's going on?"

"Grounded. Looks like we're going to grasshopper off the sandbar." He pinched his nose and moved upwind of Philo. "Any sign of Red?"

"None."

"Where can he be?"

"How should I know?" Philo said.

Aurand faced him. "You ought to. You've tracked with him more than anyone else."

Philo waved the air. "He'll be along. Red don't come out unless he feels like it."

"Well, he better be feeling like it soon. By the looks of this mess, we might need him sooner than later."

Simon Cady strolled along the desk. He had replaced his buckskins with dungarees and a long-sleeve flannel shirt to stave off the mosquitoes. He grinned as he approached Philo and Aurand.

"Get in my room and tell Jess to stay out of sight," Aurand whispered to Philo. A brief look of terror crossed the fat man's face as he passed Cady on the deck.

"Looks like we got us a little delay, Marshal."

"What do you want, Cady?"

"Want?" He dipped his pipe into a muslin tobacco pouch as he looked down at the sandbar. "Why, nothing. I want nothing. I'm just here watching the show, same as you." He drew his first puff and blew it out slowly.

The smoke hung over him in the windless air.

The rooster stoked the nigger engine with wood and tossed in a handful of lit tinder. The engine coughed to life once, then twice, before the wood caught and the engine belched nosily, nearly drowning out their words. "Looks like we'll both be delayed by this."

"How so?"

Cady drew in a deep puff of tobacco. "I need to get to Yankton, maybe farther south to find the little missing lady, and you got to off-load at Crow Creek."

Aurand looked at him and frowned. "Who said we're off-loading at Crow Creek?"

Cady smiled. "Word gets around when a manhunt is underway."

"Like I said, Cady, stay the hell out of my way."

"Yankton is as far out of your way as I can imagine."

Another roustabout joined the deckhand as they swung the long spars over the side of the boat and held them tight. The mate operated the derrick, and the cables slowly lowered the long poles into the sandbar. The small engine groaned and slowed, but the spars began inching the boat through the sandbar towards free water thirty yards down river.

Aurand caught the reflection of something on the bank, and he strained to see. At first he saw only scrub trees situated back of the river bank. Then Red Sun stepped from the tree line holding his roan mare, her white socks contrasting with the brown trees. He faded back into the trees, and Aurand turned to see if Simon Cady had spotted Red. But Cady had left as quietly as any Indian shadow.

After the *Belle of the Ball* was freed from the sandbar, Captain Merriman pointed the boat's bow into the river for the night. He came to each passenger and reported that the pitman connecting the paddle wheel to the crank had bent during the grounding. "The engineer will be making repairs during the night," he told Aurand. "Between the banging on the pitman and the noise the fireman's going to make cleaning the river's crud from the boilers, my suggestion is that you and your deputies sleep ashore tonight."

Aurand gathered his bedroll and led Con and Philo down the plank that had been dropped on shore.

"What the hell about me?" Jess said when Aurand told him he needed to stay in the room aboard the boat. "Why do I need to keep cooped up in here?"

"Because Simon Cady is still here."

"I told you, he's not here for me. I didn't do anything . . ."

"You want to take that chance? Another day and we'll be at Crow Creek."

"Maybe I ought to just sneak up on that SOB . . ." Jess drew his finger across his throat. Jess was a dangerous man in his own right. Aurand had seen him fight three soldiers at once, crippling two and sending the other one to a government grave. Yet Simon Cady was no soldier. He'd lived a lifetime of scouting and bounty hunting dangerous men by being even more dangerous himself. And cautious. Jess would have a hard time putting the sneak on Cady.

Con disappeared into the darkness while Philo gathered wood for a fire. Twenty minutes into situating their bedrolls, two shots echoed from somewhere off in the distance. And another twenty minutes later, Con returned to their campfire dangling two sage hens beside his leg. He tossed them at Philo's feet.

"What you want me to do with these?"

"Dress them," Con answered.

"Think I'm some camp cook?"

Con grinned. "With that belly of yours, I figured you did more than your share of cooking. Now get to it if you want to eat tonight."

Philo dressed the birds and stuck them on a skewer over the fire while Con cleaned his Colt. Out into the darkness, tiny campfires flickered from a dozen other passengers sleeping off the boat for the night.

Aurand bent to feel the doneness of the birds. When he looked back up, Red Sun stood at the periphery of their fire. Aurand drew his gun as suddenly as a drowning man draws a frantic breath before going under. "You ought to give a man some warning." Aurand holstered his gun.

Red walked into the full light of the fire. His Spencer rested lightly over his shoulder, and he squatted by the flames. He laid his rifle across his knees as he warmed his hands over the glowing embers. "I start by giving you warning, maybe the next man I meet I also give a warning to. And the next. Before long, I warn everyone I come across. And just maybe one of those men decides to kill me. Then you're out the best tracker in the territory."

Aurand nodded. The man's logic was flawless. Men like Red Sun — and Simon Cady — lived as long as they did by trusting no one. "Tell me where Tucker is."

Red took his belt knife and sliced a wing off one bird before sitting back on a washed-up oak log. He nibbled the meat as he withdrew a weathered map from inside his flannel shirt. "Your men went this-away . . ."

"Men?"

Red nodded. "Tucker's travelling with another. My guess is it's Jack Worman. 'Bout the only friend he has in these parts." He spread the map out and began tracing a line on the cloth by the light of the fire.

"You two get over here," Aurand commanded, and Con and Philo approached the map.

Red pointed to the rough terrain of the river bluffs west of town. "From there, Tucker and Jack began following the Bad River. Little water this time of year. Rough going for them." He finished off the wing and eyed the bird for another. "They took the hard way, but not by choice. They had to go that way."

Philo leaned over and studied the map. "You saying they went that way to make it hard for us to follow them?"

"No," Red answered. "They had to go that route because they follow Indians."

"Indians?" Philo said. "No one said anything about Indians."

"Shut up," Aurand ordered and turned back to Red. "What Indians?"

"Lakota," Red explained. "Miniconjou. Maybe one is an Oglala."

"How many?"

Red held up his hands. "Seven ponies. But they travel slow. Too slow."

"Passing through?"

Red shrugged. "Who knows? I think they think no white man will follow them. But Tucker and his friend do."

"Why?"

Red shrugged again. "You are the lawman. You tell me."

Philo plucked a bird from the fire and sliced into the breast. "Where do you think they're headed?"

"Here," Red pointed to the map with his knife. "The Badlands. They crossed the Bad River yesterday. I am certain the Lakota head for the safety of the Great Wall."

"You think we can get ahead of them?"

Red nodded. "By following the White River, we will have easier going and more water for the horses. We will have easier and faster travelling. Maybe too easy."

"Too easy?" Philo said.

Red tossed his stripped wing bone over his shoulder. "Maybe you ought to have

134

second thoughts about finding this Tucker Ashley. I have heard stories of him from the soldiers. He is not like the deserters we have hunted."

"Nonsense," Con said. "He can be taken like any other man."

Red grinned at Con and turned his back on him. "The scouts at Ft. Sully talk of this Ashley as if he were a ghost. A very dangerous ghost."

"And so am I," Aurand answered coldly. He stood and started for his bedroll. "You guys turn in, too. No telling when that crazy Merriman will get under way again. We damn sure don't want to be left behind."

Aurand spread his bedroll away from the light of the fire beside a tree stump and looked at the stars in the west. Tucker was out there somewhere: out in country where Aurand and his deputies would be hard pressed to follow him. They were suited to tracking green deserters and drunks who stuck to known trails and easy going in their escapes. He had heard of the ruggedness of the Badlands and that route Tucker took, of the hostilities and dangers waiting around every bend of the dried river beds. But Red Sun believed they had a good chance using the southern route to get ahead of Tucker and Jack.

And thanks to the *Belle of the Ball,* they'd get that jump on them. "Good luck, Tuck," Aurand said to himself. "Don't let those Lakota get you, ol' friend. I want you lively when I catch you."

CHAPTER 14

The sun beat down on the parched earth, while the constant west wind dried everything the sun missed. Tucker's mule picked its weary, plodding way among the cactus scattered along the dry banks of the Bad River. His eyes followed the thin rivulet of water as it struggled to reach the Missouri. Another year, and things might be different. Tucker and Bob Mallet had been caught in a flash flood in this canyon in the summer of 'sixty-six. Tucker had managed to hang on to a huge, drifting oak until he reached the safety of the bank. Bob hadn't been so lucky, and Tucker never saw him alive again.

The following year, while scouting for the army a mile down river, he'd come upon a skeleton, yellowed, not yet sun-bleached white. The bones had been picked clean by coyotes and cougars and hawks, and Tucker had imagined the size of the man when he'd lived. He concluded the bones were those of Bob Mallet, and he took precious time to bury Bob reverently.

Tucker looked skyward at turkey vultures circling overhead. He took off his hat, but no sweat remained inside the band, as if his head itself were rationing water. There was no danger of a flash flood now. But Tucker would have preferred one to the insanely intense heat, with the only relief the icy cold nights when the sun abandoned them.

Jack rode down the hill to the creek bank and stopped beside Tucker. He shielded his eyes as he scanned the ground ahead. "Wish that pool up ahead were real." Jack grinned through parched lips that were cracked and bleeding. "I'd jump off my cayuse and get me some swimming in. Damned mirage."

Tucker had seen the mirage, too. A half mile down the dry rock valley, Dead Eagle Creek stood shallow and stagnant. Yet Tucker knew the small pond in the shadow of the creek to be fed by an underground spring, its inviting waters cool and sweet, untouched by the filth of Dead Eagle Creek. Even from here, Tucker saw the steep walls that surrounded the pool shading the valley from the sun, slowing evaporation of the precious water.

"What kind of mirage shows trees?" Jack said.

Tucker slapped him on the back. "None. That's no mirage. That's where we're headed."

"No mirage?"

"You think those Lakota would lead us into a mirage? Even they wouldn't do that."

Jack threw his hat high into the air. He tilted his head back and hollered while he put the boots to his paint. The animal bolted, as if knowing water lay just ahead. Jack raced toward the pond, slapping the reins on his horse's neck.

Tucker smiled and bent to pick up Jack's hat. He dropped the reins and let Ben meander toward the pond at his own pace. The mule never got excited, even now, when water was so close. By the time Tucker reached the shallow pool, Jack had plunged into the shale-shielded spring. The yellow and red mudstone colored the water an off-crimson that contrasted with Jack's wet, calico shirt. But the water was good water, and Jack stood knee deep in the pond, yelling, waving Tucker in.

He started toward the pond when he paused and looked about. They had come upon it too easily. The Lakota could have led them a long way away from the pond, yet they'd made no effort to. He concluded the ponies of the two dead Indians hadn't yet reached Blue Boy. For all he knew, his warriors had successfully left Tucker and Jack scalped meals for the vultures.

Then Tucker saw the first tracks beneath where Jack had ridden headlong a moment ago — hoof prints of unshod ponies. And another, a large horse that made deeper impressions in the caked dirt. Tucker wondered about the tracks as he continued examining the sign, looking into the sun, picking up shadows the Indian ponies had made. He dismounted and studied them; they had been made sometime this morning. He and Jack were gaining on Blue Boy.

Tucker stood to leave when a mound of tiny lead balls caught his eye. He scooped them up before joining Jack at the pond.

"Jump on in!" Jack splashed water over his parched face.

"Might just do that." Tucker led the mule toward where Jack had hastily tied his horse to a large rock close to the pond. Ben dipped his muzzle into the water, oblivious to the crazy man in the middle of the pool whooping it up.

Tucker sat on an outcropping of rusty-red sandstone sparkling with fool's gold and took off his socks and boots. He wiggled his toes, relishing the relief his bare feet offered. He walked gingerly toward the pond and stepped around a clump of beggar's tick. He sat on the edge of the pool and dipped his feet in the cool water. For a moment, he forgot about this last day with no more than a canteen of water between him and Ben.

Tucker dipped his hat in the cool water and put it on. Rivulets of water felt unnaturally good running down his dirty face and sunburned neck. He soaked his feet while Jack dove under the water. He came out clutching a bulrush in his mouth.

"I'm not impressed," Tucker said. "Now if you come out of there with some water parsnips, then we got the start of a supper."

Jack disappeared into the water again. When he came up, he clutched four large parsnips that looked inviting.

"You start the fire." Tucker reached for his boots. "I'm going to bag us a rabbit."

Tucker found no rabbits, but he did find a scrawny porcupine waddling out of a stand of prairie dog weed. He returned to where Jack tended a fire and tossed the animal to him. Jack jumped back away from the hide of spines. "I started the fire. Least you can do is dress that out."

Tucker watched the nearly smokeless fire, small enough that the Indians wouldn't spot it; just large enough to cook a porcupine.

141

He sat by the fire and peeled parsnips with his Barlow knife while Jack carefully skinned the critter. "Way those tracks look, we're getting closer." He pricked himself with a quill and sucked blood from his finger. "Think those Indians' ponies made it back to Blue Boy yet?"

"I figure that's why it's been so easy for us to follow them these last days," Tucker answered. "Blue Boy still doesn't realize his braves failed. It's just a matter of time before those horses make their way back to Blue Boy's camp. I'm counting on it to make him come after us. And Lorna with him."

"Then we can get a look at Blue Boy in the flesh."

Jack tossed the porcupine's innards away from the fire and cut holes in the critter's shoulders and back legs. "Way I figure it, the next ambush won't be with Blue Boy" — he threaded a stick through the critter's legs — "any more than the last one was. We won't see him until his warriors are all dead and he's got to come after us himself."

Tucker walked to the pool's edge and scooped water into his pan. He set it on the rocks skirting the fire and dropped the cut parsnips into the water to boil. "Blue Boy needs to get Lorna to the Badlands. If he reaches it, he knows we'll never find them. Even if we manage to kill every warrior he sends after us, he knows it'll slow us enough that he'll likely make it to the Wall with her."

"If she's alive," Jack said. "We haven't found any strips of her dress for a day."

"She's alive," Tucker said. He reached in his vest pocket. He took out the small lead beads he spotted earlier and handed them to Jack.

"Lead shot. Where did you get these?"

Tucker motioned to where he had found them in a neat mound between some rocks in the trail. "Lorna left this, knowing it was as much out of the ordinary as her dress was, and we'd spot it."

"Where'd she get lead shot?"

Tucker clamped his hand on Jack's shoulder. "You visit that dancer whenever you're in town, as I recall."

"Is there a point to this?" Jack's face had begun to flush, but Tucker wasn't through embarrassing him just yet.

"Ever take her outside? Maybe for a stroll or to supper?"

"Now and again," Jack answered warily.

"And what does she wear?"

"That's kind of personal . . ."

"A dress by any chance?"

"Of course she wears a dress." Jack tested

the porcupine's doneness with his knife.

"And when the wind blows, does her dress blow up with it?"

"That's kinda' personal . . ."

"Does it?"

"No. It stays down. Just what *are* you getting at, besides nosing into my romance?"

Tucker slapped Jack's hand, and the shot spilled onto the ground. "Ladies' dresses don't blow up in our damnable wind because they sew lead shot in the hems to weight the material down. Lorna hasn't left any of her dress for us to spot since yesterday. My guess is Blue Boy found she was tearing strips and took her dress from her. But somehow she managed to rip the hem out and keep the lead shot hidden until she could leave some for us."

"So she has to be alive."

Tucker nodded. "For now at least."

That night, to the calls of a coyote somewhere on the prairie, Tucker and Jack prepared to hit the Indians' trail. He broke the grouse egg he'd found and dropped it into the boiling pot to settle the coffee grounds before pouring them each a cup.

"Got some of that molasses?" Tucker asked.

Jack fished into his saddlebag and came

away with a small jar of the sweet liquid. He tossed it to Tucker. "My coffee that bad?"

Tucker laughed. "Your coffee is always that bad. But right now, we need it stout like this if it's going to keep us awake." He looked over at Ben hobbled beside Jack's paint by the edge of the pond. They had decided Lorna could not afford for them to get more than a few hours' sleep. They needed to strike the camp while the full moon allowed them enough light to pick up sign. Still, just a few moments more . . .

"Think Aurand's on our trail?"

To Tucker's surprise, he poured another cup of Jack's coffee. "I'm sure of it. But if he's counting on that fat ass Philo Brown to cut our sign, we're home free."

Jack scrunched his nose up and tossed the rest of his coffee out. "I hear a *but* in there somewhere."

Tucker forced himself to look away from the glow of the coals. He'd soon need his night vision. "But if he's got Red Sun tracking for him, that changes things."

"I thought he was scouting for the 7th Cavalry?"

"He was, until Aurand managed to swing the territorial government into paying Red twice what the army did. Now I hear Red's running deserters to ground with Philo Brown."

"Then they *are* somewhere along our back trail." Jack whistled. "Think we can handle Aurand and Philo and Red?"

"Forget about Red — he doesn't fight them; he just finds them for Aurand." Tucker slipped on his socks and tugged his boots on by their mule ears. "Philo's dangerous in his own right but only when your back is turned. Now Aurand's a different matter. The man is pure poison-mean."

"I remember you telling me about that Indian family he killed down at Ft. Laramie."

Off in the night the coyote howled again. Close. As long as it was nearby, the Lakota weren't. And neither was Aurand. "When he was mustered out of the army in Ft. Laramie, he hung around Cheyenne. Got involved in the Vigilance Committee in 'sixty-eight to deal with the rowdies down there. Aurand bragged how he personally slapped the rump of Shorty Burn's horse and left Shorty doing the dangle of death from a telegraph pole. They killed seven or eight men in a few months, before people got fed up and put the run on them. I always thought Aurand got a taste of murdering during the war with Bill Anderson and his bushwhackers that stayed with him. How the hell he wrangled himself into a territorial deputy marshal job is beyond me."

"But you can take him if you need to, right?"

Ever since he beat Aurand that day he killed the Indian family, Tucker looked over his shoulder for him. But he didn't have to; Aurand would never shoot him in the back. He would prefer killing Tucker up close, so the last thing he saw was Aurand's smile. "Some say I'm as good as Aurand, but I know I'm not. He's faster by just enough to make the difference. But that kid who deputies now and again — Con Leigh — he's faster by far than either of us."

"Eighteen men is what folks say he killed," Jack said. "And not a back-shot in the bunch. Con faced them all."

"You mean men he goaded into a gun fight. But, with any luck, we'll come onto Lorna before they find us, and we won't have to find out just how fast he is."

They stared into the dying fire until Tucker finally stood. "You ready?"

Jack sighed and looked lovingly at the pool, the last fresh water they'd find for some time. "I'm ready, but then, I'm a mite younger than you."

"Don't let these old bones fool you,"

Tucker said as he untied the hobble on Ben's legs. "If need be — like when some Lakota are running down our throats or Aurand's nipping at our backsides — I can ride mighty fast."

Tucker led the way, looking into the moonlight for any contrast that revealed sign. The tracks were easy to follow, with the Indians making no effort to hide them. And two miles from the pond where they'd just drunk and caught some sleep, the tracks faded into nothingness, as if the Lakota's *Wakan Tanka* itself had plucked the band of renegades from the hard-packed earth.

"Problem?" Jack asked. He dismounted and walked to where Tucker squatted on his heels eying the ground.

"Blue Boy's become mighty secretive all of a sudden," Tucker answered. "Like he knows we're right behind him."

"Their ponies must have found them."

"That's my thinking." Tucker stood and grabbed a small miner's headlamp from his saddlebag. He lit the kerosene wick and walked hunched over, looking in a semicircle of light to where he saw the last tracks. He gauged the length of the ponies' strides, then looked ahead as he visualized where they would turn up next. "Go out a hundred yards and see if you can cut sign," Tucker said. He handed Jack the headlamp and pointed southwest. "Over thataway."

While Jack worked far, Tucker led Ben close in a semicircle, keeping low to the ground where moonlight would cast shadows. If Blue Boy had left anything to see.

Jack zigzagged ahead of Tucker, the light barely visible the farther Jack worked away from him. When he was a hundred yards out, Tucker shouted at him. Jack moved the headlamp in a lazy arc.

Tucker led the mule to where Jack stood in a field of dried bluestem grass. "Here," he said when Tucker had dismounted. He held a broken branch from a scrub bush. The branch had been cut, not broken. The green bark had turned brown. But the fresh bark toward the end of the branch had been abraded to white meat where the Indians had dragged the branch over their tracks.

Something fluttered twenty yards farther in the moonlight, and Tucker drew his gun. He let Ben's reins drop as he advanced toward the movement. A tiny corner of gingham material — Lorna's dress — stuck out of the dirt where it had been buried. Perhaps with her in it.

Tucker fought the urge to dig into the earth, instead taking the headlamp and studying the ground. A single moccasin print — half again as long and wide as Tucker's boot print — had been left beside the fresh dig on purpose. Blue Boy's.

Tucker could no longer contain himself. He dropped to his knees and began scooping dirt away with his hands. He expected the worst, but when he reached the bottom of a shallow trench, all that greeted him was Lorna's dress. He pulled on it and jerked it free.

Tucker stood and held the dress close, as if Lorna herself were there. He turned the dress over in his hands. Tiny blood spatters, dried days ago, spotted the bottom of the hem where it had been ripped out, probably when she tore at the fabric to get to the lead shot.

"Think Blue Boy had his way with her?" Jack asked. "If she's not wearing her dress, then no telling . . ."

"Blue Boy could have had her long before now if he wanted. Besides, Blue Boy's a Lakota. And Lakota braves are gentlemen in their own right. He might slit Lorna's throat if she showed him disrespect, but he would never force himself on her."

"Then why bury the dress here? As a warning perhaps?"

"Or as a way in which to ensure we follow

him." Tucker looked about in the night and put his hand over the headlamp reflector. "And, if that's the case, that ambush we talked about could be just around the next bend in the Bad."

CHAPTER 15

Lorna let loose of the pony's mane and scratched her shoulder under the buckskins. She took hold again when the animal dipped into a depression in the hard earth. Jimmy Swallow, riding behind her on the pony, laughed heartily. She turned her head to see his grin cross the knife scar along one cheek. "What's so funny?"

"You," he answered, with only a hint of Indian accent. "You would think this was the first time you ever sat a horse."

"This is no horse," she insisted. "This is little more than a painted mule. A real horse has a gait you can anticipate, feel its pitch and movements, so you know what it's going to do." Lorna recalled the Arabians her father raised and showed in Sioux City. Those were powerful animals, graceful, elegant, able to outdistance other horses in the surrounding counties. Lorna had been reared atop such horses. Those had been fanciful times that she yearned to return to right now: times filled with social functions, flirting, and finding fault with every eligible suitor the colonel thrust her way. And riding the Arabians across the lush grounds of their estate. As the Indian pony beneath her now loped ahead, she felt its awkward gait, the power of the animal — she was certain — to get away from the rider. The horse carrying her and Jimmy Swallow was no Arabian. But she grudgingly admitted that any of her Arabians would have died on the trail they'd ridden thus far, while this scrub pony continued tirelessly through the heat of the midday sun.

She let loose of the mane again and scratched her back, then her shoulder again before grabbing tight once more.

"Maybe you picked up some lice," Jimmy chuckled. "Or ticks."

"Neither," Lorna blurted out. "It's these clothes I have to wear. They're hot. And they're driving me crazy." She scratched some more.

"You are the one who chose to leave something for those following us," Jimmy said. "Wearing those clothes — my best buckskins — was your own doing. Besides, you will get used to them."

"Never."

153

"You have no choice." Swallow's hot breath blew over the back of her neck as he spoke. "A chief's woman cannot be seen in white woman's dress."

"I'll be no such thing." Lorna snorted. She turned just as the pony dropped into a depression, and she clutched the mane again. "If your great leader wants a woman so much, make it one of his own kind."

"He cannot." Swallow rode the pony around a deep buffalo wallow. "Blue Boy's vision was of him taking a woman to be his wife. White like his own mother."

She watched Blue Boy riding in front of them. He had taken off his shirt when the sun rose overhead, and his thick neck muscles strained as he looked about. His horse started at the bark of prairie dogs, and the Indian's forearms thickened even while he held his horse back, his muscles taut bands along his arms. His long hair flowed to just below his broad shoulders and seemed to point to his lower back. Lorna imagined what he would look like in denims and a flannel shirt, sporting a fresh haircut and wearing polished boots, taking him to one of the many dances surrounding her father's home. He would not, she concluded, be as magnificent as he was here on the prairie.

She became aware that Swallow had caught her watching Blue Boy. "Do not be ashamed." He laughed. "Most women look upon him that way."

"What way?" She tried to minimize her interest.

"The way a woman should look upon a man." He grinned. "The way you did just now."

"Nonsense." Lorna looked away and concentrated on the itching under the deerskin clothes. She so wished she had her dress instead of Swallow's clothes, which were better suited for the winter than this heat. The one who watched her constantly — the one Swallow called Wild Wind — had been told to bury her dress in the dirt. She had slipped out of it and had just managed to pull the hem apart and spill the lead shot into her handkerchief when Wild Wind approached her. She had seen his expression a dozen times, from the suitors who came around her father's estate, to the drunk cowboys and river men who came into the mercantile who hadn't visited a woman in months. Perhaps years. She told herself she would keep a watch out for this Wild Wind.

Blue Boy rode farther ahead, his head pivoting side to side, his nose testing the wind. Black Dog rode behind him, with

Wild Wind and the young warrior Pawnee Killer trailing.

The sound of approaching hooves startled Swallow, and Blue Boy jumped down from his horse. He met the two riderless horses as they ran to him. Black Dog grabbed the reins of one, while Blue Boy snatched the other's. Sweat covered the horses' lathered chests and backs, and dust caked thick on their muzzles and withers.

Black Dog ran his hand over the chest of the large army mount whose reins he held. "Hawk's."

"Yes." Swallow waited until Lorna had dismounted to hop off the mare. Wild Wind sat his horse, looking at the other ponies and at Lorna, while Pawnee Killer sat back and waited to be told what to do. If anything.

"This was Paints His Horses's mare," Blue Boy said.

"You talk as if he is dead," Lorna blurted out.

Blue Boy looked at her. His anger rose. His mighty chest muscles twitched. His face flushed the color of chokecherries, and his fists clenched and unclenched. She had only seen Blue Boy as a stoic leader of these Indians. Now she saw something else, and it frightened her.

Blue Boy handed the reins of the mare to Pawnee Killer and turned to Lorna. He seemed to be even taller as he looked down on her with controlled rage. "The men who rode those horses were good men. And now they roam the Ghost Road."

"He means they are dead," Swallow whispered in her ear.

"And you are the cause," Blue Boy gritted out between his teeth.

Lorna stepped back and ran into Wild Wind. He grinned at her and spun her back around to face Blue Boy.

"Those two warriors are as dead as if you killed them."

"Nonsense," Lorna answered, but there was no friendly face in the circle of Indians.

"The two *wasicu* who follow us killed them. That is a certainty, for these ponies would not come back here without their riders unless their riders were dead." He stepped closer, and Lorna tried stepping back. Again, Wild Wind stood close behind her. "If you had not left sign for them, they would not be able to follow. You have put us all in danger."

"Who follows?"

Blue Boy held Hawk's army horse by the head and stroked its muzzle. "Does it matter who they are? For the next time I will

157

not leave it to an old man and an impatient youngster to kill them."

Blue Boy motioned to Black Dog and Wild Wind and they stepped away from the others.

"What's happening?" Lorna asked.

Swallow chin-pointed to where the three stood talking. "Black Dog and Wild Wind will ride back the way we came. They will kill those who follow."

Blue Boy announced something in Lakota, and instantly Pawnee Killer spoke. He walked to Blue Boy and stood nose to chest, talking fast, his hands moving as if they were possessed. "Now what?"

"Pawnee Killer wants to take Wild Wind's place."

"To kill those who follow us?"

Swallow nodded.

Blue Boy spoke quietly to the young man and draped his arm around Pawnee Killer's shoulders.

"But why does he want to go?" Lorna asked.

"Pawnee Killer was stolen when just a small child from the Pawnee in a raid by some Oglala. Even though he was raised one of us, all think that he still maintains his loyalty to the Pawnee. He is a thinker, and so he argues that he has never counted coup on an enemy. He is four or five years older than me, but he has never been tested. He begs Blue Boy to allow him to go with Black Dog."

"And be killed like the other two that Blue Boy sent back?"

Jimmy Swallow's smile faded. "Black Dog has never been bested. If he departs to kill those that follow, they will die."

"Why doesn't your great leader go himself if he wants to avenge their deaths?"

"Blue Boy has other plans. Tonight he goes into Cowtown."

"I have heard of that place." Lorna scratched her neck under the deerskins. "Rough. Lawless, say some who have come into the mercantile. A place to be avoided. But why go there?"

"We need supplies. We eat coyote when we can. We drink stale water when the pools we know of have not dried up. We cannot go on much longer. We need our strength if we are to reach the safety of the Wall."

"So an Indian is just going to stroll into a white man's town and expect no one to kill him?"

Swallow grinned. "He will if he's Blue Boy."

Lorna sat with her back propped against a

large rock. Since Black Dog and Pawnee Killer left hours ago to find whoever killed the other warriors, she had sat where she could watch Wild Wind. He kept staring at her as if expecting her to summon him over. He suddenly straightened, and Lorna followed his gaze. Blue Boy emerged from the shadows, and she jumped, startled at his transformation. The low firelight flickered off his plaid shirt and dungarees. His pistol was tucked into the tops of a set of shotgun chaps, and a Bowie knife hung from his suspenders.

He stopped and turned as if modeling the white man's clothing. A white cowboy hat — a Stetson Boss of the Plains like those they had just begun selling at the mercantile — sat atop his head at a rakish angle and concealed his long braids tucked inside the hat.

She walked around Blue Boy, amazed. The hat looked like the one Tucker had just bought. Was it his? Just because the two Indian ponies came back without their owners didn't mean they weren't successful. Did Blue Boy know more than he let on? Or did Jimmy Swallow know more than he told her?

She stopped in front of him as he warmed himself by the fire. "Where did you get that hat?"

"Why do you ask?"

"There are not many like it in the territory. We have just begun selling them this summer."

"And if I say I bought it at a white man's store like the one that you used to work in? Why do you wish to know?"

"I'd say it becomes you," she lied. She suddenly became aware that she knew — just knew — Tucker Ashley, not Aurand and his band of ruffians masquerading as lawmen, was the one who followed this raiding party. Or at least she suspected it was Tucker. "How long will you be gone?"

Blue Boy looked suspiciously at Lorna. "Why do you ask?"

"I am just concerned about you, is all."

Blue Boy nodded. "I will not be long. Time enough to steal supplies from the store. And guns."

"You have guns. Why risk going yourself?" She caught Wild Wind looking at her out of the corner of his eye.

"Until Black Dog and Pawnee Killer return, we have but two guns."

Lorna had counted the guns they had. If Tucker and whoever followed with him were to attack right now, they would find Wild Wind with Blue Boy's rifle, and Jimmy Swallow with his bow and quiver of arrows to fight them off with.

"Besides," Blue Boy said, "going into the white man's town will allow me to count much coup. Our people will talk about this for many nights over winter fires."

"What then?" she asked. "Where will we go when you return?"

"To the Badlands," he answered. "Still we go to the Badlands. By the time I return, Black Dog and Pawnee Killer will have killed those who follow. And when I return, we will have provisions to get there."

"Good," Lorna lied, sinking back onto the cool dirt.

Blue Boy said it wouldn't take long to rob the store in Cowtown, but then it would not take long for her to initiate her plan. She smiled as she watched Blue Boy ride away from the camp. She kept an eye on Swallow and Wild Wind as she began secretly untying her boot laces.

CHAPTER 16

Aurand reined the grulla to a halt atop the hill overlooking the town below. From this distance, Cowtown appeared like any other dirt town that had sprung up in the middle of the prairie and that catered to cowmen and rustlers alike. In the darkness, he couldn't tell if the lights from buildings were the mercantiles or the livery or the many saloons. Certainly not a church, for the town had never met a preacher it hadn't killed or run out on a rail. Save for a small general store and livery, the town boasted half a dozen saloons, each one trying to outdo the other in wickedness and the manner in which they lifted their customers' money.

As a marshal he'd ridden this way only once, to arrest a fugitive from the army, and that had been enough for him. He knew the only folks who visited Cowtown were ranch hands and outlaws, gamblers and prostitutes. And those who loved to fight. Most of those were buried in a shallow paupers' grave in back of the town where every coyote or bobcat or wolf passing through feasted on a rotting meal.

"We going to sit here all night?" Philo asked. He swiped the back of his hand over his lips as if anticipating the whisky awaiting them. Aurand hadn't wanted to stop at Cowtown, but his deputies were trail raw and growing meaner with every passing mile. As much as he abhorred drink, Aurand knew his deputies needed a free night. They'd go down the hill, let off a little steam, and be back on the trail in the morning. Besides, they had lost Tucker's trail some miles back beside a sweet-water pond. And without Red Sun, they had no idea where Tucker was now.

"I'm needing a drink myself," Jess said

Aurand looked to Con, but the kid had already disappeared in the night.

Aurand motioned to Philo to step down. Philo handed Jess his reins and walked beside Aurand. "You're responsible." Aurand looked around Philo at Jess staring at the lights of Cowtown. "You and him go down there. Get pie-eyed and your ashes hauled. And get right back up here."

"You're not coming?"

Aurand shook his head. "Red's overdue to meet us, so I got to stay loose. When he gets here, I figure he'll tell me just where Tucker went."

Philo jerked his thumb at Jess sitting his horse. The big man smiled as he stared at the lights. "You want *me* to rein Jess in if he gets out of line?"

Aurand snatched Philo by the shirtfront stained with road sweat and dirt and pulled him closer. His breath caused Aurand to turn his head to the side. "I'm not worried about Jess. It's you that concerns me. There are boys down there that live for strangers to come riding into town just so they can plant another man in their boot hill."

"I can take care of myself . . ."

Aurand slapped Philo. Not hard, but hard enough that he knew Aurand was dead serious. "We're tracking Tucker Ashley. I need you and Jess, and we can't afford trouble right now. Get a few drinks and visit the cribs and come back here. Understood?"

Philo backed away and straightened his shirt.

"Understood?" Aurand asked again.

"All right," Philo said. "All right. But just remember, if Jess decides he wants to do something, he does it. Nothing I can do to stop it."

"You'd better," Aurand said.

"And how about the kid?" Philo asked. "I hope you don't expect me to go again'; him when he goes crazy. And you know he'll go nuts down there looking for someone to shoot it out with."

Aurand was certain Philo was right; the kid would go into Cowtown and pick a gunfight at the first chance. "No, I don't expect you to try to control Con. Just stay out of his way."

Philo mounted his horse and galloped behind Jess down the hill toward town. Within moments, the darkness had swallowed them, and all that remained was the faint noise of their horses. Soon, even that was gone, and Aurand was alone.

He tethered his horse beside a clump of grama grass and started a small fire to take the edge off the cold. He took off his hat and sat with his back against a boulder while he looked skyward to a night devoid of clouds. A full moon shone bright, yet he wondered how Red would find him in the darkness. Aurand smiled to himself; Red had found him in less light than this. And when Red appeared, he would have word on Tucker and Worman.

CHAPTER 17

Jack walked cautiously, deliberately. He held the lantern close to the ground while he kept his horse away from any sign the Indians might have left. He walked in front of Tucker, who hunched over looking into the shadows cast by the headlamp. "Stop," Tucker said. Jack stopped instantly and held the light still.

Tucker knelt and studied the ground for a moment before standing. He motioned for Jack to move the lantern right, then left. He walked to Jack and took the lantern. "Take a look-see," he said and held the headlamp close to the ground.

"They split up," Jack said.

"Looks that way." Tucker set the lantern down. "Looks to me like the main group skirted Cowtown altogether. Look here," Tucker said. He placed his foot alongside the large track and put all his weight on it. The man who made that footprint was larger and heavier even than Tucker. "Blue Boy."

"And he headed towards town." Jack sat on the ground and fished his tobacco pouch out of his vest before passing it to Tucker. "But why would some Indian chance being seen in a white man's town? Don't see him lasting more than a few moments before some drunk ventilates him."

Tucker sat cross-legged on the ground, which felt better on his backside and feet than the saddle at this stage. Their pace had been torturous since they left the freshwater pond. The Indians had left little sign, and more than once Tucker and Jack had to work their back trail to find the Indians' sign. They had tracked well into the night, switching between walking and holding the light as they deciphered the signs the Indians left. "What do you know about Blue Boy?"

Jack paused before lighting his smoke. "Light skinned. Blue eyes. Bigger'n a bear they say, and a damned sight meaner. But that's just conjecture. One thing I know from rumor is that — with the right clothes — he could pass for a white man." He nodded toward town. "But big as he is, he'd get noticed."

"Size might be to his advantage," Tucker

said as he rolled a cigarette. "A man that big rarely finds much trouble." He accepted the lucifer from Jack and lit his own smoke. "Maybe he's going down there to count coup. He'd be an even bigger legend among his people if he waltzed right through Cowtown and lived. Lakota would tell the tale around their tipis' smoke holes at night. He'd be another Red Cloud or Sitting Bull."

Jack's hands shook as he lit his cigarette. The match cast tiny shadows on his sun-cracked face. He licked lips swollen from a week under the unforgiving sun. What would have passed for smile lines were deep, gray, festering crevices of skin at the corners of Jack's eyes. He had not complained the entire time, yet Tucker knew he was suffering. "So we got to go into Cowtown after Blue Boy?"

"Not we," Tucker said. "Me. I'll have to go it alone."

"The hell you will." Jack started to stand before losing his balance and dropping back onto the ground. "You'll find more trouble than one man can handle down there looking for Blue Boy."

"I got to go alone . . ."

"I won't be able to help you if I'm not with you."

"We can't take the chance," Tucker lied.

He knew Jack was right. Cowtown averaged a killing a week during grazing season, and a shooting every night. Twice that during cattle drives. If there ever was a time Tucker needed Jack's help, it was down in the town. But he also knew Jack was in no condition for a serious fight. He needed rest, and the other Indians would be holed up waiting for Blur Boy. That would give Jack time to recoup his strength.

Tucker leaned over and patted Jack on the shoulder. "Blue Boy's band has split, and we don't know where they'll meet up again. Lorna's with the rest of the Indians, and I'll need you to find them."

Jack feebly protested, but Tucker stopped him. "You get some shuteye, and when the sun comes up, tracking them will be easier. You find out where the other Indians go, and I'll stay on Blue Boy. But don't go jumping into anything. Just find out where they are and wait for me."

After several moments, Jack nodded and watched as Tucker stood and walked to his mule. He took the canteen off the pommel and let Jack finish the last of the brackish water. He'd fill the canteen in town.

He swung on to Ben's back and rode down the hill.

■ ■ ■ ■

Tucker pointed Ben in the direction of the town and let the mule have his head while Tucker dozed. Ben picked his way through blackness partially broken by a moon peeking out of long, trailing clouds. Ben had carried Tucker so many miles, he knew Tucker's snoring and seemed to ease his gait. That's what Tucker liked about Ben, the second mule he had owned since coming to the frontier from Pennsylvania after the war. Ben could eat most anything while on the trail but never overate as horses did. He had never developed colic. And as much as Ben might crave water at the end of a long, parched stalk, he never drank to excess, never developed water founder. His small, boxy feet were the mule's secret to its surefootedness, and Tucker took advantage of that now as he caught up on his sleep.

Piano music, sharp and off-key, woke Tucker. He jerked his head off his chest and rubbed the sleep out of his eyes. A half mile distant Cowtown stood lit up like it was the Fourth of July. Except Tucker knew no one celebrated anything there unless it was successful cheating at a faro or poker game, or the celebrating of someone ventilated by another's bullet. Still, the piano music — off-key though it might be — sounded sweet to him. His mother had played the piano for the Calvary Baptist Church north of Philadelphia. As a youth, Tucker would often close his eyes while the piano music matched the singing of the well-rehearsed choir as he strained to pick out his father's baritone voice.

After Sunday service, they would join others in the park along the wild, flowing Delaware for a picnic. Mothers would knit or work on a community quilt, cackling about their hardships at home, while fathers would relate tall tales of times past they swore were true — and said so because one could never lie on the Sabbath. And sometime in the afternoons, men would sneak hip flasks from their pockets and huddle together under the guise of discussing business.

And the children. While young girls made a conspicuous effort to attract a boy's attention by playing close to them, or ruffling their frilly dresses, the boys would do their best to bump against the girls and tousle their hair before running off to the woods for fresh mischief. It was on one of these deep-woods trips that Tucker realized his fate would somehow be linked to firearms. His father had taken in a rusty single-shot Smith and Allen spur trigger at his mercantile in partial trade for a navy Colt. When the customer left the store, his father threw the rusty gun away. Young Tucker rescued it from the scrap heap and hid it under the floorboards of his room.

He'd cleaned the gun and waited until Wednesday evening, when he knew his folks attended evening services and the shop would be left to Reustas, their freeman darkie. Reustas had cast a handful of .30 caliber round balls, and the two of them had shot the gun behind the store, knocking peach cans from a board to Tucker's delight.

It was at one of the Sunday after-service picnics that Tucker and his friend Barney slipped away from the others at the park and started down the bank to the river. Tucker concealed the old pistol — cleaned and loaded — under his Sunday coat, ready for plinking. Barney skidded on the wet Pennsylvania mud and hit a large chunk of dead ash. The tree branch fell away, exposing a menacing copperhead beneath the log. Tucker was unaware he had killed the snake or that that he had even shot the tiny gun. He stood holding the smoking pistol in his trembling hand after drawing and hip-shooting the snake before it could strike Barney. Even when his father had given him a thrashing for carrying the gun, he'd been amazed at his skill. That skill would resurface later when the war broke out and he joined the Pennsylvania "Bucktails" in fighting the Confederates.

Breaking glass interrupted Cowtown's piano music, followed by a gun shot. And another. Through it all, the piano continued playing, as Tucker knew it would, for there was not a piano player this side of the Missouri brave enough to play to that crowd. There was, however, a beautiful player piano left abandoned some years before by settlers crossing the plains. A saloon owner had rescued that piano from the prairie, and it was the favorite music in the wicked town.

Tucker entered the outskirts of Cowtown and eased the thong off his gun. The saloons' lights shone bright, and yelling matched the piano music and drunks' laughter. He kept an eye on the two saloons on his left as he rode slowly past them. Across the street, a small mercantile with a livery attached to the back sat sandwiched between two more saloons. Cowtown reminded Tucker of Deadwood, without the beauty of the Black Hills surrounding it. And, like Deadwood, no lawmen had set foot inside who didn't stay for a visit at their cemetery downwind of the town. Except Aurand. He'd had *cojones* enough to run an army deserter to ground inside one of these saloons last year. Rumor filtered back to Tucker that Aurand had faced down a dozen gunnies, daring them all to be the first to draw against him. One took him up on his offer, and he'd found a permanent home in Boot Hill. The rest had stood aside as Aurand sauntered out of town with the deserter draped over his government saddle.

As Tucker rode through town, he studied the ground; it yielded nothing significant. But then he hadn't expected to see Blue Boy's tracks among all the others. He prayed he'd spot Blue Boy among the rowdies before Blue Boy spotted him.

The wind shifted, and a stench blew over him. For years herds of cattle had run through the center of town, while men visited it for the sinful offerings it provided. All those critters and men with them littered the street with their decaying waste. A line of human feces and urine could be seen a few feet away from buildings where chamber pots were tossed out every morning from cribs above the saloons. Tucker had been in Cowtown in the wet season, the filth mixing with the blood, and the rain making it nearly impossible to ride through without retching.

Ben snorted at a body lying lifeless in the street, a body large enough to be Blue Boy's, and Tucker drew in a quick breath. He had concluded that the only thing keeping Lorna alive was Blue Boy's interest in her. With him dead, Lorna might not live to see another sunrise.

Tucker dismounted and walked Ben along the street, looking around the saloons, the windows, the shadows big enough to hide a bushwhacker. Except for horses tied to hitching rails, the street was empty, the saloons packed with cowhands whooping it up. And always the piano music that never ceased, the beat matching Tucker's thumping heart as he approached the dead man.

He looked around a final time, and squatted next to the body. Ben snorted his displeasure, and Tucker held the reins tight. He hooked the toe of his boot under the dead man and rolled him over. He sighed with relief; the man wasn't Blue Boy — fortunate for Lorna, unfortunate for the *vaquero* with the single hole in his forehead, just one of the many men visiting Cowtown too slow or too drunk to prevent his own death. His pockets had been butterflied and his gun belt stripped. The boots were ripped up the sides, so they had been left.

Tucker coaxed the mule to the first saloon and tied him at the hitching rail between a mustang fighting his reins and a large dun gelding with a wild look to him. As he skirted the broken glass in front of Pearl's Saloon, Tucker knew he had little to go on. He had never seen Blue Boy, and, if Jack were right, Blue Boy looked like every other white man in the territory. Except he was unusually large, and that was what Tucker had in his favor; he'd look for the biggest man he saw and hope to hit pay dirt.

He paused at the open doors and surveyed the saloon. Trail hands stood shoulder-to-shoulder the length of a long mahogany bar, nicks and gouges and other marks of combat forever etched in it.

Somewhere to the back of the salon a woman's voice crooned off-key to the beat of a brassy clavichord. Tucker strained to see through the smoke until he spotted the girl singing behind a cage suspended over the floor. Two guards sat cradling Greener doubles on either side of her to make sure she made the next show without being kidnapped by some amorous cowboy. Tucker didn't spot another, but he was certain a third guard secreted himself somewhere in the crowd.

Tucker looked a final time before entering. The faro dealer smiled with his three remaining teeth and nodded to an empty chair. Tucker shook his head and made his way to the bar. He felt eyes on him, sizing him up, and knew the manner with which he carried himself among men such as these might determine if they singled him out for a gunfight or not. "Beer," he called to the bartender over the singer's lament.

The Mexican bartender missing one side of his scalp topped off a mug and handed Tucker his beer. It was more head than liquid, and warm, but it was better than anything he'd had this past week. "What happened to that feller out in the street?"

"He was robbed," the bartender grinned, "of his money and his gun."

"And before he ended up in that position?"

The bartender frowned as he worked wax into his handlebar mustache with his thumb and forefinger. "He was killed. No, *senor,* he was murdered. He was drunk. The other man was sober. And so fast." He pointed to the street. "Miguel was allowed to get his gun out of his holster before the other drew and killed him." He held up his hand. "I swear."

"The other was not your usual trail hand,

amigo?"

The bartender shook his head. "I have said too much already. I live because I keep to myself —"

"Was the other a very large man?"

The bartender looked around, but all eyes were on the singer, who had started taking her clothes off to the whoops and hollers of watching drunks. "This man was small. Almost as small as a boy. So young." He shook his head again. "And so fast."

"Which way did he go?"

"Next door," the bartender motioned. "To the Mud Puppy." He laid his hand on Tucker's forearm. "Do not go there looking for him, *amigo.*"

"Good advice," Tucker said, finishing his beer. "I'll go across the street to Sadie's."

"A wise decision, *senor.*"

Tucker left a half dollar on the bar, when it suddenly occurred to him what Aurand told him while he was in his jail cell. Aurand claimed to have taken three eagles — thirty dollars in gold — out of Tucker's pocket that Aurand claimed he stole from the roustabout. If that were the case, why had Aurand left him with twelve dollars and not taken that as well? Just one more thing to ask Aurand if he ran into him.

Even before Tucker walked into Sadie's

Saloon, the sound of breaking glass reached the street, accompanied by echoes of delight from cowboys inside egging on others in a fight. Tucker entered and stood off to one side. A circle of drunks formed around combatants in the center of the floor. Tables and chairs had been moved aside to make way for the fighters.

Tucker looked over the heads of the men in front of him cheering the fight on. He caught sight of a man on the floor struggling to get up. Blood stained his once-white apron from his nose, which had been mashed to one side of his cheek. Flesh showed through skin like a book that had been opened to reveal some truth. That truth, Tucker knew, was that the bartender had better stay down on the floor. "Bartender got hold of a wild one?" Tucker asked a cowboy next to him.

One of the men leaning against the wall beside Tucker glanced sideways at him as he picked his teeth with a piece of straw. "Damned fool got between that big guy fighting and another one who came in that made the bigun' there look like a circus freak."

"Some big guy, you say?"

"Big?" The cowboy threw his hand over his head, indicating the man's height. "That guy standing over the bartender picked a fight with the big guy. Lasted for one punch, and he laid that guy out." He nodded to the man kicking the bartender. "Pissed that one off, and he's been taking on all comers ever since. Bartender should have let him have his fun."

As if to punctuate the cowboy's statement, the big man in the middle of the floor reached down and took the bartender's head in his hands. The crowd cheered. Watching men demanded the ultimate.

They got it.

A crack sounded as the big man twisted the bartender's head violently, breaking his neck. The man tossed the body away, and the crowd roared its approval. The fighter stood to his full height, and Tucker drew in a breath — Jess Hammond. And, where Jess was, Aurand wasn't far behind.

Jess grabbed a beer from a man standing beside a table and downed it. He looked over the crowd through one swollen eye. Bloody flesh hung from a torn scalp over one ear. And when he shouted at the crowd, he spat a broken tooth onto the floor. "Who's next?" he roared.

Tucker started backing out of the saloon. Blue Boy had just been here. Tucker needed to find him in town, and the last thing he wanted was for Jess to recognize him.

"Who's next?" Jess bellowed again.

"Tucker Ashley," a voice called just behind him. He turned, but Philo Brown stuck a gun barrel into his back. "Keep your hand away from that hogleg of yourn." He reached around Tucker and snatched his gun from his holster. Philo jammed it into his waistband.

The cowboy Tucker had been talking with turned, and his hand fell on his own gun in a cross-draw holster. Philo leveled Tucker's gun at the man's head and cocked the hammer. "I ain't killed anyone today, little man," Philo said. "But then, today's not over yet. Scat!"

The man pulled his hand away from his gun and backed out of the door.

"What's your play?" Tucker asked.

Philo lowered his gun to waist level and jammed it in Tucker's back. "You," Philo said, his words slurred, but his demeanor as deadly as any sober man. "You're my play. See, I could kill you right here, right now. And I should for that little trick at the jailhouse."

"But I'm betting you think that'll be too quick?"

"You're smarter than you look." Philo grinned. "It would be too quick. And Au-

182

rand would be almighty angry at me for cheating him out of the pleasure of killing you. Now, if Jess there kills you in a fair fight, well Aurand couldn't fault him for that. Jess there" — he motioned to the center of the saloon floor — "is a man bent on killing someone tonight. Anyone. As you can see, he's already killed the bartender, and killing you as well would suit him just fine. Jess has been pissed since that great big feller waltzed in and knocked him out. He's been on the prod since. And you're next, ol' salt."

Philo shoved Tucker past men standing in the circle away from Jess, looking at what they must have thought was a mad bull. "Make a break for it," Philo said, "and I'll kill you outright." He shouted over the crowd, "Here's your next man — Tucker Ashley."

At Tucker's name, Jess stopped with his beer mug halfway to his lips and smiled wide. He slammed his beer onto a nearby tabletop. The mug shattered and showered the floor with broken glass.

"The gun belt," Philo ordered.

Tucker took off the belt and draped it over a chair. "Just see to it nothing happens to my gun."

Philo tilted his head back and laughed.

"Like you'll ever have need of it again in a few seconds?"

CHAPTER 18

At the ragged edge of a fitful sleep Aurand bolted upright. The hairs stood straight on the nape of his neck, and, without realizing it, he had drawn his gun. Where his head swiveled searching for what had alerted him, the barrel of his gun followed.

"No need for that," a gravelly voice said from somewhere away from the periphery of the campfire.

"That you, Red?"

"It is if you put that gun away."

Aurand holstered his gun and stood. He shook off the stiffness in his legs as Red came into the dim campfire light, leading his horse. He hobbled the mare in the grass beside Aurand's grulla, while Aurand stacked more driftwood onto the fire. He set the coffee pot atop the coals and warmed his hands over it. "Where's our man?"

"Not until I have a cup," Red said.

The iron pot spewed steam, and Aurand

took two tin cups from his saddlebag. He blew dust out of them before pouring the coffee. Red wrapped his hands around the cup to warm them and daintily blew into the hot liquid to cool the coffee.

"All right," Aurand demanded. "Where's Tucker?"

"First thing," Red said, "I want to tell you I admire the man. I know you don't want to hear that."

Aurand pinched his nose between his thumb and finger. "But it looks like I'll have to endure it."

Red sipped his coffee and looked at the stars as if formulating his thoughts. "I found a shallow grave a couple days ago."

"Graves are everywhere," Aurand said. "I've filled a few myself a time or two."

"But two Lakota in one arroyo, covered up by rocks? It took me a mite longer to figure things out, but, near as I can decipher it, those two Indians ambushed Tucker and Jack Worman. Should have had them dead to rights, them having the high ground. It should have been Tucker and Jack in those graves, but it was not."

"How's that tell me where he is?"

"I am getting to that." Red nodded to Aurand's saddle. "You got the makin's?"

Aurand nodded. He grabbed his tobacco

pouch and papers from his saddlebag and handed them to Red, who began rolling a smoke as he continued. "Right after I found the grave, I followed Tucker and Jack for some time but lost their trail . . ."

"You?" Aurand said. "Lost their trail?"

Red shrugged. "Even I do now and again when the hunted is particularly trail savvy. Anyway, I worked on ahead and saw the Indians were headed toward Cowtown, and that bothered me. 'Why,' says I to myself, 'would Indians be riding toward a white man's town?' "

"And did you come up with an explanation?"

Red frowned and patted his shirt for a match. Aurand handed Red a glowing sage brush branch from the fire, and he lit his smoke. The paper flared, catching the tobacco on fire and raining hot ashes down the front of Red's calico shirt. When he had patted the ashes out, he explained. "Made no more sense to me than it did that Tucker and Jack Worman were trailing those Indians."

Aurand felt anger rise up within him. "Just tell me where the hell Tucker is."

"Do you not want to know what man has been following you since you left the steamer?"

187

Aurand sat upright and peered into the darkness.

"Don't worry about him," Red said. "He is gone as well."

"Who's gone? Who *are* you talking about?"

"Like I said, some feller who got off the boat 'bout the time we did, be my guess. He has been hanging back, not a mile from your posse, leading his donkey like he has not a care in the world."

"A donkey?"

"A donkey."

"What the hell is someone doing with a donkey in these parts?"

"How should I know?" Red poured more coffee. "Maybe he's a priest. I just tell you what I seen."

"You get a look at him?"

"Never saw him. All I know is he is trail savvy like I'm trail savvy. He broke off following you this morning, after he watched from a butte a half mile back. Sat there for some time until the sun set, then he headed into Cowtown."

"So I don't have to worry about this feller?"

"You worry about whoever you want. All I can do is tell you how your back trail reads."

"Does my back trail tell you anything

about Tucker Ashley?"

"It tells me Tucker and Worman separated tonight. Tucker went west, following them Lakota."

"So where's Tucker?"

Red looked to the stars once again. "My guess is he is in Cowtown by now."

CHAPTER 19

Jess Hammond stood in the middle of the circle formed by cowboys, drifters, and criminals awaiting the spectacle. Jess grabbed another man's beer and downed it. He grinned at Tucker through chipped teeth and a swollen eye. His shirtsleeves were rolled up over massive forearms, and his bloody fists clenched and unclenched, a broken knuckle popping as he did so. His torn shirt revealed his heavily muscled, blood-matted chest, and one suspender dangled broken from his waist. He drew in great gulps of air, the smile never leaving his face as he circled Tucker.

Tucker had seen a man beaten to death in a prize fight in St. Louis before the war, and he always remembered it as a particularly gruesome manner of death. He knew he did not want to die that way, alone, here in Cowtown. With Lorna still a captive.

As Tucker looked around, he knew he had

no friends here. These drunks would just as soon see him beaten to death as they would like to see Jess beaten to death. It mattered nothing to them, as long as their blood rage was satisfied.

Tucker circled to match Jess's movement. Out of the corner of his eye, Tucker saw men making bets against him. Philo stood with his gun hand concealed under his vest as he took ten-to-one odds that Tucker wouldn't last two minutes. If he could have right then, Tucker would have bet all he had on himself. It would have been even more of an incentive to stay away from Jess's fists.

Philo shouted at Tucker, and he looked over at him. He held his beer high as if to toast the fight, while his gun bulged hidden under his coat. When Tucker turned back, Jess had stepped into the center of the saloon floor.

Tucker circled until he spotted the back door visible through the crowd. He filed it in his mind as he met Jess in the middle of the circle of cowboys. He sized Jess up, and he didn't like the size. Though Tucker was several inches taller, Jess had him by thirty pounds of muscle. And the man felt no pain. But Tucker also knew he was sober, and Jess was not. If he could move to Jess's left, away from his power side where his swollen eye was closing, Tucker might have a chance. Either way, he didn't have time for a dragged-out fight. He needed to find Blue Boy before he fled town.

But if the cowboy he talked with earlier was right, Jess was vulnerable — Blue Boy had laid him out with a single punch. Tucker prayed for such an opening just as Jess stopped circling. Finished sizing Tucker up like professional fighters do their opponents, Jess came straight at Tucker.

Tucker lashed out with a left jab that landed flush on Jess's jaw but didn't slow him down, and he followed up with a straight right. Jess moved at the last moment, deflecting the blow, and threw his own punch. Tucker felt the blow too late to roll with it. It landed on his cheekbone, and he staggered back against the circle of drunks. Hands propelled him forward. He lost his balance and stumbled right into a stiff jab that felt as if Jess had hit him with a right. And then he did, and Tucker dropped to the floor. He wiped blood from his split lip and looked up. Jess accepted a beer offered by a spectator, giving Tucker time to stand. He bent over to catch his breath. He had seen what Jess did to the bartender when he was unable to toe the line, and he wanted no part of Jess's hands on his head.

Jess motioned for him to stand. Tucker gathered his legs under him and sprang at Jess. He head butted him in the stomach. Jess doubled over. A storm of putrid air rushed out of him, and Tucker jerked his head up violently. The blow caught Jess on the point of his jaw, and his head snapped back. Jess's eyes rolled in his head, and Tucker lashed out with a wicked left hook to Jess's swollen eye that floored him.

It was Tucker's turn to accept a beer from an onlooker, and he downed it in one gulp. The crowd cheered Tucker, and cowboys looked to Philo, the big mouth who had given ten-to-one odds on Jess.

Jess struggled to his feet as he wiped blood from his closed eye. He pawed with his left jab, judging the distance. Suddenly, the stupor left the big man, and he feinted with a right cross. Tucker moved out of the way of the punch and ran into a hard left hook, then a right uppercut that jarred his jaws and chipped a tooth. He flew back, his legs flailing the air, and hit the floor. Jess bent over Tucker and grabbed him by the front of his vest.

"Now we finish this," Jess said and hit him on the chin. Tucker's head snapped back, hitting the wooden floor. Jess pulled him closer and hit him in the face twice. Three times. Tucker gradually became immune to the pain. Like a wrestler's second wind, he realized that the life was being beaten out of him by the big man who straddled him.

Tucker watched the blows, timing them, and . . . moved his head just as Jess swung hard. The blow whizzed past Tucker's ear, and Jess's fist hit the floor. Knuckles broke, and Jess hollered in pain. He reared back to hit Tucker again when Tucker brought his knee up and rammed it into Jess's groin. The air whooshed out of him, and he dropped to the floor. He clutched his crotch and writhed in pain.

Tucker struggled to his feet and accepted another drink, glad the fight was over . . . when Jess stood on teetering legs. One eye had swollen shut, and his nose lay flattened off to one side. He bellowed like an old bull stuck in a mud wallow and charged. His arms pinwheeled the air, and Tucker side-stepped to Jess's blind side. When he staggered past, Tucker set himself and swung hard. The blow caught Jess flush on the temple, and his momentum carried him for two more steps before he crumpled to the floor. His head hit a chair, and he came to rest face up, unconscious.

The crowd grew silent for a moment, then cheers reverberated inside the saloon.

Cowboys gathered around Tucker. They patted him on the back and thrust all manner of beer and rotgut at him, wiping blood off his face with their multi-colored bandanas. Through the crowd, Tucker ducked and looked around. He spotted Philo elbowing his way through the drunks toward the door. One hand rested on his covered gun, the other ready to pull his coat aside for a fast shot.

"The law's here!" Tucker shouted.

The cowboys paused.

"Over there," Tucker pointed. "The fat man in the gray duster's a deputy marshal."

Cowboys grabbed Philo, and Tucker's gun fell from his waistband. Hands prodded Philo, pulling back his vest and revealing his tin star. Like crazed dogs, they turned angry at a lawman invading their sanctuary. Philo struggled against the crowd that closed in tighter by the moment.

While the rowdies busied themselves with Philo, Tucker bent and grabbed his gun. He stuck it in his holster still draped over the chair and backed away. He strapped the gun on as he made his way toward the back door. Just before he escaped the saloon, he looked over his shoulder at Philo being kicked and beaten, and at Jess, still unconscious on the floor.

Tucker staggered into the cool night air and began running toward the livery. If Blue Boy were still in town, he would be there or at the mercantile; guns and horses were all that would interest him here. Besides, Tucker was in no shape to brave the other saloons looking for him.

He reached the end of the alley and started between the Last Chance and the livery stable when a voice behind him called his name. He froze.

"Tucker Ashley," the voice called once more. No emotion, only a still coldness that Tucker long ago learned belonged to those comfortable with killing. "Turn around, Ashley."

Tucker turned around to meet his challenger. He recognized the kid, from his fancy pointed boots to his hat that was a size too big for his small head. Con Leigh stood with his feet apart, one hand touching his low-slung holster, the other hand resting on a gun in a concealed shoulder holster. "Been waiting a mighty long time for this." He smiled.

CHAPTER 20

Red Sun added another thick piece of sage brush to the fire. "If Tucker goes to Cowtown, he might not make it out."

"Especially if Philo sees him." Aurand grabbed his saddle blanket and shook the dust out before setting it on his horse. "He is still mad that Tucker made a fool out of him."

"Where you going?" Red asked as he sat contented on a rock sipping coffee. "Not into Cowtown, I hope."

"Got to get to Philo. That damned fool might just try on Tucker himself without waiting for me."

"Philo will be all right. He's got Jess there with him."

Aurand laid the front and rear cinches out of the way. "Philo would if he managed to get around to back-shoot Tucker, he'd be dead." Aurand moved the breast collar and stirrups away. "And Jess is pretty good with a six-gun, but he's no Tucker Ashley. Then if there's Jack Worman watching his back . . ."

"I told you Jack and him split up."

"All the more reason to get into Cowtown." Aurand fed the latigo through the front cinch ring and tied a Texas T to hold the saddle in place.

"Sit a moment," Red said.

"Don't have time."

"A few minutes more won't hurt none."

Aurand sat and poured the last of the coffee into his cup.

"When I was a youngster our band winter-camped at the base of the Shining Mountains." Red laid twigs on the fire. "There hung at the higher tree line this mule deer with the most amazing rack you ever seen. I wanted that buck so bad, I could taste him roasting over the fire. And I wanted to kill him before some travelling Nez Perce did."

"There a point to this story?"

"I'm getting to it." Red spat a stream of tobacco juice five feet, and it splattered atop a rock. "What I'm getting at is, I stalked that buck winter and summer. Just when I thought I had him figured out, he threw me a curve, and I would not see him for months." Red downed the last of his coffee. "And *that* is the point of my story."

"That you never bagged the buck?"

"Oh, I bagged him all right, after several years of hunting him. The older he got, the cagier he got. My point is that he was a lot like Tucker and you: just when you think you have him figured out, he will do something unexpected."

Aurand slipped the cup into his saddlebags and stroked the muzzle of his grulla. "I got him figured out enough that I'll find him."

"That buck," Red said, standing and tying his bedroll across his saddle, "never tried hurting me. He wasn't Tucker Ashley. You find that man, you watch your back side, 'cause he will do the unexpected."

Aurand gathered the reins in his hand and swung into the saddle. He started for the hill leading down to Cowtown when Red whistled. "One more little thing: that young kid — Con Leigh — you got deputying for you . . ."

"What about him?"

"I was sitting the mare out there in the dark watching your camp when I seen Con ride out by his lonesome."

"Is that important?"

Red Shrugged. "Only if you don't want all your deputies in Cowtown at once. 'Cause that's where the kid went, too. And if I was a betting Indian, I would wager he'll run in to Tucker sooner or later."

"That's what I'm afraid of." Aurand dug his spurs into the gelding's flank.

"You better hurry afore Con finds Tucker," Red yelled after him.

CHAPTER 21

Lorna awakened to the sound of an approaching horse. She sat up and drew the elk-skin robe around her as if protection from the unknown. Jimmy Swallow, who never seemed to need sleep, stood from where he sat beside the fire. Wild Wind approached Swallow and spoke something in Lakota. They broke up, and Swallow ran for the safety of a large boulder as he notched an arrow on his bowstring. Wild Wind cocked his rifle and lay down behind a clump of sage brush just outside the light of the campfire.

The pony came into view. At first Lorna thought it riderless, until light from the campfire threw odd shadows over it. She jumped in horror as she recognized the dead man tied over the horse with strips of rawhide. His head bounced against the pony's side with every step. Swallow ran from the boulder as the pony galloped into camp. He grabbed the reins, and the horse reared its head back against the horsehair bridle. He spoke soothingly, and the animal looked at Swallow with a wild-eyed stare.

Wild Wind laid his rifle on the ground and ran to the body laid over the pony's back. He held his head up: Pawnee Killer. Black blood caked onto his chest from a gaping hole, and a knife stuck out of his back. Wild Wind pulled the knife free, and Lorna gasped. The knife was no trade knife, but a quality brand sold only at her mercantile back home. Tucker had bought such a knife from his monthly army pay this spring. But then, they had sold many such knives. Had Tucker killed Pawnee Killer?

Lorna stepped back from the horse as she hugged herself. Pawnee Killer had looked upon her with a respect that transcended their language barrier. His voice never rose when he talked to Jimmy Swallow about her, and he never threw her a lewd look, as did Wild Wind. Although he was among those who kept her captive, she felt grief looking at the young man's dead body.

Swallow and Wild Wind spoke for long moments before Wild Wind ran to his saddlebags on the ground beside his pony.

Lorna approached Swallow cautiously. She averted her eyes from Pawnee Killer, but she found herself peeking around Swallow to look. "He has been shot through," Swallow said, anger in his voice for the first time since she had known him. "Those who follow have killed him."

"And the other warrior who went with him?"

"Black Dog?" Swallow said. "I am certain he killed whoever killed Pawnee Killer."

Lorna sucked in a breath. Tucker's knife confirmed it was he following her and not Aurand or any of his deputies. How he'd escaped the jail, she could not imagine. What she did know was that Tucker would continue following them until he could rescue her. Unless he were already dead. "Where is Black Dog?"

Swallow cut the rawhide straps securing Pawnee Killer to the pony and eased him to the ground. He looked in the direction the pony had come from. "I do not know. But this is serious."

Wild Wind returned, carrying a floppy, felt cowboy hat and handed it to Swallow.

"What is happening?" Lorna said.

Swallow gathered his hair and tucked it under the hat. Wild Wind spoke in Lakota, and Swallow turned to Lorna. "I need to go into Cowtown and find Blue Boy."

"Why?"

Swallow nodded to Pawnee Killer. "That makes three of us dead in a short time. And He Who Follows may be near. We need Blue Boy. He will tell us what to do next."

"Why do you have to go into town?" Lorna nodded to Wild Wind. "Why not him?"

Swallow fumbled around his saddlebags and came away with a red flannel shirt. "Someone has to go. And he told me to."

Lorna looked at Wild Wind, who stared back with a look that chilled her. With Jimmy Swallow gone, she would be alone with Wild Wind. "Why not him?" she asked again. "Why doesn't he go into Cowtown?"

Swallow brushed her hand off his arm. "Like Blue Boy, I can pass for a *wasicu*. And I speak your language."

He buttoned the shirt while he looked around a final time. He grabbed his bow and quiver and started for his pony. Lorna ran after him and grabbed his arm again. "Don't go."

He shrugged her hand off. "I have to."

"But your pony, your bow . . . people will see they belong to a Lakota."

"I will tether him at the outskirts of town and leave my bow and quiver there as well. I will walk the rest of the way into Cowtown."

"Please, don't go."

Swallow faced Lorna and eased her hand away from his arm. "Wild Wind will take good care of you, and Black Dog is sure to ride in any moment. I will be back with Blue Boy soon. Then we can leave this place."

Swallow swung into the saddle in one smooth motion. Before Lorna could let out a fearful breath, he had ridden into the night.

Lorna returned to the fire while she kept Wild Wind in her peripheral vision. She piled branches onto the fire. It flared up and popped when the tree sap burned, and she drew the elk-skin robe tight around her. She watched Wild Wind circle the fire before dragging Pawnee Killer to the outskirts of the camp. He spoke something in Lakota and grinned at her. She ignored him and bent to the fire as if the flames would protect her. She looked casually around for anything she could use for a weapon. Could she wield a rock with enough force to protect herself? Or a brittle tree branch? There was nothing, and she would have given half her mercantile for Tucker's knife, now stuck in Wild Wind's sash.

He walked to a clump of sage brush and broke off a branch. He sauntered back to the fire and stood across from her, the flames causing his grin to look even more malevolent than usual. He spoke to her, but she ignored him. He spoke in Lakota again, as if she should understand what he said, and she looked away. He yelled at her and slapped his leg with the switch. When Lorna failed to respond, he stepped around the campfire toward her.

Lorna looked frantically around the camp, but there was nothing to use as a weapon, nothing that might slow Wild Wind down.

He walked to within an arm's length of her and used the branch to raise the bottom of her robe. She skidded back and wrapped it tighter around her. Wild Wind yelled. He snatched the robe off her and threw it aside.

Again he grunted in Lakota and rubbed the inside of her thigh with the switch. For the first time, Lorna was grateful she wore Swallow's buckskins and not her dress. Her fortune was short-lived, as Wild Wind rubbed her thigh again. When she slapped the switch away he pushed her to the ground. She backpedaled in the dirt, trying to get away from him, but he advanced on her. A guttural sound erupted from his throat, and he threw himself on top of her. "Get off me!" But Wild Wind was like a wild wind, untamable.

She buried her nails in his cheek. He

yelled in pain. He sat up, and his hand went to his bleeding face. Lorna skidded away from him, but he slapped her hard across the face. Her head hit the ground as he threw himself on top of her again. His hand clawed at the top of her pants. The drawstring broke away in his grasp. She struggled. Hit him on the back. The neck. But there was no slowing his lust as he worked the trousers down her bare thighs.

A *whoosh*ing in the night overshadowed his lustful grunts and Lorna's fearful screams. A thud caused Wild Wind to stop. He rose off her and stiffened, a perplexed look crossing his face, when another *whoosh*ing sound accompanied another thud. His face contorted in pain, and he tried to speak, but frothy blood leaked out of his mouth, over his shirtfront and onto Lorna's thighs a heartbeat before he collapsed on top of her. Twin arrows stuck out of his back.

Jimmy Swallow walked out of the shadows and approached them. He shook his head and laid his bow on the ground beside the dead warrior. He grabbed Wild Wind and pulled him off Lorna. Even away from the light of the fire, she saw Swallow blush when he looked upon her nakedness. He turned around abruptly. "Cover yourself."

Lorna trembled. Swallow had saved her from disaster by mere moments. Her hand shook as she pulled the pants up and fumbled for the rawhide drawstring. She tied it tight, as if she expected Wild Wind to come back for another try. "I am dressed," she said, a plain statement to the man — more like a mere boy — who had saved her from the horrors she had heard happened to captives of Indians.

Swallow turned around and bent to her. She jerked back, but he seemed not to notice as he wrapped the robe around her shoulders. "You saved me. My life, even. He would have . . ."

Swallow put his finger to his quivering lips as he looked a last time at Wild Wind's corpse before adding wood to the fire. He sat cross-legged on the ground and stared silently into the flames for many minutes before turning to face her. "I should have asked: are you hurt?"

"I am fine," Lorna answered. "Thanks to you. How did you know . . . ?"

"For many days now," Swallow began, "I have seen how Wild Wind looked at you when Blue Boy was not around."

"But he forgot about you watching him?"

Swallow nodded. "I am sure he cared little what I saw — him a seasoned warrior, while

208

I am but a . . . boy. I was fearful tonight what might happen if I left you alone with him. So I doubled back and hid in the dark."

Lorna leaned over and laid her hand on Swallow's arm. "You are more man than anyone else in your band."

Tears wet his eyes, and he looked away. "I have counted coup before, but Wild Wind is the first man I have had to kill." He shook his head. "His death will be looked on with dishonor around campfires at night."

"For saving the life of your leader's . . . woman?"

Jimmy Swallow looked off into the distance as if he could see Cowtown several miles away. "Blue Boy is down there, and I fear for him. He has been gone so long." He chin-pointed to Pawnee Killer's body lying off to one side of the camp. "And He Who Follows has killed another one of us."

"Perhaps it is best if I am left to go my own way."

Swallow looked at Lorna with a sadness she couldn't understand. "Perhaps. But it will be Blue Boy's decision what we are to do with you. It is up to him. And to He Who Follows."

CHAPTER 22

"Been waiting for this a long time," Con Leigh said. "Aurand's not around to stop me."

"And if he were?"

"Then I'd kill him first." Con smiled. "But he's not. It's just you and me."

"Here, with no one to witness it?" Tucker began to back away, creating distance. Most fast guns he'd encountered were good for a short distance, where they relied on speed, not accuracy, preferring the closeness of the kill, the look of their opponent's eyes as they pumped lead into him. "You'd be a big man if folks knew you killed me in a fair fight."

Con's voice broke with the intensity of what he was about to do. "Folks will know it soon enough, witness or not. What is important is there'll be no Tucker Ashley after tonight."

Tucker talked, stalling, inching backwards, working feeling back into his bloody hands, which had begun to stiffen. "Isn't one dead man enough for one night?"

"That cowboy in front of the saloon?" Con chuckled. "Just another man who thought he was fast."

"Way folks tell it in the saloon, you goaded some trail hand drunker'n hell into a fight. Even sober, he wouldn't have stood a chance. You're some big man, aren't you?"

"I've about jawed all I intend to," Con said. "Time to get this over with."

"I agree." Tucker inched backwards, now twenty yards away from Con. " 'Cept it won't give me much pleasure in killing a man sporting a woman's name. Connie."

Even in the dim light of the back of the Mud Puppy, Tucker saw Con's lip twitch, saw his jaw muscles tighten. "No one calls me that."

"Except your momma, who's calling your name about now. Connie. Did I mention I had an aunt named Connie?"

Con began to shake. His hand snaked to the gun in the shoulder holster Tucker knew he packed. And Con drew.

Tucker crouched and grabbed for his own gun.

Before Tucker cleared his holster, Con got off his first shot. Anger and distance affected him, and his bullet kicked up dirt two feet in front of Tucker.

Tucker drew his gun. His motion smooth. His breathing controlled. Turning sideways and blading himself. Making himself a smaller target as Con's second shot tore into Tucker's shirt and grazed his shoulder.

All time slowed for Tucker. Con thumbed back his hammer. He bent his arm alongside his torso. He shot from the hip again. A window behind Tucker shattered with the miss.

Tucker brought both hands up locked around the big Remington. Found his front sight. Let the slack out of the trigger. And shot Con Leigh center chest.

Con sank to his knees, still holding his Colt. He grunted and struggled to raise his gun as Tucker fired again. His second .44 slug tore into Con's heart, and the little man slumped forward, lifeless.

Tucker kept his gun on Con while he walked toward him. He rolled the dead man. Con starred back at Tucker with eyes reserved for the dead. Tucker breathed a heavy sigh. He shucked out the two empty cartridges and replaced them with fresh ones before he holstered his gun with trembling hands.

Tucker wiped the sweat-mixed blood from his eyes. He started for the livery when shots erupted from the direction of the mercantile. He ran toward the shots. He rounded the corner of the saloon as an old man staggered toward him. "He gut-shot me." The man collapsed in Tucker's arms. Blood seeped from a hole in his stomach, the stench of the wound tangy in Tucker's nostrils.

Men poured out of the saloons, guns drawn, willing and ready to kill anything, anyone. They ran to where Tucker cradled the man's head in his hands. "Who shot you?" Tucker asked.

"Big guy," the man answered. He coughed once, and bloody froth splattered Tucker's shirtfront, mixing with his own. "Broke into my store. Caught him." The storekeeper coughed again, and Tucker wiped blood off his cheek. "Stole rifles. Ammunition. For God's sake, he shot me when I tried to stop him."

Tucker turned to the sounds of drunks running toward them, vengeful figures in the night, the taste of blood already with them from killing Philo Brown. "Who was he?"

The storekeeper gagged. Blood trickled from the corner of his mouth, and he shook his head. "Big guy. Bigger than any here. Rode west toward the Badlands. Funny."

He spat up a chunk of lung. "He yelled something at me in Sioux."

Tucker looked up. The crowd was nearly upon them. "How many guns . . . ," but Tucker realized the shopkeeper had gone limp in his arms. He eased the man's head to the ground and stood to face the crowd. "Storekeeper said five, six men stole guns and rode south toward where your herds are grazing."

Tucker watched the cowboys fumble to untie their reins from the hitching post. One cowboy fell from his cayuse and hit his head on the hitching rail. None of the others lifted a finger to help but left him lying. They were on a killing mission as they rode out toward the south, opposite the direction Blue Boy had gone.

Tucker walked around the corner to where he'd tied his mule. Thick dust hung in the air as the cowboys rode away to avenge the storekeeper's death. Away from Blue Boy's tracks. Away from the Badlands and the Great Wall.

He caught a faint shuffling sound behind him. He drew his gun and shot in one smooth motion. An Indian, his knife poised over his head, buckled over. He clutched his chest and looked up at Tucker with eyes disbelieving before he fell to the street, dead.

Tucker crouched next to the body. One of Blue Boy's men, then, sent after Tucker to avenge the others.

Tucker spotted an Indian pony hobbled between two saloons, and he bent and hoisted the Indian over his shoulder. He knew just what he had to do. After this night, Blue Boy would have to come after him. And he'd have Lorna with him.

CHAPTER 23

The morning sun shimmered off the prairie as Blue Boy rode into camp. He carried two new rifles and enough ammunition to continue his own private war with the whites. And the food. What little he managed to grab before the storekeeper staggered dreamily out of his room might keep them for half a day. Perhaps less. In that he had failed. They'd had little luck with game along the trail, and he cursed He Who Follows for that, forcing him to ride the most difficult route toward the Wall. And forcing him to go into the white man's town.

His dun snorted an alarm a moment before Blue Boy, too, smelled the odor of putrid blood, and he reined up short. He squinted as he recognized two bodies lying on the ground — Wild Wind and Pawnee Killer, bloating black in the heat. Blue Boy jerked his rifle from the scabbard and racked a shell. Silence. He cocked an ear but heard no life in his camp.

He urged the horse ahead at a slow walk while he studied the ground. When he arrived at the place where the dead men lay, a shuffling sound reached his ears, and he pivoted with his rifle. Something fluttered just on the edge of the camp, and he walked the horse closer. A head popped up from behind some sagebrush, then dropped back down. A moment later Jimmy Swallow stood and looked at Blue Boy. There was no smile in his greeting; nothing to indicate the boy was glad his leader had returned. There was just a sad silence that was unusual for Swallow. He bent and helped Lorna stand.

Blue Boy dropped to the ground. "So there has been trouble while I was in the white man's town?" He slung his rifle over his shoulder. "Was it He Who Follows?"

Swallow eyed the gunny sack, and Blue Boy dropped it at his feet. Swallow bent and rooted around the sack until he found a can of peaches. He ran his knife around the rim of the can to open it. He handed it to Lorna, who took a sip of the juice before handing it back. "Pawnee Killer came into camp draped over his pony," Swallow said. "This was sticking in his back." He handed Blue Boy the knife Wild Wind had taken from between Pawnee Killer's shoulder blades.

"He Who Follows did not have to plant this" — Blue Boy turned the knife over to inspect it — "into Pawnee Killer. He has thrown down a challenge. I shall think about what to do next." Blue Boy looked at the corpse. "He was such a gentle soul. I often thought . . ." Blue Boy stopped and thought of what he was about to say. Telling another that your fallen friend was not suited to be a warrior was a huge insult. "I often thought that he would have made a great chief one day," he lied.

He nodded to Wild Wind. "And did He Who Follows kill him as well?"

Swallow looked away.

Blue Boy took Swallow's chin in his hand and turned the boy's face toward him. "What happened to Wild Wind?"

"I killed him."

Blue Boy stepped back. For the first time since starting out with his men, Blue Boy was unsure how to take this. His band had fought amongst themselves over perceived injustices with one another. But it had never resulted in death.

"I shot two arrows into his back."

Blue Boy's pulse quickened. Black Dog hadn't returned, and Blue Boy had lost three members of his band to his enemy. Now another one over an argument while he was gone. His hand shook from what he knew he must do. He drew his knife and stepped toward Swallow. Blue Boy drew his knife back. Swallow stood immobile, awaiting his fate, when Lorna jumped between them. "I don't know what you two just said, but I was here when Swallow killed Wild Wind." She faced Swallow. "Tell him."

Swallow remained silent while he stared at the ground.

She looked up at Blue Boy. "If he won't tell you, I will. If Swallow hadn't killed Wild Wind, he would have . . . had his way with me. I tried to fight him off, but he was too strong. Swallow protected me."

Blue Boy turned Swallow's chin up to him again. "Is this true? Did Wild Wind try to take her?"

"It is true," Swallow said. "He had been watching her for days, waiting until he was alone with her. I would not have been able to fight him off; he was too strong. I could do nothing else to help the woman."

Blue Boy felt the urge to kick Wild Wind. Had he been so preoccupied envisioning the life he would have with the woman that he'd been blind to Wild Wind's lust for Lorna?

"Do we bury Wild Wind and Pawnee Killer?" Swallow said at last.

Blue Boy looked at his back trail. There would be some cowboys among all those drunks in town sober enough to work out his trail. And they would follow to avenge the death of the shopkeeper. "We ride," Blue Boy said. "We cannot give them a proper burial along the Ghost Road. *Wakan Tanka* will understand. It is because we wish to survive and reach the Great Wall that we leave them."

Blue Boy stood, eying the way he had come. Swallow said that Pawnee Killer's pony had ridden into camp during the night, but where was Black Dog? He must have run into trouble with He Who Follows. As much as Blue Boy wanted to await his friend's arrival before they struck camp, he knew Cowtown and those death-hungry cowboys would be on his trail. They had to leave. Black Dog could catch up with them.

He Who Follows had caused him more than a little sorrow. His warriors had all been loyal to Blue Boy, even Wild Wind, when his lust didn't swell up within him. Each man had pledged his loyalty to Blue Boy, and in turn he vowed to always protect them. Yet the man tracking them had undermined his trust with his band. Three warriors dead by the hand of He Who Follows, and Wild Wind dead because of his own uncontrollable urges.

It stops here, Blue Boy said to himself. *I will lead what is left of my people — and my woman — away from the cowboys who would avenge the storekeeper's death. And when that danger has passed, I will hunt you and kill you, He Who Follows. And then I will seek the sanctuary of the Great Wall.*

CHAPTER 24

Aurand rode into town expecting drinking cowboys and prostitutes working overtime. He expected bartenders with their pockets fat as they gathered up dead men from the street, stripping them of whatever they could find to sell. Instead, there were ghost towns livelier than Cowtown, and he wondered if he had the right place. "Where the hell is everyone?" Red asked.

The sun was just rising, and there should have been cowboys passed out all along the street. A red-boned hound trotted out of a saloon, and Aurand drew his gun before he saw it was a dog. "You ever knowed it to be this quiet here?"

"I've been coming here off and on for nine, ten years," Red said. "Mostly to get my ashes hauled." He nodded to the cribs over the saloons. "And every time it is so wild, so dangerous, even I second-guessed myself last time whether or not I ought to have come here. But never like this."

They pulled up in front of Sadie's Saloon and tied their horses to the railing. Empty whisky bottles and broken beer mugs littered the floor of the saloon. Black blood spilled from some recent fight stained the center of the floor. Two tables lay smashed, and a chair still stuck into the plaster wall above the bar where it had been thrown. Like the street, Sadie's was as empty of living people as any cemetery.

Aurand walked around the bar and grabbed two mugs from under a broken mirror running the length of the room. He filled each with foamy beer and slid Red's toward him when someone descended the stairs carrying a shotgun. Aurand whirled on his heels and drew. Red dove under a table for safety.

"Who the hell's down here?" a raspy voice called out.

Aurand knelt behind the bar and aimed his gun in the direction of the stairs. An old woman descended the steps as she led with her shotgun. Her pink drawers were big enough to fit Philo, and her flannel shirt showed tobacco stains down the front. She spotted Red under the table and pointed her gun at him when Aurand called out, "Don't do that."

She jumped, and Red yelled at Aurand, "Don't get her jittery. That shotgun's pointed at my butt."

Aurand held his gun on her. "Just point that thing at the floor," he ordered.

"You first. I don't trust you . . ."

"Territorial marshal," Aurand announced.

"Now I really don't trust you."

Aurand cocked his gun, and the sound reverberated off the bullet-pocked walls beside the staircase. "I've got one with your name on it, old woman."

"Oh, all right." She tossed the shotgun on the floor, and Red jumped. "Tell your brave partner it's not even loaded."

She hobbled down the last few steps and waddled around the bar. Red stood and grabbed his beer while he eyed the woman cautiously. She nodded to their mugs and snickered. "Mostly foam," she said and poured herself four fingers of whisky from a bottle under the bar. She downed breakfast and eyed the bottle for dessert. "Sadie." She slammed the glass down. "My old man left me this dump when some cowboys strung him up for making fun of Texans." She squinted at him. "You really the law?"

Aurand pulled his vest back and showed her his tin star.

"Where the hell was you last night?"

"Problems?"

"You ever see it this quiet here?" Sadie asked.

"Can't say I have." Red walked around back of the bar and warily took the bottle of whisky from her. When she didn't object, he poured himself a shot and nursed it. "You're good enough to be a bartender, old-timer." She winked at Red. "And I need a bartender."

"He quit?"

"Some fool made him quit," Sadie said. "Killed him in a fight last night. Just before the mercantile was robbed and the owner murdered." She squinted at Aurand. "If you're the law, do some law business."

"What do you want me to do?"

"Find the killers, for starters. Folks figured Clive at the mercantile got hisself killed by some big guy . . ."

"Big guy?" Aurand said, motioning several inches taller than he was. "That big?"

"Oh, honey, that wouldn't even touch this man. He was a whole lot bigger than the man what murdered my bartender, even." She nodded to the shotgun. "I put that on him. Tied him up while he was still passed out from that last fight. Some of the boys helped carry him to the meat locker out back. He's all trussed up with that partner of his who damn near got killed. Some fat fool claiming to be a lawman. You gonna' take him and string him up?"

"You are the law, after all," Red said and winked at Sadie.

Aurand took Red by the elbow and led him off to the side. "I can't be saddled with prisoners now that I'm this close to Tucker."

"So maybe they die when they try to escape." Red looked around Aurand and smiled at Sadie. She shoved in plug tobacco between gaps in her teeth. "Wouldn't be the first time for that, now would it?"

Aurand turned back to Sadie. "All right, show us your prisoners."

She led them out back where a meat house stood, sawdust packed tightly around the seams to keep things cool inside. She took off boards across the door and swung it wide. The two men inside shielded their eyes from the sun as Aurand stepped aside. "Come on out."

Jess helped Philo stand, and they stumbled to the door. He started to speak when Aurand ordered him to shut up. "You got some food for these prisoners?" he asked Sadie. "Maybe some water we can clean them up with?"

"And maybe you got some money to pay for it?"

"The territorial auditor will reimburse you for your expenses," he said and shoved the men toward Red. "And fifty dollars a head for capturing them."

"In that case, honey, take them into the saloon, and I'll bring some meat and wet towels."

Jess had consumed his second bowl of buffalo stew, not even complaining how hard it was to chew now that he had two less teeth to do so with. Philo, on the other hand, bitched about everything, from the way his neck hurt from the rope the cowboys had cinched around it, to the broken ribs he picked up when they jostled him toward the telegraph pole last night. "And you couldn't even keep Tucker under wraps long enough for me to get here?" Aurand said.

Jess wiped his mouth with the back of his hand and blew bloody snot into a napkin. "I tried my best. But he didn't fight fair."

"As if you ever fight fair?" Aurand said. He tapped the table, and Philo stopped sopping up stew with his biscuit. "And what the hell's your excuse?"

"Don't have any. Like Jess said, if Tucker had fought fair, he would have been laid out waiting for you, and I'd have been a whole sight richer than I am now."

"If anything's happened to him . . ."

"Could have, for all we know. Con Leigh found Tucker last night in back of the livery."

Aurand stood abruptly. "Why didn't you tell me Con killed him?"

"Relax," Philo said. "Tucker's still alive. Way they tell it happened last night, Con got the short end of the stick."

"You telling me Tucker outdrew Con?"

Philo nodded, his mouth full of soggy biscuit. "No one saw it, but it must have been one hell of an interesting gunfight. Someone drug Con's body to the edge of town and left it."

Aurand sat back in his chair, rubbing a headache. Con dead complicated things. He hadn't wanted the kid to die so suddenly. But even less, he hadn't wanted Con to find Tucker and kill him. "Where's Tucker now?"

Philo looked at Jess, who called to Sadie for another bowl of stew. "He ain't in Cowtown, that's for certain."

"You sure Tucker killed Con?"

"Just what we heard when Sadie kept us locked in that meat locker. Some men talking how they found Con Leigh dead with two .44 holes in his chicken chest."

"And you said Tucker wasn't fast." Red nudged Aurand.

■ ■ ■ ■

"Tell me again just what shape Tucker was in when he beat hell out of you?"

"Well, he didn't do it fair," Jess insisted.

"I don't care if it was a fair fight or not," Aurand said. "I need to know how bad you hurt him."

"Jess hurt him good," Philo said. "If he hadn't got a lucky shot in, Jess would have killed him."

"Damned lucky you didn't," Aurand said. "Like I told you two peckerwoods, Tucker is mine. Now, did you injure him bad enough to slow him down?"

"I think," said Jess, "that the one you ought to ask if Tucker was slowed any would have been Con."

Sadie came out of the back room. She stood with her hands on her wide hips and stared at Aurand. "You gonna' take these two in?"

Aurand stood. "We're headed out now."

"Well, don't leave town until you catch Clive's killer."

When they arrived at the mercantile it was locked, and the sign read: *Closed Due to Death in the Family.* Aurand cupped his hand against the glass and peered in. A light flickered in the back room, and he knocked on the door. When he got no answer, he banged harder until he heard footsteps approaching. A woman pulled a curtain aside. "I'm closed," she said and dropped the curtain back.

Aurand rapped louder this time, rattling the door on its frame, and the woman once again peered out at them. Aurand pulled his vest aside so she could see his badge. She unlocked the door and stepped back. Aurand led Philo and Jess into the store. "Thank God you've come." The woman dropped her head on Aurand's chest and began sobbing.

He pulled her away. "That your husband got killed last night?"

She wiped tears with the sleeve of her nightshirt and nodded to the sitting room. A body — presumably the shopkeeper's — was laid out on a mourning table. "Clive. You will find the man who murdered him, won't you?"

"We'll try," Aurand said and introduced his deputies. The woman took a step back as if disbelieving two men who looked as dead as her husband could be deputies. "They were worked over by the crowd last night," Aurand explained.

The woman nodded; the only explanation she needed. "Please find the killer."

"First, my men need fresh clothes. Guns. Belts. They were stolen last night."

"And I could use a new pair of boots," Philo added.

She pointed to the storeroom.

"Go shopping, boys," Aurand said and sat on a bench beside her. "Did you see the man who broke in?"

She nodded and shuddered as fear visited her once again. Her eyes became wide, and her lip quivered as she told Aurand about the robbery and murder. "He broke in. Biggest man I ever saw. Had to stoop to get through the doorway. He began filling a gunny sack with rifles. Ammunition. He'd started taking some canned goods when Clive confronted him. The man shot him. Just that quick. And continued filling the sack until he heard men running thisaway."

"Would you recognize him again?"

She paused as she thought. "It was dark, and I didn't see his face so good. Just his size. But . . ."

"But what?" Aurand asked.

"He might have owned a big Chestnut gelding. White blaze on his forehead. And a donkey that Clive boarded at the livery for him yesterday."

"But you don't know if they belonged to your husband's murderer?"

She wrang her hands as she thought about last night. "I just don't know. The onliest reason I think it was his is they are gone from our livery this morning."

Jess and Philo emerged from the back room dressed out. Jess wore a black bowler more at home in Boston than the Dakota Territory. It matched his pointed boots that reminded Aurand of the dandies he had killed on cross-border raids in Kansas and Missouri during the war.

Philo had dressed more sedately, with wide suspenders holding up a pair of the new denims out from St. Louis. He, too, wore new boots, but laced up like those worn by infantry soldiers at Ft. Sully. He packed a new pearl-handled Smith and Wesson top break like those Aurand favored.

He thanked her and started for the door when she stopped him. "Do you wish to pay for these items?"

"If you can make a list," Aurand said, "I will see to it that the territorial auditor pays you the first Tuesday of next month. For now, we need to get after that murderer if we are to ever catch him."

They walked outside, Philo and Jess stepping carefully in their new boots. They followed Aurand as they headed for Sadie's Saloon. "There's a territorial auditor that'll pay for this stuff?" Philo asked.

Aurand looked over his shoulder. The new widow stood at her doorstep looking after them, just out of earshot. "Hell if I know. But it beats paying for it ourselves. Now go get Red," he told Philo.

"Where is he?"

"Upstairs with Sadie. Seems like they got a lot in common: old age."

It took Red most of the morning to decipher Tucker's sign. "Looks like a stampede outta here last night, heading south," the old man said. "Don't know what's that all about, but it's lucky for us. Only tracks I see are Tucker's over an unshod pony's."

"There's that damned Indian element again," Philo said. "He's been following some Lakota since he broke out, but why the hell is he?"

"More importantly," Aurand asked, "can we catch Tucker any time soon?"

Red smiled and bit off a corner of plug tobacco. "He has to travel slower than we do. Those pony tracks — even though they make a deeper depression than normal — are harder to spot than shod horses. We'll catch up with Tucker" — Red looked to the

sun and shielded his eyes — "by the time
the sun sets tonight."

CHAPTER 25

Tucker reined his mule to a stop. He climbed down from the saddle feeling far older than his thirty-one years. His swollen cheek throbbed where he'd caught that first heavy blow from Jess last night, and he had to strain through a partially closed eye to study the ground. Two knuckles of his gun hand were broken and bruised, and he blew bloody snot out of his nose. He bent to the pony tracks while he looked back into the sun to catch shadows. A single unshod hoof, a mere scuff on the hard dirt, leapt out at him. Perplexed, he led Ben while he studied the ground. The track wasn't Blue Boy's large horse. Did another of Blue Boy's band go with him into Cowtown?

He stood and stretched before walking hunched over again. Since last night when he lit out of town, he debated whether to find Jack or go after Blue Boy and his band. His first choice would have been to find

Jack. Tucker worried about him, with the shape he'd been in last night, and he needed to mend. Tucker needed to recuperate, too, from the beating Jess Hammond gave him at Sadie's Saloon. But as bad shape as Tucker was in right now, he was worried that Lorna was worse off, and he decided to keep following the Lakota. Unless Blue Boy found him first.

Tucker bent to the tracks. They had become more pronounced, the rider making little effort to hide his sign now.

Tucker mounted Ben. He coaxed him forward at a fast trot while keeping an eye on the ground. As the pony tracks led him between two large boulders, Ben snorted, and his muscles stiffened. Too late, Tucker recognized the ambush site. He kicked free of the stirrups just as an arrow reflected the morning sunlight. It emitted a sickening sound as it penetrated his leg and pinned him to the saddle. He fought for consciousness, the pain shooting high up his leg, when he heard another twang of a bowstring. He jerked back, and the arrow breezed past him. It struck Ben in the neck, and the mule dropped to the ground.

Ben rolled onto his front quarters, and Tucker rolled with him. He grabbed the shaft of the arrow and broke it off, the ar-

236

row head still stuck into his saddle. He fell away from Ben as he tried getting up, but the mule rolled onto his back. Blood spurted from the wound, and Tucker knew Ben didn't have long.

A black-braided figure rose from the outcropping and raised his bow. Tucker clawed at the gun in his holster and snapped a shot that struck the Indian in the shoulder. Tucker steadied himself for a follow-up shot, but the warrior had dropped behind cover of a boulder.

Tucker low-crawled toward Ben while he kept an eye out for his attacker. Another arrow caromed off a rock a foot in front of him, and he scrambled for the safety of a rock formation.

He sat with his back against the rocks, taking stock of his predicament. His rifle was shattered and still in the scabbard under the dying mule. His canteen had been crushed when Ben rolled over on it, the water soaking into the dirt. He had only five shots left to battle Lord knew how many Lakota, and he didn't know where Jack was. He'd depended on his friend so many times; Tucker needed his help once again. If he were able himself. He hadn't found any sign of Jack's horse and could only conclude Jack might already be dead. Perhaps at the hands of this same Indian.

Tucker chanced a quick look around the rocks. Something fluttered in the wind — a shirt, perhaps a coat. Tucker ducked back behind the rock. He estimated the distance to the shirt to be twenty yards. No great distance when one didn't have an arrow sticking out of your thigh. A nearly insurmountable distance when one did.

He looked at the other side of the rocks to where the ground dipped away, reminding him of the arroyo he had used to his advantage when the Lakota ambushed him and Jack by the river. It wasn't as deep as the one that concealed him then, but it was closer — to within crawling distance. It was the only chance he had, for he knew that soon his strength would leave him, and he'd be at the mercy of the Indian.

He took off his bandana and wrapped it around his leg to stabilize the stump of the arrow shaft still in his leg. He held his Remington in front of him like a divining rod as he low-crawled to the depression. He dropped down into it, expecting more arrows to fly his way.

He lifted his head ever so slightly. The Indian's shirt fluttered in the wind, and Tucker knew he hadn't been spotted yet. Ten yards separated him from his attacker now. At this range, it didn't matter if he faced arrows or guns — either would be just as lethal.

He tried standing, but the pressure on the arrow caused him to sit back down in agony. His breathing came in shallow gasps. His hand trembled from the pain, and he wasn't sure if he could shoot straight when he needed to most. He sucked in a last gasp of air and crawled on his knees the last ten yards, rolling onto his stomach when he cleared the rocks where the attacker waited. His Remington came to bear on a shirt draped over a sagebrush branch. His attacker had fled, leaving the shirt and a bow with four arrows in the quiver dropped beside the shirt.

Tucker lay still and calmed his breathing before gathering his knees under him. He studied the sign left by the Indian. Blood showed where his attacker had waited before backing through the rocks to his pony. The Lakota had led his horse away, and the droplets of blood became larger. He had broken off his attack. If he'd stayed any longer, he might have bled out. The Indian would flee to Blue Boy.

Tucker snatched the shirt off the bush and grabbed the bow and the quiver of arrows. He dragged himself under the shade of a boulder and looked about. He grabbed a broken branch from a dead cottonwood and settled back. He cut his trouser leg until it cleared the shaft of the arrow and examined his wound. There was just enough of the shaft sticking out of his leg to grab.

He wrapped his bandana around the shaft several times and stuck the branch into his mouth. He pulled hard, and the shaft came out of his leg. He grunted against the intense pain and jammed his bandana in the hole to stop the bleeding.

When the pain subsided enough for him to crawl, he made his way to Ben. The mule had bled out, and Tucker closed the animal's eyes before working his saddlebags from under him. He cut the cinch rope from his saddle and stuffed it in his bag.

On the far side of the clearing, the rocks made natural shade, and Tucker crawled under the overhang. With his cinch rope, he secured the cottonwood branch and the rawhide quiver on opposite sides of his legs to make a temporary splint that would take pressure off his wound. When he finished, he sat up and assessed his surroundings. A shallow valley dropped off just below him. He spotted a stand of buffalo-berry bushes, the closest thing with moisture in it he'd have any time soon.

He could remain where he was, but he was afraid that Blue Boy's band or Aurand and his deputies would easily find him. The valley offered a natural refuge that would confound the Lakota trackers, but only for a short time. And if Aurand still had Red Sun with him, that changed things — the man was relentless until he worked out a track. At the most, Tucker had mere hours before he was found. Less if he remained here.

He grabbed the stone and painfully stood. He slung his saddlebags and the Indian's bow over his shoulder and hobbled down into the valley.

It took Tucker the better part of an hour to make it to the bottom of the valley where the bushes stood. He parted the silvery leaves to get to the scarlet berries. It could have been worse, he thought. He had his knife and five rounds in his revolver. He had the bow and quiver the Indian had left, and that could prove useful. He had used a Blackfoot bow many times to bag small game, but this was a Miniconjou bow, with more pull. He prayed that if the time came that he needed it, he would have the strength to pull it back.

He finished picking all the berries his hat

would hold and sat with his back against a rock formation at the base of a sandstone overhang. He rationed his berries at first; then, ravenous, he quickly depleted his supply. When he finished, he licked his stained fingers and looked about. He recalled a trip into a rugged valley such as this at the edge of the Badlands last summer, leading Major Wells's G Troop in pursuit of a band of Hunkpapa Lakota they would never catch up to.

In such a valley at the end of another unsuccessful day, the troopers whined about their discomfort and their misfortune, while Tucker went off exploring the loose ground. He'd found bright red garnets lying on the surface of the ground, striking blackish-green jasper, and nearly perfect tourmalines. Those he'd gathered and brought back to Lorna. It was the first time he offered her a gift, and she had smiled at such a simple gesture. Even now the thought invaded Tucker's memory, and he wondered if she was safe, wondered if Blue Boy was taking care of her on this roughest of trails.

Movement off to one side caught his attention. He kept his head steady while he moved only his eyes. A scrawny jackrabbit scurried toward the berry thicket, unaware that Tucker watched. He slowly took the bow off his back and tested the sinew string before notching an arrow. It hefted well, the iron trade arrowhead fitted to the shaft with just the right amount of balance. As the rabbit turned, it presented Tucker with a side shot, and he let the arrow fly.

He crawled toward where the jackrabbit kicked, impaled to the ground by the arrow. Sharp rocks tore through his dungarees and bloodied his legs. When he reached the rabbit, Tucker twisted its neck, and he returned to the safety of the overhang. He fished a match from his saddlebags and, praying for the first time since childhood, hoped that this one rabbit would give him enough strength to continue. And to find Lorna.

CHAPTER 26

Tucker awoke to the soothing sounds of steady rainfall. He crawled over sharp rocks as he made his way to the edge of the outcropping. How long it had rained he was uncertain. But he knew from experience that the Badlands clay would soak up whatever water offered it and make walking and moving about double hard. Even standing could present problems on the gooey, slick mud. Still, he knew he had to move if he was to find Lorna.

He crawled back under the rock and lay with his head against his cave. He closed his eyes. Just a moment longer, he thought. Just a moment longer, and he'd gather strength enough to look for Lorna.

And the steady rainfall lulled him to sleep.

Tucker bolted upright. Had it been the rain that had awakened him, or had it been something else? He turned his head, watching and listening. His small campfire had been extinguished after he'd eaten the rabbit, so he was certain no one spotted it. And, until a moment ago, he had felt secure hidden under the rock.

Across the valley, the bank gave away to the hard rain and plunged mud into the rising water, exposing yellow-tan and rusty-red mudstone shale beneath the dirt. Creeping jennies uncurled their long tendrils as they reached their parched pods toward the rain. Yellow wallflowers collapsed with the surrounding mud, their buds like tiny ships floating away on the water toward the narrow end of the valley. Tucker realized the rain would soon reach torrential proportions and flood the valley in a dangerous flash flood, including the rock outcropping that had been his protector for the last six hours. Had the mud-sliding rock awakened him, or had something else, just outside the safety of his cave?

He slung the bow across his back and grabbed on to the side of the rock to help him stand. He hobbled to the edge of the cave. The rain had intensified since he'd fallen asleep, and it pelted the side of his face. Mud walls slid into the raging river of the Badlands flash flood. He would have to traverse a narrow ledge from where the outcropping protected him and go along that ledge to where he could crawl ten feet up the slippery bank. But he would have to do it soon. Already the water had risen high enough to erode the bank directly beneath him. If he was to make his move, it would have to be now.

Pain from the festering arrow wound caused him to double over, and he nearly lost his balance as he teetered on trembling legs. The thought of walking farther on that leg sent chills through him. The thought of being carried away by the flash flood was even more chilling. He'd already had to fight for his life during one such flood, and he was certain he'd run out of chances.

He crawled toward the edge of the outcropping when he froze. Sounds of things not heard in nature filtered through the rain, sounds that came from directly overhead. He strained but heard nothing. He began crawling out of the cave when the snort of an impatient pony rose over the sound of the thunderstorm. Tucker strained to hear, but the noise of the flood overrode any other sounds around him.

He lay on his back, stifling a cry of pain when his leg hit the ground. He inched to the edge of the cave. He heard the clomp of feet and muffled words between men, and

Tucker became aware he stared at the flank of a Sioux war pony. He scooted out another foot and saw a moccasined leg dangling over the horse's back.

The effort to crawl had exhausted him, and he sucked in great gulps of air before crawling out farther. Warriors sat astride their ponies as they talked. They were looking for him, and he thanked God that the storm concealed his tracks and his presence.

He retreated into the cave and looked across the gully. The water had risen a foot since he'd crawled out to spot the Indians, and the torrent angrily chipped away at the soft bank beneath Tucker's cave. Another two feet, he estimated, and the water would be high enough to trap him inside.

Another snort of a pony, and he chanced another look. The war party talked amongst themselves. One waved the air toward the far bank of the river. They became silent and slowly rode off, and Tucker was certain other Lakota hunted him in other parts of the canyon. It was only a matter of time before one spotted him and moved in for the kill. But he also knew that if he stuck with those Indians, they would lead him to where they held Lorna. The thought of a crippled man on foot following Lakota on horseback made him laugh. But he had no other choice. If he could stay on them and bide his time, he could steal a horse when he had the chance.

He took the bow and used it for a crutch as he stood. With a last look at his cave, he slung his saddlebags over his shoulder and stepped away from the outcropping. Mud clung to his feet, and he brought each foot up with a sucking sound as he walked. Another step, and he used his hand to help his bad leg up the slippery bank. He grabbed onto a willow root sticking out of the bank, but the ground gave way. The uprooted tree tore from the side of the hill. It fell into the water and raced on by as suddenly as a man blinks an eye.

Tucker's crutch give way, and he fell. Slick gumbo sucked him toward the torrent. Sliding. Slipping. First one leg, then the other dropped over the side of the bank, and he clutched at rocks with bleeding hands. The water soaked his boots, rising higher. He dropped his saddlebags, and his last thoughts were of Lorna.

A cottonwood trunk caromed off the opposite bank, coming straight for him when strong hands clasped his collar, tore through, then another hand grabbed an arm. He felt himself being dragged up the bank, away from the river. His head grazed a cactus, and stickers imbedded in his cheek as someone pulled him across the muddy ground.

Strong hands dropped Tucker onto the wet ground overhead. He shielded his eyes with his hands and looked down the bore of a rifle.

CHAPTER 27

Jimmy Swallow grabbed his bow and notched an arrow as he scurried toward a boulder. "I hear him coming, too."

The rain had begun again, soft at first, then harder, nearly masking the sound of the approaching horse.

Blue Boy nodded and grabbed Lorna by the arm. He led her toward the safety of a group of three boulders and set her on the ground.

Lorna jerked free. "I'm not one of your other wives . . ."

Blue Boy's face had assumed the look he got when danger neared. "Do not leave this place."

She rubbed her arm while he grabbed his rifle and crouched behind a rock.

The hoofbeats fast approached, the rider not caring if he was heard. He rode through the natural boulder doorway, and Blue Boy yelled to Swallow. "Do not shoot your arrow!"

Blue Boy ran to Black Dog, slumped over in the saddle, and grabbed the reins of his pony. Water dripped down his scuffed cheeks, yet he still forced a smile. *"Hau, tahanski."*

Blue Boy eased him off his horse. The rain had washed his shirt nearly free of blood, but the flannel fabric remained pasted to the bullet wound in his shoulder. Blue Boy led Black Dog to a cottonwood stump under the protection of a rock ledge and laid him down.

Jimmy Swallow ran to Black Dog. "You have been shot."

Black Dog looked up through glassy eyes. "You have learned something about being a warrior." He grimaced. "You can tell when a man has been shot. Good."

Blue Boy grabbed medicine out of his saddlebag and used his knife to slice Black Dog's shirt away. "Get the woman," Black Dog said, and Swallow ran to the boulder to bring Lorna back.

"He Who Follows" — Black Dog said as Blue Boy spread the wound apart to look at it — "killed Pawnee Killer."

"We know," Blue Boy said. He grabbed a concoction of sage and chokecherries and worked them into a paste. "Pawnee Killer's horse brought him faithfully back here."

Black Dog looked around the clearing pelted by rain. "Where . . . ?"

"His pony brought him into our camp a few miles over there" — Blue Boy chin-pointed to the east — "with this stuck in his back." He handed Black Dog the knife that had been stuck in Pawnee Killer.

Black Dog nodded. "It is the one who follows. His eyes see where they should not."

"Not now —"

"We followed his tracks to the white man's town," Black Dog interrupted with an urgency in his voice. "Pawnee Killer went to the north end of the town. I rode south of Cowtown to find the white man's sign. I heard two quick shots in the direction of where Pawnee Killer had ridden. By the time I got there, all that was left was blood-sign telling me Pawnee Killer and his pony were gone."

"How this then?" Blue Boy motioned to Black Dog's injured shoulder.

"I set an ambush even He Who Follows could not have spotted. I notched an arrow. Let it go. But He Who Follows jumped from his mule, and the arrow flew past him and into the mule. I killed his mule, and He Who Follows shot me." He grimaced as Blue Boy stuffed the sage poultice into the bullet hole. He looked about for something to stop the bleeding when Lorna approached, walking beside Swallow. "I have my . . . underthings. They are white and made out of the cotton plant. I can rip enough material for a dressing."

Blue Boy began to tell Swallow to follow her into the brush so that she did not run off. But he realized she would not shirk her duty at a time like this. She was developing into a Lakota woman after all. "It will make a good dressing. Please," Blue Boy said.

The rain had increased, but they were in no danger of being washed away. Under the rocks of their high camp, the ground was dry, and Blue Boy had built a small fire to warm Black Dog. "We will have to leave, Swallow and me."

"Going after He Who Follows?"

Blue Boy nodded. "Sticking his knife into Pawnee Killer's back was an insult we cannot ignore."

"And the woman?" Black Dog asked.

Blue Boy looked into the far corner of their outcropping. Lorna sat with her back against a rock, knees bent, hugging them as she rocked back and forth. "She is in no shape to leave. Besides, she has a one-armed

Lakota to watch her."

Black Dog swatted Blue Boy on the arm, but there was little conviction in his punch.

Blue Boy tied the strip of petticoat around Black Dog's shoulder and neck when Swallow ducked under the rock. "The ponies are ready."

"Go," Black Dog said. "I will watch the woman until you return."

Blue Boy laid more branches onto the fire before duck-walking to Lorna. "Will you be all right here with Black Dog?"

She motioned to the wounded man. "He is no Wild Wind. I feel safe here with him."

Blue Boy resisted the urge to kiss her good-bye. There would be time enough for that later. "Take care of my friend."

"I will," Lorna answered.

"And thank you again for tearing your petticoat for a bandage."

Lorna didn't answer but looked from Black Dog to the opening of the cave, as if she had other ideas.

CHAPTER 28

Jess Hammond grinned at Tucker through chipped teeth and winked with his swollen eye. Beside him, Philo Brown stood with his floppy hat pulled over his eyes against the rain pelting his face. He picked his teeth with an "Arkansas toothpick" and drew it across his throat as he smiled.

"Why'd you save me?" Tucker shouted at them over the roar of the thunderstorm.

"Because I told them to." Aurand's hat was pulled low, and water dripped off his nose. "I want you dead, Tuck ol' salt. But I aim to do it myself. You killed Con back in Cowtown, and that doesn't set right with me. You beat hell out of Jess —"

"He got lucky," Jess blurted out.

Aurand looked sideways at Jess and shook his head. "And you almost got Philo here lynched." He squatted next to Tucker. "I thought all I wanted was you dangling at the end of a rope. Now I realize I want you at the end of my pistol sights." Aurand slapped Tucker's wounded leg. Tucker gritted his teeth in pain, but he did not give Aurand the satisfaction of yelling. "Looks like you should have ducked a mite quicker when some Indian shot you."

"Look." Tucker struggled to sit up. "I'll face you. Just you and me. With a town full of witnesses. But only if you let me go to find Lorna Moore."

"Lorna Moore's out here?"

"Lakota took her from town."

"I told you I figured Blue Boy's bunch has a woman with them." Red Sun ran his hand over one of his mare's white stockings. He stood up straight and arched his back. The rain beat down on his bald head, but he seemed to be impervious to the storm. He pulled his hat low and wiped water from his eyes. "I could not imagine Blue Boy taking one of his women on this raid. I figured it was that missing shopkeeper."

Aurand scanned the far ridge they'd just come from. "You mean one of those two Indians sitting on that ridge over yonder was Blue Boy?"

Red nodded and retrieved papers and a pouch of tobacco from his pocket. He bent over against the rain and rolled a smoke.

"My guess is Lorna's daddy put up a reward for her," Tucker said. "Let me go, and I'll give it all to you when I bring her home safe."

Aurand seemed to be weighing Tucker's proposition when a smile creased his face. "Wouldn't matter if the reward was twice that. The only reward I want is you standing tall in the street."

Aurand nodded to Jess, and Tucker turned his head in time to see a rifle butt smash squarely on his chin.

Tucker fought for consciousness, but the last thing he saw before he went under was the grimace of hatred crossing Aurand's face.

Tucker awakened from a fitful sleep. His chin throbbed from Jess's rifle butt. A large welt had formed on the side of his jaw, and dried blood caked his chin stubble. He remained silent and listened. The rain had stopped, and the only thing he heard was sap popping from a nearby campfire.

He opened his eyes and shielded them from the morning sun as he looked about. Shackles secured his legs together, and the swelling of his injured leg seemed to have diminished. That was the one small thing in his predicament to be grateful for.

He stood and hit the end of a chain wrapped around a cottonwood log five feet away. He thought at first that Aurand had left him chained here, when he spotted a form lying ten yards off in some reed grass. His snoring rose and fell with the pitch of the wind, the sound muted under the man's floppy hat. "That you, Red?"

The snoring stopped.

"Least you can do is get me a swig of water."

Red pushed his hat on the back of his head. He propped himself up with an elbow and shook his head. "You're a mess." Red stood and walked to packs sitting beside the fire. "Never thought it would be so easy to get the drop on Tucker Ashley."

Tucker rattled the chain. "I'm kind of handicapped. Pass that water over."

Red handed Tucker a deerskin water bladder and stayed well away from the end of the chain. Tucker took a shallow sip first to lose the raw in his throat, then a longer pull as he considered this to be the last water he'd have for a time. If Aurand were here, Tucker was certain he would have overridden Red's generosity. "Where's Aurand and the others?"

Red broke off a chew of his plug and pocketed the rest. "Aurand and Philo rode out for meat. Philo saw a herd of prong-horns fleeing that gully washer we had."

"And Jess?"

"Out there." He waved his hand over the prairie. "He seems to think those Sioux have doubled back and are looking for our camp." Red laughed.

"But you don't believe it?"

Red spat a string of tobacco juice that the wind took dangerously close to Tucker's head. "With last night's rain, those Lakota couldn't find buffalo tracks in this mud, let alone men holed up here." He waved his arm around the campsite shielded by boulders and thick sandstone spires. "No, if they find this camp it will be with the help of their *Wakan Tanka*. And a lot of luck."

Tucker stretched his arm toward Red and handed him back the water bladder. "What's Aurand got planned for me?"

Red set the bladder beside a saddle and squatted in front of Tucker. "Aurand aims to see you dead. But he wants what he calls a fair fight."

"One on one?"

"One on one."

"But Aurand knows even on a good day I couldn't beat his draw." Tucker rubbed the stiffness out of his leg and massaged his broken knuckles, which had bruised black.

"And it seems like it'll be some time before I have another good day."

"Does not matter to him."

"So all he really wants is for me to be able to stand up long enough for him to put a slug in my gut?"

"You do have a grasp of your predicament." Red turned back to his saddlebag. "So I guess the least I can do is doctor your leg some more."

"So he can kill me quicker?"

Red ignored him and rooted in his beaded possibles bag. He came out with a tin cup and a small deerskin pouch. He untied the pouch and withdrew another, smaller one. He sprinkled powder into a cup before he dribbled water over it and mixed the paste with his finger. "You ain't going to try anything on ol' Red, are you?"

"I will if I get a chance," Tucker answered.

"That's what I figured." Red unsheathed his knife and stuck it in the ground beside him. "Insurance." He knelt close to Tucker and set the cup on the ground. "Bring your leg closer."

Tucker felt his leg hit the end of the chain, and he gingerly dragged it closer to where Red could work on it. Red pulled the cloth away from the wound and peeled some hide stuck to Tucker's trousers. "Sorry," Red said.

"And I'd like to think I'm sorry about Con," Tucker spoke between gritted teeth. "But I'm not. Heard you and him hunted now and again."

Red shrugged as he examined the arrow hole. "Just once when Aurand saddled me with the kid. We did not exactly develop a lasting friendship." He mixed the poultice with his finger. "So I will lose no sleep over your gunfight with him. The kid knew he could go any time if he met someone faster." He looked around as if people lurked about to hear him and lowered his voice. "My opinion? The kid deserved an early grave. Lord knows he sent enough men to theirs who were no gun hands." He nodded to Tucker's leg. "Or men not quite up to a fight. So I'm not losing any shuteye over his demise."

Red dribbled water over his bandana. He cleaned the dried poultice he'd applied before and dripped water over the stitches he'd put in. He scooped fresh poultice from the cup and smeared it over the wound with his finger. Tucker gritted his teeth and stiffened with the pain. Red wiped excess blood and poultice off on his pant leg before he wrapped a bandana snugly around the leg.

He stood just out of Tucker's reach and looked down at him. "Just so you know, I don't hold no grudge agin' you. When Aurand kills you, I will not dance a happy jig over your grave."

"That's mighty white of you," Tucker said. He leaned back against the rock and massaged his leg. "Least you can do is tell me if you heard what happened to Jack Worman?"

Red spat his tobacco out and reloaded his cheek with fresh plug. "Now that's kind of funny. Ironic, them educated people would claim. When the cowboys lit out after the killer of that shopkeeper — I imagine it was you who gave them the wrong directions — some hung back. When they spotted Jack —"

"Jack was in Cowtown?"

"He was there looking for you, be my guess. When those cowboys who stayed in town spotted Jack . . . well, they was looking to string somebody up."

"You're saying Jack's been lynched?"

"I never seen it myself," Red answered. "But the way Sadie at the saloon tells it, Jack was a stranger they did not recognize. It would bother them none if they hung an innocent man as long as someone paid. Old

Clive was a popular man in Cowtown." Red bit off a chunk of jerky and chewed on the side opposite his tobacco. He tossed Tucker the jerky. "That must be some woman you're chasing after."

"What do you know of her? Is she all right?"

"Whoa." Red held up his hand. "I ain't seen her since I bought that box of rifle ammo in her store last month. Only thing I know is she is with Blue Boy's band."

"You sure she's still with him?"

"Son," Red said, "I was tracking Indians when you were an idea in your daddy's mind. Of course I am sure. No one makes deep tracks like that murdering bastard."

"So you know she is alive?"

"She was two days ago."

"You seen her?" Tucker pulled at the chain.

"I said I ain't," Red answered. "Just her sign where they camped off Bear Lodge Creek. By the looks of the tracks, there is some buck always close by her. My guess is they guard her almighty close." He caught the jerky Tucker tossed back. "But she was alive."

Tucker fell back against the rock. *Lorna's still alive. Still fighting.* He looked over at Red, who had stood and walked back to his bedroll. *I've got to get away.* Far enough away from Aurand and his bunch, but close enough that Blue Boy could pick up his sign. For Tucker had no doubt that Blue Boy would want to avenge the death of the braves Tucker had killed. And he'd find Tucker's trail. He was counting on it.

Chapter 29

Early into the afternoon Tucker awoke to a horse riding hard into camp. *Only a fool or someone desperate rides a horse like that in this heat,* he thought. He sat up as far as his leg chain would allow to get a better look at the rider. Tucker turned to speak with Red, but he had disappeared into the brush.

When the rider topped the hill south of their camp, the unmistaken swollen face and broken nose of Jess Hammond reflected the light. He fixed his gaze on Tucker as he slowed to a fast walk. When he reached the center of the camp, he stopped his horse beside Tucker. The animal shook his head, flinging lather onto Tucker's face. "You all alone now?" Jess asked.

"Not hardly." Red emerged from wherever he had been hiding. "Just that I wanted to see who the fool is come riding hell-bent for election into camp."

Jess dismounted. "Aurand says he's mighty

worried about those Lakota."

"What's to worry about?" Red laid branches across the coals and blew on the fire to flare it up. "They are long gone for the Great Wall. Knowing Blue Boy like I do, he's taken his white woman with him, and they're at the bottom of the Badlands by now. He's probably mighty impatient to break in his new bride."

Tucker tried to stand but fell against the chain. Red looked at him and smiled. "Nothing personal, but you know the score with these Sioux. Having multiple wives. Hell, that ought to make you feel good, knowing that woman of yours is alive and just waiting to please her new husband."

Tucker drew in deep, calming breaths as he fought against his pain and anger, and the thought of what suffering Lorna must have had to endure thus far. Red was right: Tucker had known almost from the start that Blue Boy took Lorna that night from her room to make her his newest wife. And once they reached the safety of the Wall, they would wed in the custom of the Lakota.

Tucker thought back to the woman abducted by the Lakota who had escaped two summers ago. Tucker had talked with her at Ft. Pierre after her escape. The men had treated her well. Exceptionally well, in some instances. It had been the competing women and the other women in the band who had torn at the soul of the captive. The Crow and Pawnee women — natural enemies of the Lakota — had been picked apart by the badgering and the back-breaking work and beatings at the hands of other tribal women, but it had been the white woman who had been mistreated by Sioux women the most. Tucker knew that — with Blue Boy to protect her — Lorna could live out a satisfying existence. Until he went on a war party or hunting foray away from camp. Then the abuse would resume.

"Red's right." Jess grinned. "By now, that Indian's sharing a tipi with her and breaking her in proper."

Tucker lunged at Jess but hit the end of his chain. Pain radiated from Tucker's bad leg all the way through the rest of his body.

"Calm down, Tucker," Jess said. "Maybe there is some hope yet. Maybe Red here'll pick up those Indians' trail."

"What that?" Red set a coffee pot over the fire.

"Aurand wants you to find Blue Boy and his band. Aurand's waiting at Rocking Chair Creek for you. He says to find where they went and come tell him pronto."

"Why not you?"

Jess smiled and took out his pocket knife. He began picking what teeth he had left. "Us city boys wouldn't last more'n a day out there looking for Indians. Aurand needs someone who can work a track."

"Aurand wants me to find Blue Boy?" Red's hand trembled as he filled his cup. "Now?"

"He does."

"Most folks who have found Blue Boy didn't live to tell anyone where he was."

Jess laid a hand on Red's thin shoulder and squeezed hard. "But Red Sun could find him. Aurand wants that woman found. He don't care so much about those Sioux."

Red shook off Jess's hand. "Why the interest in that woman all of a sudden?"

Jess shrugged. "Guess Aurand's realized he better get her back. Wouldn't look good for a territorial marshal to ignore an abducted citizen." Jess winked at Red. "Or maybe he's been thinking of that reward money. Either way, you better saddle up and find those Indians."

"Someone has to watch Tucker."

"What's to watch," Jess said. "He's chained up. I'll stay until you come back."

Red tossed his coffee onto the ground and started for his horse. He paused and looked down at Tucker with sadness. "Good luck," he said and walked into the brush. Although he couldn't see it, Tucker knew the old man had his horse tethered apart from the camp. A few moments later, hoofbeats riding away from the camp grew fainter.

Tucker turned his attention back to Jess. He stood on the other side of the campfire and began taking off his gun belt. "Aurand never wanted Red to scout for Blue Boy, did he?"

"You're smarter than you look." Jess dropped his Bowie beside his gun belt and rolled up his sleeves. "I wanted another crack at you. You didn't dance fair the other night in Cowtown."

"Aurand will kill you if I'm found beaten to death."

"So the little man will be mad. By the time he finds your body, I'll have hopped a stage to California and won't ever see Aurand again."

"It angered you that much that I beat you the other night?"

"Let's say I never been beat before."

"You forgetting about Blue Boy cold-cocking you in the saloon?"

Jess frowned. "If I thought we'd have any chance to find that Indian, I'd take him on, too. Point is, he's not here, and you are."

"You that afraid of me?"

"Afraid?" Jess stopped rolling his shirt-sleeves up. "How so?"

"You want to fight me while I'm shackled to this tree, and with a bum leg to boot?"

Jess paused and seemed to mull that over. He fished a key out of his pocket and tossed it to Tucker.

Tucker unlocked the leg irons and dropped them on the ground beside him. He massaged circulation back in his leg where the shackle had rubbed his ankle red and raw. "And my bum leg?"

"I'll try not to hit it." Jess grinned. He stood in the middle of the clearing, flexing and unflexing his fists as he waited for Tucker to toe the line. Tucker continued to massage feeling back into his leg as he tested his weight on it. Red's medicine had worked, but Tucker's leg still felt as if a coyote had gnawed on it all night.

He limped to where Jess stood waiting. Although it had only been a few hours since the rain stopped, there was little left to indicate there had been a nasty storm. All that greeted Tucker was the hard ground and a man bent on beating him to death.

Tucker toed the line, careful not to put too much weight on his bad leg.

Jess smiled through broken teeth, his

tongue flicking past spaces in his gums like sentries peeking around a fort's walkway. Jess had learned something from their last fight. He began to circle well out of Tucker's long reach.

Tucker tried turning to match Jess's movement, but each time he turned to face the big man, his weight shifted and pain shot up his wounded leg.

Jess smiled, and Tucker knew he'd figured out how to prolong Tucker's agony. He circled first one way, then the other. Each time he turned to match Jess's movement, Tucker nearly cried out in pain.

Suddenly, Jess slid to one side and flicked out a jab that caught Tucker flush on the cheekbone. It wasn't a hard blow, but it rocked Tucker, and he staggered back. He wasn't sure he could stand another shot like that, when Jess proved him right. A left hook landed on Tucker's jaw. His head snapped back, and he felt himself falling backwards. His head hit the hard ground with a vengeance, and pain shuddered all the way down to his toes.

"Don't move so fancy now, do you boy?" Jess stood over him. "Get up. We ain't done dancing."

Tucker remained on his back. He pawed sweat out of his eye as he focused on Jess, who bent over Tucker and hoisted him to his feet. Jess let him loose, and he began circling Tucker again. "I owe you," Jess said and landed a jab on Tucker's eye. He stumbled back. As Jess came in for another, Tucker landed an uppercut that rocked Jess back. Tucker moved toward him for a follow-up blow, but his leg buckled. He just caught himself from falling down and turned to face Jess.

"You do have some spunk left." Jess flicked two quick jabs meant to harass Tucker. They connected to his nose and watered his eyes. "You could have got me and Philo killed in Cowtown." A quick jab landed above Tucker's eye, and blood dripped into it from split skin. He staggered back and threw a roundhouse. Jess moved back, and Tucker fell to the ground.

"And this is for that nasty little headache you gave me." Jess kicked Tucker's bad leg. He tilted his head back and laughed when Tucker writhed in pain.

He rolled over and caught sight of the bedroll where Jess had tossed his knife and gun. Twenty feet away. Might as well have been twenty miles away, unless Tucker could work close enough to grab either.

He stood on wobbly legs when Jess lashed out with a right cross. Tucker pulled back;

the blow caught him on the side of the head. He rolled with the punch and allowed himself to fall down, closer to the bedroll. One more punch to mask his moves, and he'd be close enough to grab Jess's gun or his knife.

Tucker stood bent over as he sucked in breaths. "You hit like an old woman," he told Jess and braced himself for the charge he knew would come.

"Woman!" Jess bellowed. With his fists flailing in the air, he hit Tucker in the stomach with his head. The force of Jess's charge drove Tucker back twenty feet. And within reach of the gun.

Jess landed on top of Tucker. As he swung a hard right at Tucker's head, Tucker grabbed a rock and hit Jess on the forehead. Jess screamed in pain, and Tucker rolled over onto his stomach. He gathered his good leg beneath him and sprang for the bedroll. He landed beside it as Jess hollered again when he realized Tucker's plan.

He grabbed for Jess's Remington, but Jess clamped his hand onto Tucker's arm and smashed his hand into a rock. He let go of the gun, and Jess snatched it from him. Tucker lunged for the knife, but Jess rolled out of slashing range.

Jess sat back on his haunches and turned

so he could focus on Tucker out of his good eye. Jess smiled a toothless grin as he leveled his gun at Tucker's head. "Aurand will think it came down to you coming at me with a knife, and I had to defend myself."

Tucker stood and crow-hopped on his good leg. "Who'd believe that cockamamie story?"

"Only one who has to is Aurand."

"I thought you were going to California."

Jess grinned. "That's when I hadn't run into this little scenario. Even Aurand would believe I had no choice, you wrestling my knife from me and all after Red unlocked your shackles."

"So you admit I'm too much a man for you to fight fair?"

Jess turned red, and his gun hand trembled. "Let's just say no one else will know." He cocked his gun.

Tucker held the knife in front of him like a shield.

Jess smiled. He pointed his Remington at Tucker's head and took up the trigger slack.

The shot reverberated off the surrounding rock. Tucker slumped over while he checked himself for holes. Jess looked down at an exit hole through his chest. He fired his gun into the ground beside Tucker and fell face first into the dirt.

Simon Cady walked out of the brush and into the clearing, leading his small brown donkey tied to the pommel of his chestnut's saddle. "Hold these," he said and handed Tucker the reins.

Tucker took hold of the reins while Cady slid his Spencer back into his saddle scabbard. "Bet you wonder why old Simon saved you." He squatted beside Jess's body. Though he was twenty years Tucker's junior, Cady easily hoisted Jess onto the donkey's back. "You figure it out yet?"

Tucker shook his head. He had never met Cady, but his reputation as a scoundrel preceded him. Few people with a bounty on their heads lived to tell how the trip to the law went with Cady. He had scouted for the army — old scouts told tales around campfires. He had been with Chivington in Colorado when the state militia had murdered unarmed Arapaho at Sand Creek in 'sixty-four. Some even thought Cady set the whole thing up. And bad legend had dogged him ever since.

"Jess Hammond here's got a sizeable bounty on him. Man's been working for Aurand Forester, but on the side he's been robbing and killing all around the territory."

"How'd you find him?"

Cady took rope out of his saddlebags and

walked around his donkey. "Aurand is so predictable. I began following him knowing he was after you. I knew he'd need every criminal working for him as a deputy if he were to best the likes of Tucker Ashley. I knew he'd *have* to meet up with Jess somewhere." Cady took out a pipe and filled it with tobacco. "I almost had Jess the other night in Cowtown, when you spoiled my fun by beating him in front of a hundred witnesses."

"Excuse the hell out of me for surviving."

Cady brushed the air as if telling Tucker it was all right. In the end. "Aurand thought I was after the bounty offered for that little lady from the mercantile."

"Aren't you?" Tucker leaned against Cady's horse to steady himself. His arrow wound had opened up again, and sticky warm blood oozed down his leg. "Aren't you after her for the reward?"

"Friend," Cady said as he cinched the rope tight holding Jess's body onto the donkey, "I don't go after women. Some folks say I have a propensity to kill my prey." He shrugged and walked around the animal as he snugged Jess's body to the pack frame. "If there's a bounty on your woman, let someone else collect it. I'll stick to my kind of hunting. Besides" — he turned Jess's leg over to look at his new boots — "sometimes the man I hunt wears my size." He laughed. "A bonus, don't you think?"

Tucker debated if he could mount Cady's horse before he realized it. But the Spencer within Cady's reach told Tucker that was a bad idea.

Cady took the reins from him and seemed to be reading his mind as he motioned to the rocks. "If you can sit a horse with that bum leg, Jess's gelding looks like he's willing. He's grazing over yonder." He motioned to a nearby hill. "And you have my permission to take his gun." Cady swung a leg over his horse, and it groaned with the weight. He started away from the camp when he stopped and turned in his saddle. "If you're still foolish enough to go after Blue Boy, I saw him looking for you during that storm. I'm thinking he's hanging out closer to the Badlands about now. Waiting for something. Just this side of the Wall."

Tucker watched Cady disappear down a hill and then turned to Jess's bedroll. He grabbed the gun belt and put it around his waist. But it was too long, so he slung it over his shoulder before tucking the Bowie into Jess's belt sheath.

Tucker walked to Jess's horse and ran his hand along the gelding's muzzle as he spoke softly. He gathered the reins and swung his bum leg over the side and into the saddle. Pain shot up all the way to his head, and he felt himself become lightheaded. He took deep breaths as he fought to remain conscious. He couldn't let himself go under right now. There had been Cady's Spencer firing, followed closely by Jess's pistol shot. A man might speculate where a single shot came from. Two shots, and whoever heard it would know where it originated. The gunshots would warn Aurand that there had been trouble in his camp. But at least it would tell Blue Boy where Tucker was.

Tucker was counting on that.

Chapter 30

Blue Boy reined his horse up sharply. He sat motionless on top of a rise as he cupped his hand to his ear. Two shots. Coming from the east. Close.

Black Dog stopped his pony beside Blue Boy. He had pried the slug out of Black Dog's shoulder, and it hung in a makeshift sling made out of Lorna's petticoat. When he and Swallow had ridden back to camp without finding He Who Follows, Black Dog was up and insisting he come along on the hunt. "I heard it, too." Black Dog sniffed the wind like a coyote. "I think it came from the east."

Jimmy Swallow pulled up the rear. He walked his pony towards Blue Boy and Black Dog.

"You hear shots?" Blue Boy asked. "Or are Black Dog and me losing our minds?"

"I heard them," Swallow answered and chin-pointed to the northeast. "They came from that way."

"I do not think so," Black Dog said. "The ones that I heard came from there." He pointed. "Straight east."

"I think they came from the east as well." Blue Boy turned to Lorna riding in front of Swallow. "What direction do you say the shots came from?"

"The shots came from the northeast. Swallow is right." Lorna looked into Blue Boy's eyes. "Swallow is young. You two are . . . older. Perhaps both of you have been hit on the head once too often, and that cost you your hearing. All I know is the shots came from where Swallow said."

Blue Boy digested what Lorna told him. Perhaps Jimmy Swallow's young ears had heard better than his and Black Dog's. "What else can you tell us about the shots?" Blue Boy asked.

Swallow puffed out his thin chest. "I know that one was a rifle and the other a pistol. And at least one was a *wasicu.*"

Blue Boy looked down at the young warrior. "And how did you come up with that wonderful conclusion?"

"Only a white man carries a short gun into this hostile place. He would not last long if his life depended on a pistol."

Blue Boy thought of Swallow's logic.

Perhaps a chief could learn from the littlest of braves who followed him. "I think you are right, and He Who Follows just fired off a shot. We will start in the direction you heard them."

Black Dog trotted his horse beside Blue Boy, and he nodded to Lorna. "She slows us down enough. If we go after He Who Follows, the Badlands may elude us after all. And perhaps the woman will seize her chance to escape."

"Enough!" Blue Boy hunched over and stroked his horse's withers as he spoke to Black Dog. "Whoever that man is, he has killed many of us. If we do not avenge the deaths of the others, their dishonor will rest on our heads."

Black Dog sat tall on his pony, his arm in his sling, looking as if he cared little for the outcome of their conversation. "He Who Follows does so to free her." He pointed to Lorna. "It is for that reason you want him dead. She has the white man in her heart. Killing him will never release her to you."

Blue Boy looked at Lorna. Even after a hard week on the trail, she still carried her defiant look as she sat the pony in front of Swallow. "In time, she will come to love the life of being a war chief's woman. In time she will grow to think only of me. Not of

He Who Follows. Now go and eat. It may be the last meal you have for some time."

Blue Boy sat his dun on a high hill overlooking a shallow valley leading northeast. His stomach growled, yet he ignored it. There were other things on his mind as he studied the terrain. They were close to the Badlands. How close, he was never sure, for they were unlike any other mountains. His people thought of them as mountains growing into Mother Earth. They did not rise up like the Shining Mountains of the Arapaho, or the majestic peaks of the *Paha Sapa,* the Black Hills. The Badlands offered stone fingers and granite and shale as the only warning to their harshness. Travelers rode into those mountains at their peril, and many did not return. The sunken mountains came upon unsuspecting travelers as suddenly as the frequent flash floods down her valleys. Perhaps Black Dog was right. Perhaps he should forget He Who Follows and ride into the safety of the Badlands with his woman.

He turned to watch the others seated around a fire roasting rabbits and a quail Swallow had killed. He wondered if he were doing the right thing as a leader of his band. What band he had left. But if he fled to the safety of the Great Wall now, his people would tell how he had pursued the white man. And had allowed him to live even after he had killed so many of Blue Boy's warriors.

He left them and rode along the hillside. He had gone not a hundred yards when he topped a hill, and suddenly the Badlands loomed before him. He reined his horse to a stop as he sucked in a breath. He knew they had been close, yet he always reacted the same way when he saw them and the Wall that protected the Lakota. The Great Wall lay scooped out of the earth before him. Hundred-foot spires jutted up from the ground that seemed to be peppered with the white man's popcorn: pea-size clumps of dried gumbo that would trip a horse up and kill its rider on the way down.

He recalled old men telling stories as they warmed their hands by the fire in the center of their winter lodge. They told of vast herds of *tatanka* being driven over the cliffs of the Great Wall to their deaths. Those buffalo had given their life so that the Lakota *Oyate*, the Seven Council Fires of the Lakota Nation, should live and flourish.

His thoughts drifted to the French trappers, and to the raid White Swan had led four summers ago, the man still dangerous in his old age. Those warriors relentlessly dogged the trappers as they picked their way down the long and treacherous, steeply winding, narrow trail. The Frenchmen had lost two of their party to falls from the trail, and two more from lack of water. White Swan's Miniconjou had caught them halfway across the barren desert at the floor of the Badlands. *"Les mauvaises terres à traverser,"* they cried. "Bad lands to travel" — right before they met their deaths at the hands of White Swan's Lakota.

Blue Boy knew from growing up around the white man that most could not endure a trip across that sunken desert. Wherever he looked, he saw the shimmering waves of mirages of false hopes, rivers and ponds that did not exist except in the mind's eye. A land wicked enough to confuse even the best of men.

He continued to gaze across that familiar land and felt that special serenity found only in visions. Peace could come to him and Lorna. They could live the natural life of the Lakota. Only there followed a white man who tugged at the shirtsleeves of Blue Boy's elusive peace. Black Dog was right, of course. His friend often displayed wisdom possessed by those much older than he. It was true that Lorna slowed them down and that he could not free her. He had taken her as a hunter takes a prize elk, something to display above the smoke hole of the lodge. And it was true that if they ran for the Wall now, they could evade He Who Follows.

Blue Boy sighed deeply and turned his horse around toward his camp. He knew what he must do.

Blue Boy rode east into the bright sun. He had said his morning prayers, thanking the four winds and Mother Earth and the sky. And he thanked *Wakan Tanka* that there were no clouds to mask the shadows of the white man's tracks. He studied the ground, while the others walked behind him, not wanting to disturb sign left by He Who Follows.

At a fetid stream trickling from yesterday's storm, the white man had dismounted. He had led his horse while he walked around. He had limped around the clearing on a foot he favored, even dragging his lame leg across the ground at times. Blue Boy said a silent prayer that the man would live long enough to feel Blue Boy's blade enter his chest.

Blue Boy had watched Lorna out of the corner of his eye most of the morning as she rode with Jimmy Swallow. She seemed to know that they had turned back to hunt her man. She hadn't even glanced Blue Boy's way since they mounted up after their meal. During the night, she had hobbled their ponies with the strings she had taken from her boots. A vain attempt, she had admitted, meant to slow them down. And one that had cost them only as long as it took to slice the boot strings off the ponies' legs.

Blue Boy turned his attention back to the white man's tracks, when he stopped abruptly. He dismounted and squatted next to where a second track impressed itself over the tracks of He Who Follows. Black Dog rode up to where Blue Boy knelt. "Another begins to follow the woman's man."

"And riding hard." Blue Boy motioned to tracks going in the direction of He Who Follows, as distinct as if he had put up little sign posts along the way. "At this rate, we will catch up to him within hours."

"Unless this new hunter finds him first," Black Dog said.

Blue Boy felt rage well up inside him. He hadn't come this far, and taken his band away from the sanctuary of the Badlands, to be thwarted by someone out to kill the man. *His* man.

CHAPTER 31

As Tucker rode to the ridge overlooking Medicine Root Creek, his leg began to stiffen. He grabbed the saddle horn tightly and lowered himself gingerly to the ground to stretch his muscles. Any other time in his life, he would have dismounted fifty yards back and low-crawled to the ridge. But his strength was slow in returning, and he wasn't sure he could have crawled that far. He needed rest, he knew. But he also knew he was on to Blue Boy's tracks, and rest wasn't an option.

Simon Cady's shot that killed Jess Hammond would alert the Indians, he was certain, if they were still within the sound of the gunshots. Sending the young warrior back to Blue Boy with a knife stuck in his back would be the last straw. Blue Boy had to be hunting him. And Lorna would be with Blue Boy.

Tucker needed a place to make a stand.

He constantly checked his back trail these last few miles. Even though he had made no attempt to cover his tracks, he hadn't seen the Indians, and that worried him. How many warriors did Blue Boy have left? Tucker had killed four, but how many more rode with him? Did he have enough to send other braves to kill him while Blue Boy fled with Lorna to the Badlands? Tucker pushed the thought from his mind. The knife in the back had been a challenge Blue Boy would not leave for the others to settle.

Tucker continued searching the valley that lay some miles to the east of the Badlands, a desolate country that could be every bit the killer a desert is. Unless you knew where to ride safely, the ledge you rode on might well fall away with the weight of your horse. You had to know where the few pools were secreted amongst the rocks, and how to forage for what food lay buried in the ground. The Lakota knew that. Tucker had ventured into the Badlands some years ago on a scouting mission. He had only gone a day's ride when he turned back. His report to the army had been brief: do not send your troops in there after fleeing Lakota.

Tucker watched until he was satisfied no one waited for him below before he mounted. He nudged Jess's horse down the shale hillside. The gelding jarred him as it tried to get its footing. Tucker had become spoiled riding mules over the years he had been out West. Ben's boxy feet were better at maneuvering tight places and slippery ground than were horses' hooves. Even Indian ponies. Often Tucker would let Ben have his head, and the mule would take the logical path to the bottom. He'd always known better than Tucker which route to take. And on this steep descent, he missed Ben even more.

A sage hen gave flight, roused from her sanctuary behind sparse brush, and the horse bucked, then bucked again when a doe antelope burst from a hidden arroyo. Tucker fought to keep the horse under control. Ben would have never been bothered by the grouse or the pronghorn. And neither would other mules Tucker had ridden.

He got the horse under control and coaxed it down the steep embankment. The horse had almost made a mistake and bolted with the antelope and the sage hen. And Tucker hadn't spotted them in time, and that had been his mistake. Right now — expecting Blue Boy's warriors to come riding down on him — he could afford few mistakes. But he was almighty tired and hurting from his leg wound, from cracked ribs from his fight with Jess, and from festering cactus spines still embedded in his leg. A mistake at the wrong time now could cost him his life. And Lorna's.

When he reached the bottom of the valley sheltering Medicine Root Creek, the horse hunched again and headed for the trickle of brackish water. Tucker coaxed the gelding toward a dead cottonwood lying along the muddy bank beside the puddle. While the horse drank, Tucker stepped out of the saddle and onto the log. The pain in his leg jarred him, yet it had diminished from yesterday. He silently thanked Red Sun for the Crow's medicine.

Tucker knelt upstream from the horse and used his hand to scoop the stagnant water into his hand. He thought only of the water and dismissed the putrid odor as he drank from his hand, then another and another. He put his bandana over the canteen spout to filter out the silt and filled it. It would have to do until he found fresh water. If he didn't and had to drink from the canteen . . . the thought repelled him. But Lorna being with Blue Boy and his band repelled him even more.

Suddenly, the horse jerked its head up, turning his ears, testing the air. Tucker long ago learned that a horse was every bit as good as a dog on the trail for alerting a man of trouble. He studied the gelding. Something had concerned it. Was it another pronghorn or sage hen? Tucker hoped so, but he also knew the horse had alerted to something that didn't belong. It had alerted to men.

Tucker slipped the thong from his gun and checked the loads — the first time since he'd taken Jess's gun and ridden away from Aurand's camp, and that worried him, too. He should have checked the gun at his first opportunity. His leg was causing him to make more mistakes he couldn't afford, with Lorna's life in the balance.

Tucker belly-slid over the creek bank toward a dry dirt wall. He breathed out of the side of his mouth, careful not to dispel any dirt and reveal his position. He looked in the direction the horse had looked. Nothing.

He shielded his hand to the sun, but saw nothing except . . . a small tendril of smoke arose from the direction he had ridden. He strained to see more, but the smoke had blown away as quickly as it had crossed Tucker's sight. Indians often broke from the trail long enough to eat in mid-mornings. But Indians — especially Blue Boy's band

— wouldn't grow careless enough to start a fire that failed to dissipate its smoke. Still, he remembered the bones found at the side of the trail when hunting Blue Boy. Someone in his band had been careless then. And they might — with a week of hard riding and evading and fighting — be making more mistakes in their exhaustion. Such as failing to capture their smoke.

He watched the horse. It had returned to watering, and Tucker was confident whatever had spooked it was now gone.

He stood and shuffled toward the horse. Time to move.

Tucker grabbed onto the saddle horn when a branch broke behind him. Then another.

He drew the gun and pivoted behind him. His leg buckled. He fell to the ground, and his leg hit hard on a rock.

The pain shot higher, more intense than before, his head swimming like a Badlands mirage. His vision faded as he tried to focus on a lone figure approaching him. The blur lasted only a moment before he went unconscious.

CHAPTER 32

Red Sun rode his mare up to where Aurand and Philo had stopped for the morning. They sat in front of flickering flames watching a sage hen cook over coals. Red stepped down from his pony at the edge of the camp and walked the rest of the way. "You want to find Tucker Ashley?"

Aurand prodded the meat with his knife. "Damned fool thing to say. If I didn't want him, I wouldn't have started this little outing a week ago."

"Then I'd put out that fire. Tucker's just savvy enough to see it. And he might find you first."

"But the meat's not done yet." Philo squatted in front of the fire and dug a knife out of his pocket. His swollen lip had blackened, and his eye remained matted shut from the mob's beating in Cowtown. "What do you want us to eat — raw meat?"

"Suit yourself," Red said. "Not me who

wants to find Ashley."

Aurand tossed a cup of coffee onto the fire. It crackled and hissed in protest and went dead a moment later.

"What the —"

"Red's right," Aurand said. "We don't want Tucker spotting it."

"You believing that old man?" Philo reached over and gathered fresh firewood from a pile.

"Red's been right all the other times." Aurand kicked the pile of branches on the ground beside Philo. "I said we can eat the meat raw if we need to. Anything to catch that bastard." He turned to Red. "What did you figure out?"

Red tipped his canteen over his head before taking a deep drink. Philo reached over, but Red jerked the canteen back. "Where'd you get fresh water?" Philo asked.

"Where *did* you get fresh water?" Aurand repeated.

Red chin-pointed down into a long valley a mile away. "There is a spring down thataway. I got to cutting sign for Tucker, when I ran into Indian tracks . . ."

"How many?"

"Three ponies," Red answered. "Or I should say two unshod ponies and one white man's horse. They got the woman with them riding along with a brave. They are looking for Tucker, too, I figure, but I do not believe they have picked up his scent yet."

"And you have?"

Red bit off a plug of tobacco. He ignored Philo's outstretched hand and pocketed the plug. "It will not be long before they find his tracks. Tucker is making no effort to hide them." He laughed. "Even Philo could follow his sign."

"So you picked up Tucker's tracks?"

"I did."

"Then why the hell didn't you follow him?" Aurand said. "Wing him or cripple him long enough and come get us?"

Red's eyes narrowed, ringed by deep lines. "You know our arrangement — I find them for you. I do not fire a shot. That is your job."

Aurand nodded. Since hiring Red to track army deserters from Ft. Sully, and the occasional robber dumb enough to get caught, Red had proved just what he claimed: that he was the best tracker — Indian or white man — in the territory. "I'm no fighter," he told Aurand that first day when he'd hired Red. "I am a lover," Red had announced through a grin that spanned few teeth. Sadie at the Cowtown saloon could attest to that.

"How far?" Aurand asked as he watched Philo brush coffee and dirt off the half-cooked bird.

Red looked in the direction he had ridden from. "We might be able to catch him by tonight, the morning at the latest. That is, if Blue Boy does not find him first."

Philo stuffed his mouth with a chunk of half-raw meat. "At least there's only three Indians after Tucker."

"And the woman's bound to slow them down," Aurand added.

"You are forgetting," Red said, spitting a string of juice five feet over that just missed a lizard scurrying to the safety of a rock crevice, "that one of those Lakota is Blue Boy."

Philo shrugged. "So we kill him if we get the chance."

Red shook his head. "Has nothing I said this past week penetrated your thick skull? Blue Boy is credited with a hundred enemy killed. And that is just other Indians. Hard telling how many settlers and soldiers he has murdered." Red looked to his back trail once again. "That is the last man I want to meet on a moonless night."

CHAPTER 33

Tucker gradually became aware of a figure moving about. He kept his eyes closed, kept a stillness about him that might mean his life. A fire flickered close. Sparks of dry kindling crackled close to him. He lay on his side that covered an empty holster, and his wounded leg was propped up on a bedroll.

He cracked an eye. The campfire was mere feet from him, and a figure moved in the light's periphery ten feet away. Tucker opened his eyes just as the man moved toward him. Tucker's head snapped up. He struggled to stand, but gentle hands eased him back down.

"Easy, Tuck. You ain't going nowheres." Jack's grin told Tucker that — at least for now — he was safe.

"I thought you were dead," Tucker said. He rolled over. "Strung up in Cowtown. How'd you get here?"

"Whoa," Jack said. "Let's get something in your gullet before I answer any questions."

Jack helped Tucker sit and propped a saddle behind his back. Jack took meat off the fire and sliced it before dropping it into a metal plate and handing it to Tucker. He eyed it suspiciously. "Coyote?"

"Bobcat," Jack answered.

Tucker shrugged and closed his eyes as he savored the meat. It seemed so long since he'd eaten anything that the bobcat tasted as good as any buffalo steak he'd ever had. When he finished the meat, he grabbed some wild onions popping on a stick over the fire. "How'd you come on to me?"

"First, Cowtown." Jack poured each a cup of chicory and sat on a rock in front of Tucker. "I got to worrying about you being there all by your lonesome. Figured you needed help. So I rode in anyways —"

"I thought we'd agreed you were in no shape to help."

"That was you agreeing with yourself." Jack nudged Tucker. "Couldn't let my ol' pard face those cowboys alone. Anyways, some of those cowboys didn't run off with the others you suckered. Some held back. And when they seen me sitting there in that saloon . . . well, they placed it upon themselves that I was a little too calm. That I was, in fact, the one who killed that shop-keeper. So they held me until the rest of those rowdies came back. Had a vigilance trial they called it. The next day I was to be run up a telegraph pole when the ol' gal who owns Sadie's Saloon busted through the crowd. Seems like the shopkeeper's widow told her the man who killed her husband was almost too big to fit through the door." Jack smiled. "First time in my life I was grateful I'm a runt."

"But how'd you know it was my tracks you was following? Ben was arrow-shot, and I had to take Jess Hammond's horse." He told Jack how Jess had sent Red Sun on a wild-goose chase just so he could beat Tucker to death, and how Simon Cady had decided at that time to harvest his wanted man. "You knew Ben's track. His gait. On Jess's horse you wouldn't know it was me."

"I didn't right off." Jack passed his canteen to Tucker. "I finally found where your mule had been killed, and I started working things out from there. I followed your tracks until I come onto Simon Cady. Damn fool singing like he didn't care if he attracted every Indian in the territory. Jess's body was tied across Cady's donkey. We got to talk-ing, and I got to tell you, that man made the hairs on my butt stand at attention, he was so creepy."

"How so?"

"Asking who I was," Jack answered. "Wanting to know if I'd ever had a price on my head. When I told him all I was doing is trying to find you, his hand came out of his coat with a sawed off Greener double I never spotted. He pointed with Anastasia — that's what he called his shotgun — to the west and wished me luck. It didn't take me long to get clear of Cady."

"See anything of Aurand? He's got Philo and Red with him." Tucker licked onion juice off his fingers, and Jack handed him more.

"I haven't yet, but I suspect they're out trying to find us right now."

Tucker felt Jess's empty holster.

"I cleaned it some after I found you." Jack reached over to his bedroll and grabbed Jess's Remington. Just like the one Tucker carried.

Tucker checked the cartridges before he holstered the gun. He slung the belt over his shoulder and tried standing, but he fell back onto the ground. He rubbed the fresh bandage encircling his leg.

"That leg will take some time to mend up." Jack propped Tucker up against the saddle once more.

"Don't have time to wait till it heals. I got a feeling those Indians will be coming up any time, as sloppy as I've been leaving sign for them to follow."

Jack took out a tobacco pouch and began rolling two smokes. "That's the oddest thing." Jack lit the cigarettes and handed Tucker one. "As obvious as you've been, Aurand should have caught up with you by now, too. Especially with Red with them. Nobody confuses a trail on Red."

"Unless he wants them to."

They finished their noonday meal, and Jack rubbed sand over the tin plates before stuffing them in his saddlebags. "How's the leg feel now?"

Tucker flexed it and found being off it for a few hours had helped the pain and the stiffness. That and Jack's doctoring. "See any infection while you were in there?"

"That's another surprising thing. It looked clean."

"I can thank Red and his Crow concoction for that." Tucker had been wounded at Antietam. A ball had penetrated his shoulder, passing through and through. In that Confederate prison he'd spent the rest of the war in, Tucker had seen many other Yankees come in wounded less severely, yet they soon died from infection. "I ought to be good to travel in the morning."

"You asking me or telling me?" Jack said.

"Does it matter where Lorna's concerned?"

"I suppose not," Jack said as he unrolled his bedroll. "If you think you can make it on your own."

Tucker wrapped a blanket around his shoulders. "You leaving?"

"Got to," Jack said. "I need to ride out. See if I can pick up any sign of Blue Boy. I don't want to be a sitting duck when he comes onto us. Or when Aurand figures out Red's been leading them in circles."

CHAPTER 34

Aurand climbed off his horse and held the reins while the gelding drank from the drying creek bed. The Badlands this time of year could be hell on earth. With the storm two days forgotten, the ground had once again begun to crack from the heat. He should have been grateful for what cool water the creek provided. Instead, he was just frustrated that they hadn't come across Tucker yet.

Philo stood back from the creek bank and let his horse drink while he resisted the urge to sip the water himself. After long moments, he dropped onto his knees and scooped mud from the trickling creek. When he came up, silt was pasted across his face and into his scraggly beard. He stood and looked about. Red stood beside his horse as it cropped at some grama grass on a hillside twenty yards away. Philo looked at Red and turned his back as he bent to Aurand. "I think we got problems," he whispered.

"What kind of problems?" Aurand asked.

"Get rid of the breed. We need to talk."

Aurand had worked alongside Philo for years. He knew every emotion, every weakness, every strength in the man. He'd grown to trust Philo's judgment when on the trail, even if he didn't trust him when he was drinking. As he looked at Philo, he knew whatever he had to say was serious. And he couldn't risk Red hearing it.

"Red," Aurand called out, and the scout led his mare to where Aurand and Philo stood. "Go out and see what you can wrangle up for meat."

Red checked the sun's angle. "Kind of early for supper, ain't it?"

Aurand shrugged. "It won't be long, and we'll catch up with Tucker. We can afford the time to eat a good meal."

Red unsheathed his Spencer from the saddle scabbard. "I think I saw a small herd of mule deer a couple hills over."

Philo waited until the white socks of Red's mare had disappeared over the hill before talking. "Red's been playing us for suckers."

Aurand filled his pipe and patted his vest for a lucifer. "How so?"

"He's leading us around in circles."

"Oh bull—"

"Look," Philo said, "I'm not the tracker Red is. But I'm no slouch, either. Even Jess could have followed the tracks Tucker's been laying down" — Philo made the sign of the cross — "as obvious as they are."

Aurand squatted on his heels, and motioned for Philo to do the same. "Here's where we are." He drew in the dirt with his finger. "Where's the last time we cut Tucker's sign?"

Philo scraped an X in the dirt. "Just south of where we were camped. And where Jess lit out."

Aurand felt his anger rise. When he and Philo had returned with camp meat, Jess was gone. He took his bedroll and saddle, his horse, and even his saddlebags with him. He didn't intend to return, and Tucker had escaped. When Red came back from scouting the region for Tucker, he had told them that Jess lit out to parts unknown. And somehow Tucker had got hold of a horse. His escape was speculation among all three, and they tossed it around that Tucker might have surprised Jess and taken his horse and that Jess had gone after Tucker on foot. Or stolen another horse somewhere. Speculation. But Aurand had the feeling Jess would not be returning. He was no coward, but Aurand knew he was no trail hand either.

After he found and killed Tucker, Aurand planned to stop in Cowtown. He suspected Jess just might be there whooping it up with the rest of the drunks.

"Well, boss, do you want me to kill Red when he comes back?"

Aurand thought that over. Red Sun had scouted for Aurand since he'd been appointed deputy marshal, but he knew the man's loyalties lay only with himself. If Red were leading them in circles, perhaps he had designs on that reward money out for the woman. Or the reward outstanding for Jess. Hell, Aurand thought, if he and Philo found Jess in Cowtown, perhaps they'd collect the reward out for him themselves. It'd be the last time Jess Hammond deserted anyone. "When Red comes back into camp, I want you to look almighty normal. Say nothing. I want to gauge his reaction when I confront him. If he won't come clean as to why he's leading us around like a couple fools, then feel free to kill him."

Philo smiled a toothless grin and took out his knife. "I'll talk to Red real slow like when the time comes," he said as the bright light reflected off his blade.

CHAPTER 35

Tucker fell into a deep, healing sleep where Lorna invaded his dreams. He rode toward her, the ruffles of her white wedding dress flapping against her wrists as she spurred her Arabian toward him. Tucker dismounted and ran to her with arms wide. She showed neither hunger nor that she was harmed in any way. She was hungry only for Tucker's embrace.

His sleep became fitful. Blue Boy and Aurand appeared on either side of Lorna. Blue Boy's face was painted black, silver lightning bolts adorning either cheek. He dwarfed Aurand as he rode his grulla, guns in both hands, and Tucker could look down the barrels of both pistols.

He awakened abruptly to the sharpness of a blade breaking the skin across the front of his throat. He opened his eyes, calculating if he could kill his attacker before he bled out. He eyed Jess's holstered Remington five feet away. It might well have been fifty feet away.

He looked into serious, dark eyes, ringed with the wrinkles of a man who has survived for longer than Tucker had been alive. Those deadly eyes met Tucker's, eyes behind a mask that held Tucker's life in his hands with the jerk of his blade.

Then the knife came carefully off his skin, and Red Sun backed away. He sat on his haunches and stared at Tucker. "Couldn't take any chances with you." He sheathed his knife. "Even injured, I can think of no other man I would hate going agin' than Tucker Ashley. Except maybe that Blue Boy."

"What's with . . . ?" Tucker motioned to the buckskins, the Crow's blue-beaded belt and leggings different from the trail-worn dungarees he'd worn before.

"I figure I have been living with the white man too long," Red said.

"And Aurand?" Tucker said. "Is he just a hill over, ready to come busting in with guns firing on your signal?"

"He would if he knew I was here with you."

"I don't understand." Tucker sat and eyed Jess's gun. But he knew he wouldn't need it this night against Red. "You scout for Aurand."

"Not anymore." Red brought a tobacco pouch out of a small, beaded bag on his belt and began rolling a smoke. "I knowed Aurand was evil mean, and I guess I was lookin' for a reason to get clear of him." He grabbed a smoldering twig from the fire and lit his cigarette. "Who owned that donkey back at Aurand's camp?"

"Simon Cady."

Red's hand shook. "I wondered how it came to be that an unarmed man killed Jess Hammond. No offense, but I did not figure you could get the job done being without a gun, the shape you were in. So Cady killed him for the reward, did he?"

Tucker nodded. He sat with his back against the cottonwood root. "He saved my life, though I'm certain it wouldn't have bothered Cady none if Jess had killed me before he got him." He flexed his leg. "How'd you figure it out?"

"Jess's gelding favors his right front leg," Red answered. "Not so a man would notice — certainly not Aurand and Philo Brown — but enough that I knowed Jess's horse was gone because something happened to him. Only thing logical is that you got the drop on him, took his horse and gun. With no body, I figured somebody carted it away. So I led Aurand and Philo around in a wide circle to give you time to mend up."

Tucker laid branches and dried sage twigs on the fire. "Why would you do that?"

"Ever been around Lakota?"

"Some Hunkpapa took me in one winter after a buffalo gored me."

"Then you ought to know they treat their women fine. But it is when the menfolk go hunting or warring their captive women suffer the most."

"I've heard that. Still doesn't explain why you helped me out."

"Sure it does." Red flicked the rest of his butt into the fire. "That Blue Boy is one murderous Lakota. There in 'sixty-two in Minnesota, he got caught with the rest of the Sioux killing white settlers in town. Why he never got strung up with those Santee Sioux is beyond me. He has had a hatred for white men ever since they locked him in that prison. I think he hates whites even more than he hates us Crow." Red shook his head. "I made a terrible decision scouting for the white man once before. Down Colorado way when I found those Arapaho at Sand Creek."

"So you know Simon Cady from there?"

Red trembled. "We both scouted for Chivington. I wanted to lead the militia in circles just like I did Aurand and Philo, but

Cady would have none of it." Red's mouth turned down with sadness. "I told myself ol' Red is never going to do that again. Even if it is hunting Lakota. Aurand can find Blue Boy on his own. Though if he found Blue Boy, he might not live to brag about it." He stood and nodded to the brush just outside of the camp. "Now you can tell your friend out there he can come in and warm himself."

"Jack?"

Red shrugged. "I do not know his name, but I suspect he has a gun leveled at me right now."

Tucker called to Jack, and he emerged from the shadows.

"You can put your gun down," Tucker said, and Jack lowered the Henry.

"I will be putting some miles between me and Aurand." Red's back popped when he arched it and stretched. "I got the feeling Philo got on to me a few miles back. He is just tracker enough that I figure he worked it out I was leading them around by the nose. Aurand told me to go kill supper. Except Red is no fool. The first time I step foot back in their camp, I would get drilled through and through. By now they know I am not coming back."

"What of Blue Boy?" Jack asked. "Is he

over the Great Wall by now?"

Red paused for a moment, looking up at a hawk overhead as if the answer were there. "That is another odd thing. Blue Boy has lost most of the band he took with him on this raid. He confounded me whenever he could, then all of a sudden, when he was close to reaching the Badlands and safety, they turned back." Red hitched his belt up over his thin hips. "If I am working Blue Boy's trail out right, he is making a run back this way. And he has got that woman with him."

"You sure she's still with Blue Boy?" Tucker asked, praying for the second time in a week.

Red dipped into his possibles bag looped around his shoulders and came out with a closed fist. He dropped a dozen tiny lead balls onto the ground. "She has left some of that nearly every time they stop. She is alive, all right, and she is a keeper if she thinks clear enough to keep leaving clues."

"How much time until they find us?" Jack asked.

Red shrugged. "They will be here by morning. You two will have your hands full — I suspect both Aurand and Philo will get here the same time as Blue Boy and his band. It ought to be interesting."

Red walked to where his pony stood tied to a boulder. He bent and lovingly ran his hand over the mare's white socks. Then he straightened and gathered the reins when Tucker called after him. "Thanks."

Red stopped but didn't turn around. "I would do the same for any man who would have a chance to kill a murderer like Blue Boy." He untied his horse.

"Where you headed?"

Red chin-pointed to the north. "Back to my people. I figure if I go through Canada, I will make it to the Shining Mountains without Blue Boy or Aurand finding me."

The moonless night quickly engulfed Red, and the only thing Tucker heard was his hoof beats riding away from camp. His leg felt stiff, but the pain had subsided, and he was able to hobble around the camp. He stopped in front of Jack, who had set a coffee pot over the coals. "This isn't your fight," Tucker told him. "If you took off now, you'd be able to catch the steamer north from Yankton in three days' hard riding."

Jack pulled the loading tube out of his rifle's butt stock and counted his rounds before replacing the tube. "I'll not miss the best fight either of us will have for some time by hightailin' out of here. We've been in some scrapes, you and me, and this will be another one to tell the grandkids one day."

"Difference with this one," Tucker said, "is we've been able to re-tell the other battles. I'm not so sure we'll be around to brag about this one."

"Maybe we could call on the Lakota's *Wakan Tanka.*"

"At this point," Tucker said, tying Jess's gun belt around his waist and securing it with a cinch rope, "I'd call on the devil himself if I thought it'd keep us alive long enough to find Lorna."

CHAPTER 36

Lorna rode the mare Blue Boy had brought for her when he returned from scouting last night. Where he found it she'd never know, but she suspected he'd stolen it like he stole everything else he had. The mare had a nice, even gait, though it wasn't like her father's Arabians. And it wasn't as handsome as the Arabians, though its white socks contrasted with the pony's tan coat. But the pony suited her fine just now. She was just glad to be off Jimmy Swallow's horse.

Blue Boy had said nothing when he came back to camp this morning leading the mare. He'd dropped the reins at Lorna's feet, and she knew he expected her to keep up. She caught herself more than once checking their back trail, calculating if the pony could outrun Blue Boy. The little horse would never be one for speed, and she'd dismissed the thought. Blue Boy apparently wasn't worried. He had sent Black

Dog and Jimmy Swallow up ahead to find Tucker, leaving her to ride alone. Either Blue Boy thought he could catch her should she bolt or that she had no desire to leave.

What she couldn't dismiss was the thought of Tucker following, for it must be him trailing them and killing the warriors Blue Boy sent to stop him. She caught herself thinking more and more about him as the days passed, even as it seemed she was destined to live out her remaining years as the wife of a Lakota chieftain.

She remembered comparing Maynard Miles to Tucker whenever he came into the general store. Maynard was stable, having worked with her father to build up a string of mercantiles along the Missouri, while Tucker was much like most animals in this rugged and dangerous country — happiest when roaming the prairie and mountains. Maynard would be a steady provider, while Tucker's meager income depended on the whim of the US Army. Maynard would teach their children proper manners and the ways of the gentleman, while Tucker would teach them the ways of the wilderness.

But for all Maynard's fine attributes, she knew she didn't love him. She loved Tucker, although not a single word had passed between them that suggested romance. Sure, he had brought her wildflowers that he'd picked from fields nearby. But then he often picked such flowers for the ladies at the Bucket of Blood. He had given her gems he found along the trail somewhere. And walking her home at night from dinner was just the gentlemanly thing to do, with all the rowdies and roustabouts working the docks. How often she had wished he would chance a kiss, or brush his hand across hers, or whisper special feelings for her. But he had not. And, looking back, she thought of Tucker as more timid schoolboy than the army scout with the nasty reputation as a wild gun hand.

And, looking at Blue Boy, she'd become more confused as the days wore on. She'd begun to feel stirrings — like a woman feels for a man — gradually appear as her days around him wore on. She began thinking of him not so much as her captor, but as her suitor; not as one who had abducted her from her room, but as a romantic conqueror claiming his prize.

She looked at his back, broad and rippling, until he turned his head, and she dropped her gaze. When he turned back, she chanced another look. He proudly sat the large dun gelding that seemed too small for him, despite being sixteen hands tall if it was an inch. He wasn't at all like the savages she came to know over soldiers' and cowboys' talk in the store. He was not dirty or deceitful, not uncouth or uncaring. He was, she admitted to herself some days ago, an impressive man. He stood a head taller than Tucker, who was tall by western standards. Blue Boy's hair hung about his powerful shoulders. She wondered about the deep scars and nicks across those shoulders and concluded they must have happened in battle. She even supposed — in another time, another place — she might be attracted to the leader of this band of renegades. What was left of them.

Sounds of horses approaching, riding hard and riding noisily, echoed off the shale rocks and boulders, and the riders came into view. Black Dog clutched the reins of Swallow's paint as he rode beside the young warrior. Swallow lay slumped over his pony and bounced hard. Blood smeared the animal's withers. Black Dog reined their horses in front of Blue Boy, who shielded his eyes from the dust their horses kicked up. Black Dog spoke Lakota and waved his arm in the direction they had come from. He gestured to Swallow, who clutched his stomach. Flies had gathered around fresh blood, and Black Dog swatted at them.

"We are in need of more strips of your petticoat," Blue Boy said to Lorna.

She looked about for a place to drop her buckskins and tear off cloth. "Is Swallow hurt badly?"

"Bad," Blue Boy said. "Black Dog says a bullet passed through his side."

"Black Dog has been hit, too."

Black Dog talked as he waved the air with his good arm.

"Just a few pellets from a white man who cannot even shoot his own shotgun well," Blue Boy translated.

Lorna walked behind a boulder and dropped her trousers. When she emerged from behind the rock holding torn fabric, Blue Boy had eased Swallow onto the ground, while Black Dog cut his shirt away and dribbled water over the bullet wound. "What is happening?" she demanded. She had learned in recent days that she was immune from any abuse or anger from Blue Boy and had become quite bold with him. "What did Black Dog say?"

"Over there" — he gestured to the east — "several miles that way, some white men ambushed them."

She drew in a quick breath. "Was it the one who has been killing your warriors?"

Blue Boy's mouth drooped, and he looked away. "No. It is not He Who Follows that shot Swallow. Black Dog said it was the one — the leader of the white men — that we saw back in the river town."

"Back in my town?" Lorna asked. "Who did you see back there? What happened that Black Dog would remember the man today?"

"It was white man's business that night."

She stepped closer and craned her neck up to look him in the eyes. "Tell me."

Blue Boy sighed while he looked on at Black Dog dressing Swallow's wound. "While we waited for . . . your light to go out of your room, two men came upon a sleeping drunk in the alley behind the saloon."

"And?" she prodded when he'd stopped talking.

"One large man — but not as large as me, and he was fat. He wore a star. He bent to the sleeping man, who woke up, and they struggled. The fat man put a knife to the sleeping man's neck. The smaller man yelled, but it was too late: the big man had already cut the drunk's throat. The fat man went through the dead man's pockets, while the other one watched for anyone coming. Then they left the dead man and found another drunk sleeping outside the saloon. They carried him to the jail."

"And Black Dog is certain of this?"

Blue Boy nodded. "He thinks the one they carried to the jail is the one who shot him three days ago. He thinks it is He Who Follows."

Lorna laughed. Her happiness transcended her discomfort from the days on the trail. "You've just cleared Tucker Ashley. This proves he didn't murder that roustabout. Your testimony could . . ."

Blue Boy put his finger to her lips. "I care not for any white man. I did not care that night. I do not care now. The man they shut up in that jail will have to clear his name without me." A broad smile crossed his face. "If he lives. The men who ambushed Black Dog and Swallow track He Who Follows." He gestured across the prairie. "A mere wind's breath over there. But we are close, I think. By the time of this *honwe,* this new moon, your man's scalp lock will hang from my pony's neck — along with the others who follow him."

"And what of me?" she asked. "What will happen to me while you are off fighting these men?"

"What would you do," he taunted, "if you were Blue Boy?"

"I would let me go."

He laughed. "You would not. If you did that, I would warn the others. No, if you were me you would lash you to something — a boulder perhaps — where you would be safe from the battle. Yet not free to warn them."

Lorna gestured around the barren prairie. She knew she would not survive long in this sun. "And Blue Boy would tie his . . . woman here to suffer?"

"There is shade ahead," he answered simply and bent to Black Dog. They spoke for a moment as Black Dog finished wrapping Swallow's stomach with Lorna's petticoat. Blue Boy stood. "He will live to count coup on the *wasicu.*"

Black Dog stood and handed Lorna what was left of her petticoat.

"But he is only a boy," Lorna blurted out. "How many more young men that you lead must die because you want to keep me?"

"Swallow is a warrior." Blue Boy reached into his saddlebag. He came away with a small pouch and opened it. He shook powder onto a flat rock before he trickled water over it and began to mix the war paint. "For me to deny him the chance to kill his enemy would be worse than anything he would experience in battle."

323

Blue Boy began to paint lightning bolts on his blackened face with silver tint. Lorna looked frantically around, and for a fleeting moment she once again considered escape. She needed to warn Tucker; to tell him the Indians hunted him. She needed to tell him Blue Boy had identified Philo Brown as the one who knifed the roustabout, while Aurand helped him carry Tucker to jail. But she also knew that wherever she fled to, the Indians would be on her. They might give her a brief start before tiring of the game and riding after her.

So Lorna dutifully sat her mare and waited until Swallow had been doctored. She fell in behind Blue Boy and the others as they rode away to fight Tucker. And those who hunted him.

Lorna watched Blue Boy ride his horse out of the shallow depression that had once been a creek and disappear over the next hill. She had struggled briefly when Black Dog secured her hands to the dead cottonwood root until she realized the leather thongs would not break. She settled onto the dried creek bed, shielded from much of the sun by large boulders. To her right lay whitened bones of some animal, buffalo or deer perhaps, and a coyote-picked backbone of some kind of fish. She strained to look over the bank when she spotted tracks of a wolf, maybe a coyote, and she wished Blue Boy were still here.

He had been brutally honest with her. He told her that Black Dog had picked up the tracks of her man no more than a mile from them. "By the time the moon rises, I will have his scalp hanging from my belt," he told her. She canted her ear in the direction the warriors had ridden. In the stillness of the morning, she was certain she would be able to hear sounds of the upcoming battle.

Exhaustion overcame Lorna, and she stretched out her legs. She laid her head onto the cottonwood and slept. How long, she was uncertain. And she was uncertain when the distant rumbling of storm clouds to the west began to echo ominously off the shallow walls of the creek.

CHAPTER 37

Aurand looked at where the Indians fled through a boulder field as he squatted beside Philo. He stuffed fresh shells into his shotgun, and laid it on the ground beside him. He gathered kindling and started a fire for coffee. "Think they'll be back?"

Aurand broke open the top of his .44, and spent cartridges popped out. He thumbed fresh ones into the cylinders before snapping the action closed. "They weren't expecting us, and I think we peppered them pretty good. If I were them, I'd be off licking my wounds and forgetting about us."

Philo broke off a piece of tobacco and stuffed the rest in his vest pocket. He bent and blew on the fire. "Indians don't like to be caught short. Fast as we shot, they're probably telling their pards back in camp there was a dozen of us."

"I wounded one — might have killed him — so I'm not sure how much talking he'll be doing." Aurand stood and peeked around the boulder. The two Indians had been too busy looking at the ground, following sign, when they rode unawares toward him and Philo. And too late the raiding party ran into the ambush Aurand and Philo set. "I'm just wondering if Red put them onto us."

Philo stood and turned his back to Aurand while he unbuttoned his trousers. "Not that one. He'd rather gnaw off a leg than help a Lakota." Philo shook and buttoned up. "Although I am wondering how Red knew we were onto him."

"That's just what I asked myself," Aurand said. "You and Con tracked with him the most. Got to be real friendly with the breed, I suspect. Suppose you tell me how he knew we were going to ventilate him once he rode back into camp."

Philo looked up at Aurand. "You think I tipped him off that we were planning a surprise party for him?"

"All I know," said Aurand, drawing his gun and holding it loosely beside his leg, "is that Red never came back to camp. Let us say it seems suspicious."

Philo spat a stream of juice that hit the fire with a hiss as loud as any rattler. "Any time you want me to leave and go my own merry way — let you track Tucker your ownself — you let me know. In fact" — Philo stood and cradled his shotgun under his arm as he walked toward his horse — "I ought to do that anyways. Everyone who sticks around you on this little trip's gotten killed."

"Now you wouldn't leave your old bud all by his lonesome out here." Aurand cocked his gun and Philo froze. He turned slowly. "I was just supposing." He held up the hand without the shotgun. "No reason to get all riled up for that. I want Tucker as much as you do."

Aurand smiled and holstered his gun. "Then let's see what those Indians were so interested in, studying the ground like they was doing."

Philo slipped his shotgun into the saddle scabbard and untied his horse. Aurand took the reins of his grulla and fell in behind Philo as he studied the ground. Aurand wasn't as certain as he'd been a moment ago that Philo wouldn't cut and run. The fat man had always been happiest when he could ambush some unsuspecting trooper fleeing the army, or a hapless fool with some petty territorial warrant out for him passed out on the trail. But the odds had been even with those two Indians. And Philo wasn't accustomed to even odds. Something in Aurand wanted to kill the man right here, in the Badlands, and blame it on those Sioux passing through. But right now he needed Philo. Even though he was no Red Sun, Philo was the only tracker he had at the moment.

Philo walked with his head bent toward the ground as he shuffled out of the boulder field toward where they first saw the Indians. "There!" Philo dropped to one knee and studied the tracks. "That's the same track we come onto earlier. Except now they're riding single file. And making no effort to hide it." Philo stood and brushed dirt from his knees. "Shod horses, both. Gotta' be Tucker and Worman. My guess is either they're getting careless, or they figure there's no chance anyone will still be on their trail."

"It's smart to rule out the first." Aurand stood in the stirrups and shielded his eyes with his hat. "I doubt Tucker Ashley ever gets careless." There were dozens of ideal ambush spots, countless chokepoints in the direction their tracks went. "We just got lucky Tucker was hurt the last time we got the drop on him."

They followed the tracks for another half mile when Philo reined up short. He slipped the thong from the hammer of his pistol and pointed to tall boulders. The tracks led through them fifty yards ahead. "I don't like those rocks up ahead, Aurand. I'm thinkin' we ought to go around that bunch of boulders. Pick up their trail on the other side."

"No, I think we should follow those tracks straight between them."

"I'm telling you," Philo said, "There's more places among those rocks that they could wait for us. It wouldn't be smart."

"Duly noted," Aurand said. "But we're going straight through. You go first, and I'll follow you."

"You son-of-a—"

"Go on." Aurand drew his pistol and pointed it at Philo. "We're wasting daylight."

CHAPTER 38

Jack checked that his Henry was loaded, then ran the loading tube out of the butt stock again. "You've checked that thing four times already," Tucker said. "Put it down."

Jack looked to Tucker, then to his rifle before setting it against the rocks he hid behind. "Guess I'm getting nervous. This waiting is killing me. You think they'll find our tracks?"

Tucker caught himself checking Jess's Spencer. Again. "We made tracks so plain even Aurand could follow them. But he's got Philo with him, even if he can't."

"No other way, huh?"

Tucker thought of that. Since burying his knife in the back of that young Indian three days ago, he knew that the gauntlet had been thrown down for Blue Boy. And Blue Boy knew it, too. Revenge would cause him to come after Tucker and risk losing Lorna. "Only thing that's sure to attract Blue Boy is the sound of white men fighting."

"If Blue Boy's still within earshot," Jack said.

"Then we have a gambler's chance that he'll hear the shooting when the time comes." Tucker took a pull from his canteen before he passed it to Jack. "If he makes it to the Great Wall, the Badlands might as well be a thousand miles away for as much luck as we'd have finding him and Lorna."

"We could try following them if this don't work." Jack wiped his mouth and handed the water back.

Tucker shook his head and looked out at the shimmering heat waves coming off the rocks, off the sandstone, forming odd shapes that made him do a double take. Men could walk straight at them in this mirage and blend in with the other shimmering shapes out there. "I've been into those Badlands before and had to turn back. The Lakota have been going in and out of there for centuries, and they know where the watering holes are any given time of year. They know which game they might run on to, and where to find grass for their ponies. White men don't. No, if Blue Boy doesn't answer this challenge and heads there instead, Lorna will just be lost to me."

"I just hope Blue Boy and Aurand don't

get here at the same time."

"So do I, Jackson." Tucker used the side of a boulder to stand. His leg felt better, but it cramped easily, and he walked the knots out of his muscles. He looked off into the sandstone spires, some reaching higher than a telegraph pole. A dust devil kicked up fine dirt as it meandered its way across the ground and disappeared in the creek bed. Lorna was out there somewhere, and he worried on her. She had been raised in the sanitary environment of fine mid-western stock. She was the only person he knew who had been to a university. But she had been thrown into the middle of circumstances that would have killed most able men. And if he believed Red Sun when he trickled the lead shot onto the ground, she was still leaving clues.

"Storm brewing," Jack said. He tested the wind with his nose. "Powerful one if I know my storms."

"The last thing we need," Tucker said as he limped about, "is a storm to mask Aurand and Philo riding into our trap."

Tucker stashed his canteen under a rock so a stray bullet wouldn't hit it and made his final check around their ambush site. They had the high ground looking down onto prairie on three sides. Only their left flank — devoid of rocks or boulders — could not be observed well. That area dipped down into a long ravine they couldn't see into.

Below their position lay a meandering creek bed. Like so many other creek beds in the Badlands, this one had last seen water some years ago. But the approaching storm with its gong of thunder every few seconds and lightning that streaked across the sky and occasionally touched down would soon change that. Tucker prayed that the storm would come after Aurand and Philo made their move.

Tucker closed his eyes and rubbed a headache away. He almost welcomed the pain that kept his thoughts from his leg. And from Lorna. This had been the longest ten days he could recollect. He'd been on trails longer scouting for the army. But the only thing at stake then was finding the enemy. Or not. He had spent the last ten days wondering if Blue Boy would come after Tucker or continue down the Great Wall with Lorna. Had he gambled wrong? He hoped not, and he hoped the Indians wouldn't be all the way into the Badlands before he realized his folly.

Jack drummed the tree trunk with his fingers, their long-ago signal that danger approached. Tucker froze and followed Jack's gaze. A rider approaching fast kicked up a cloud of dust a hundred yards away heading between the boulders.

Tucker eased himself beside Jack and both men shouldered their rifles. "Lone rider," Jack breathed. "Riding that grulla a whole lot harder than he should in this heat."

Tucker squinted through the rising heat waves that distorted horse and rider. They were still indistinct shapes, but the grulla looked like Aurand's horse. Tucker made out the shape of the Montana Peak Aurand always wore pulled down and shading his eyes. "He's riding here like he knows just where we are," Jack said, "And wants a fight." He turned to Tucker. "You don't have to fight Aurand, you know."

"I'm no fool." Tucker knelt on his good leg. "But I'm no coward, either. If it was just him and me, I'd pass on it. But with Lorna out there . . . well, this gunfire will surely bring Blue Boy."

"If he's within earshot," Jack said, and rested his rifle over a rock.

"Hold your fire until he's close. We'll only get one clean shot, and we'd better make it good."

"Only thing that worries me is, where's Philo?" Jack said.

Tucker lowered the rifle from his shoulder. Philo would never abandon Aurand — the man was as loyal as a stray hound, even if he was a scoundrel. As Tucker rubbed the mirage away from his eyes and concentrated on the rider coming in fast, he realized he was far larger than Aurand.

As the horse neared, the rider looked up for a brief moment, and Tucker saw Philo spurring Aurand's grulla. "That's not Aurand!" Tucker yelled at Jack. He turned toward the deep ravine when a voice called out, "Hold it now." Aurand stepped from the gully with a pistol in each hand. "You fellers put those rifles down on the ground. Real slow."

They laid their guns down, and Tucker turned to where he could watch Philo riding into their ambush site. He wore Aurand's floppy hat, and he stripped it off as he reined his horse to a stop beside him. Philo clambered down from the grulla and ran to stand beside Aurand. "That worked just like you figured."

Aurand smiled and waved his pistol at Tucker and Jack. "Shuck those horse pistols. Careful like, so I don't have to shoot you before I want to."

Jack dropped his gun first, while Tucker was slower in unhooking Jess's gun belt. Aurand spoke to them, but a clap of thunder drowned him out. "I said kick those rifles over thisaway."

Jack nudged his rifle toward Aurand with his boot. He bent to pick up the rifle, when an arrow flew just over his shoulder and bounced off a boulder in front of him. Another twang of a bowstring, and Philo ran for cover as an arrow skidded off his holster. He dove for cover just as two Indians broke from the ravine. One notched and shot his arrows faster than the other Indian fired his rifle. Aurand hip-shot both guns at once, and the small warrior — almost effeminate in appearance — dropped his bow, his elbow shattered — and scurried for the safety of the ravine.

Tucker dove for his six-gun, snatched it, and rolled away as an arrow dug a deep furrow in the dirt inches from where he'd stood. He fired two quick shots at a figure that melted behind some rocks.

Thunder clapped as loudly as their gunshots, and Tucker looked around for Jack. He lay behind a boulder with an arrow sticking out of his foot. A painful grimace creased his face, but he held his gun ready to shoot anything that moved.

A sharp crack of thunder disoriented Tucker for the briefest moment, then a bullet grazed his neck. Sticky blood oozed down his chest, mixed with rain that began as the shooter ran out of the ravine. Tucker looked up at the largest Indian he'd ever seen.

He'd finally met Blue Boy.

Instantly, the legend heard over campfires and the fears of men telling tales welled up inside Tucker, and he froze, immobile, as the Lakota raised his rifle. Things turned slowly for Tucker; Blue Boy took aim. His knuckles whitened on the trigger. At the last minute, Blue Boy swung his rifle Jack's way. He ducked behind a boulder as Blue Boy's round kicked up dust beside him.

Another crack of thunder brought Tucker around. He fired as he rolled behind Jack's boulder, the pain in Tucker's leg returning in spades. He leaned his back against the rock and opened the loading gate. He peeked around and watched for Indians as he shucked the spent cartridges and thumbed fresh ones in. "How's the foot?"

"How the hell would you feel if you had an arrow stuck out of your boot?"

Tucker quick-peeked around cover then pulled back. "I saw only three Indians."

"But they're in a better position than us." Aurand skidded in the dirt beside Tucker and waved his hand at Philo, who ran hunched over and nosedived behind the boulder. A bullet hit the dirt and drove rock fragments into Tucker's cheek. He looked over at Aurand, and for a moment their differences were forgotten in their mutual desire for survival.

"That young one took a good hit," Jack said. "The one with the bow."

Aurand peeked around the rocks. "I shot him yesterday. I figured he'd be worm food by now."

"Apparently not," Tucker said. "Still leaves three, and it's just a matter of time before they work their way to the top of that ledge" — Tucker pointed across the clearing with his pistol to high rocks overlooking their position — "and get a clear view of us. Then all they gotta' do is start firing. If they don't hit us directly, they might get lucky, and a ricochet might get any one of us."

Silence. Except for the rain that started in earnest and the thunder that threatened to break eardrums, there was silence. "Think they left?" Aurand asked.

"What do you think?"

"You're the Indian expert here," Aurand said. "You tell me."

"If he won't, I will," Philo said. "They're out there, all right. Just waiting for us to make a mistake. Then —" He drew his finger across his throat.

"Somebody's got to draw their fire long enough for us to move to better cover over there." Aurand pointed to a large boulder with a higher vantage point. "Someone quick."

Tucker grabbed his leg. "I would if I could, but I'm not up to running. And Jack," Tucker said, nodding to him, "still has an arrow stuck in his foot. You can damn well bet he'll be no sprinter."

"Leaves only the two of us," Aurand said.

"Us?" Philo said. "Hell, if you don't notice I can barely walk fast let alone run." He jiggled his sizeable belly. "If I go out there I'll get —" Philo stopped, and the color drained from his face as if the torrent of rain were washing the blood right out of his florid jowls. "I'll get killed."

Aurand held his gun on Philo. "Well, I'm sure not going. And Tucker's right — all Jack can do is hobble. I'll be damned if some Indian's going to kill Tucker for me." He grinned. "That leaves you, Philo. Besides, you got those new fancy boots from the store in Cowtown that'll help you run. Now get ready."

"I'm not going —"

Aurand cocked his pistol and jammed it into Philo's side. "You'll have a better chance with them than with me." He bent to Tucker and yelled over the sound of the storm. "When Philo runs out there guns-a-blazing, you'd better help Jack to that bunch of boulders 'cause he don't look like he's doing so good."

"I'll do all right," Jack said.

Tucker straightened and helped Jack stand. He draped an arm around Tucker's shoulders. "And just where the hell will you be?"

"I'm going to lay down as much firepower as I can," Aurand answered. "And hope to keep their heads down. With their concentration on Philo, it just might work." He tapped Philo on the side of the head with the barrel of his gun. "When I say so, hobble like the wind, old man."

"You son-of-a—"

"Now!" Aurand shoved Philo hard. He stumbled, lost his balance, and caught himself. He zigzagged as well as he could across the clearing while he fired wildly in the Indians' direction. Tucker half-ran, half-dragged Jack to the safety of the large boulder when thunder mixed with gun shots echoed off the rocks and spires. Lightning struck the ground close enough that the hairs on Tucker's neck stood at attention. And just before he and Jack dropped behind the boulder, he saw Philo jerk spasmodically as bullets impacted his chest, his back.

"Where the hell's Aurand?" Jack blurted, his teeth clenched against pain.

Tucker caught his breath and peeked around the boulder. The top of Aurand's hat just stuck up from the rock they had just left. "He didn't run with us. Guess he figured we'd get lucky and take out those Indians."

Rifle rounds hit the ground in front of them, and Tucker searched where they came from. The young Indian's bloody arm dangled helplessly, yet he still rested a rifle across a clump of sagebrush. "I make that forty yards."

Jack chanced a look. "More like fifty."

Tucker looked at Jess's rifle being rained upon in the clearing, and he cursed Aurand.

The Indian shot two more slow, deliberate shots. The rounds kicked up dirt as he walked his rounds in on them. Tucker lay on the ground and rested his gun hand on a large rock. Fifty yards. He'd shot that distance at small game. But that was with his own gun. This was Jess Hammond's. Still, it was the same make. Same caliber.

Tucker cocked the hammer and picked up the sights. He brushed rain water out of his eyes and ran his finger through his hair to get it off his face.

Another shot. Rock splinters drove into Tucker's cheek.

He took out the trigger slack.

Exhaled.

Tickled the trigger. Twice. Three times, thumbing the hammer back until the gun was empty.

A .44 round hit the warrior chest high. He slumped over the bush, still clutching his rifle.

Blue Boy ran toward their boulder, and Jack shot at him. The bullets kicked up mud behind Blue Boy as he disappeared behind some rocks.

"Give me some .44s," Tucker yelled at Jack. "I'm empty."

Jack rolled onto his side and fished into his pocket. He fumbled and dropped the cartridges in the mud. As Tucker clawed at them, an Indian rushed him. Tucker realized he'd never load his gun in time, and he dropped the rounds in the mud. He faced the Indian as a knife blade sliced across Tucker's shoulder. The Indian moved in, but Tucker lashed out with a right cross that caught the Indian on the jaw and drove him back.

Tucker drew Jess's Bowie and crouched to meet his attacker. It was the one who'd ambushed him, the one he'd shot two days ago. He circled Tucker when he noticed his bad leg. He grinned wide, even though one arm hung in a sling of . . . a woman's petticoat?

He flicked out his blade. Tucker stumbled back. But not before the Indian's blade cut a shallow furrow through his shirt and across his stomach.

The Indian circled. Tucker stumbled to keep up while thunder drowned out the sounds of battle behind him, and lightning lit up the storm-dark sky.

Tucker feinted to his right. The Indian — short and stocky, with far less reach than Tucker — thrust his knife at Tucker's gut. He threw a hard right that caught the Indian on the nose. He stood blinking for a moment, trying to focus on Tucker, when Tucker took a step closer and plunged the blade to the hilt in the Lakota's stomach. He shuddered and grabbed onto Tucker's hand. Tucker ripped the blade upward and pushed the dead Indian off his knife. He fell face up as rain water washed the blood from his dying eyes.

Tucker stood for a moment looking at his enemy. He had died an honorable death, but one that Tucker had no time to pay respect to as he became aware that Jack's firing had stopped. Tucker turned to the sound of hoofbeats fading fast as Blue Boy rode away. His horse kicked up huge clumps of mud, and Jack raised his Henry. Tucker knocked the rifle away, and the shot went wild. "Why the hell you do that?" Jack said. "It was my last round."

"He can't lead me to Lorna if he's dead." Tucker staggered to his horse when a bullet kicked up mud between his legs.

"I said stop right there," Aurand yelled above the sound of the storm.

Tucker favored his bad leg as he turned and faced Aurand, who leveled one of his guns at Tucker's belly, the other still holstered.

"You going to shoot me now, in cold blood? Is that how it's going to be, Aurand?"

Aurand wiped water from his face. "Kick Jack's rifle out of the way."

"I'm empty anyway," Jack said between clenched teeth. He looked up at Tucker. "I'm all right. Just do what you gotta' do."

"Step over here in the clearing, Tuck."

Tucker walked to where Aurand stood, feet apart, prepared for a fight.

"Now you holster that gun slow," Aurand said. "I don't want it be said that Aurand

Forester murdered Tucker Ashley in cold blood."

Tucker holstered the gun and eyed the .44 cartridges Jack gave him still buried in the mud twenty yards away. "Lorna's out there," he shouted over the storm. "And Blue Boy's the only one who knows where she is. If I don't follow him now . . . in this rain there'll be no tracks for me to follow."

"I couldn't care less about her," Aurand said. "Turn around and face me, or I'll shoot you where you stand. We've jawed enough."

"I'm empty." Tucker pointed to the other side of the clearing. "My cartridges are in the mud over there."

"Then get them. And be mighty careful when you turn around. I want to see that pistol holstered when you do."

Tucker stumbled to where he'd dropped the cartridges and kept Aurand in his peripheral vision. "Who was that roustabout Philo robbed and murdered?" Tucker shouted over his shoulder.

"Just some slob unlucky enough to be passed out where Philo could spot him. I'd say I was sorry we pinned it on you, but I'm not."

Tucker gambled that Aurand wanted to brag to those who might listen after this day that he had faced Tucker Ashley in a fair fight. He gambled that Aurand wouldn't back-shoot him, and he kept him talking.

He bent to the muddy rounds. He wiped them on his wet shirt as he stumbled farther away from Aurand. Another stumble, another few feet. Tucker estimated he was now twenty-five yards from Aurand. An unheard of distance for the marshal. A normal distance for Tucker.

He wiped the mud off the shells and blew water off them before slowly feeding them into the cylinders. He holstered, feeling how Jess's gun rode in the leather. Jess had been no gunnie — the Remington sat too far into the holster for Tucker's liking. It would slow his draw even more. The only advantage he had was Aurand himself. Tucker knew how Aurand concealed a .36 pepperbox in an inside pocket, one that his opponents never expected. It was quick but suited to gut-shoot a man at arm's length instead of halfway across this clearing.

Tucker looked skyward. The rain pelted his face, and he opened his mouth. He let the water run down his parched throat, and he drank deeply of the rain-fresh air. A Shoshoni shaman had once told him that a man feels life the fullest right before death. Tucker thought of that as he raised his hands and faced Aurand.

Aurand smiled and holstered his Smith and Wesson. "I'll even keep my hands off my guns." Aurand's hand snaked inside his vest.

Twenty-five yards, Tucker thought, maybe more. Too far for Aurand's pocket pistol. He realized it, too, and started walking toward Tucker. "This is going to pleasure me, ol' pard, seeing you gut-shot —"

Tucker grabbed for his gun.

Aurand did, too, and beat Tucker's draw by a heartbeat. Aurand's hand came away clutching his little four-barreled gun, and he fired. His bullets cut furrows into the mud ten feet in front of Tucker. Aurand threw his hide-out gun in the mud and drew his Smith and Wesson.

Tucker bladed himself to make a smaller target when Aurand's next round plowed into the mud at Tucker's feet.

Tucker brought both hands up and picked up his sights.

He took up trigger slack.

Aurand fired.

Tucker's gun jumped in his hand.

Aurand's bullet creased Tucker's shirt.

Tucker's .44 hit Aurand center chest with a dull thud heard even over the noise of the storm.

Aurand stood motionless, dead although he didn't know it yet. His pistol drooped as he clutched his chest. He sank to his knees and cursed Tucker as he walked towards him. Aurand's gurgling death throes sickened Tucker, as they always did when he killed a man. Aurand sucked in his last breath and fell face up, the rail forever pelting his lifeless eyes.

"Some shot," Jack called to him. "But I would have gotten it off quicker."

Tucker hobbled to Jack and knelt beside him. "You all right?"

"Get the hell out of here," Jack yelled and waved in the direction Blue Boy rode. "Go!"

Tucker patted Jack on the back. "I'll be back for you." He staggered to where they'd hobbled their horses, the pain in his leg so much less than the pain in his heart if he couldn't find Blue Boy.

CHAPTER 39

Lorna heard her terror long before she saw it. The water surged down the gully where she was tied to the dead cottonwood. The torrent carried rocks and branches, the bones of some dead animal, a decayed trunk of some settler who tried crossing the prairie with too many fancy things. It caromed off the bank just under where Lorna struggled against the leather rope. She screamed, but the water, the rain, and the thunder drowned out her voice, and she could not even gather enough voice to pray to her God to save her.

An uprooted cactus the size of a cat crashed against her. Barbs stuck in her leg, and she screamed louder. She struggled against the rope that bound her to the tree she could never move. Her strength ebbed as she thrashed against the water and debris pounding the bank and the tree trunk. The water was up to her chest now. Rising. She tried maneuvering to keep the tree between her and the water assaulting her. But the rope held.

The water rose.

The storm drowned out her cries.

Her Lord had forsaken her.

CHAPTER 40

The thunderstorm pounded the Badlands gumbo into a slippery, gray goo. Tucker spurred the horse up a bank. It slipped and went down, rolling over onto its side and trapping Tucker's leg. He felt the stitches tear loose, but he held tight onto the saddle horn. He knew the gelding had to right itself. It did, catching its footing, and stumbled erect as Tucker coaxed the horse up the bank.

He caught sight of Blue Boy's dun as it disappeared over a hill a hundred yards distant. He'd chased Blue Boy for a quarter hour and was gaining. The Indian's horse, though a magnificent animal, carried tremendous weight, and it was beginning to slow.

Tucker's horse stumbled in a water-filled prairie dog hole, and he struggled to stay in the saddle. The ground that had been as hard as any brick used to build a house an hour ago had been turned into a soggy bog.

Tucker dug his boots into the horse's flanks and rode up a steep embankment. Twice the horse slipped in the mud, and twice Tucker hung tight, prepared to kick himself free if he needed to. But the animal kept its legs under it and reached the top. The rain poured down at a steep angle, pelting Tucker's face and neck with hard raindrops. He shielded his eyes with his hand and looked for Blue Boy.

Nothing. Tucker sucked in a breath. Lorna was out here somewhere. God knew where she was, or what the Indians had done with her. All Tucker knew was that only God and Blue Boy knew where she was, and he'd better not lose sight of either one.

Movement at the bottom of a hill a quarter mile away. Blue Boy rode his horse at full gallop toward a rapidly filling creek bed. Tucker spurred his horse after him, riding the rim of the hill overlooking the creek below, gaining on the Indian.

Tucker's heart stopped a beat; he'd lost sight of Blue Boy.

Then Tucker caught movement at the bottom of the creek bed, beside a partially submerged cottonwood.

A figure thrashed wildly in the water.

Lorna.

Even at this distance and wearing Indian buckskins, he recognized her. She frantically beat her arms while she fought to keep her head above the rising torrent that crashed debris against the tree that held her.

Tucker dug his heels into the horse's flank, and it bolted, running headlong toward the creek bank. It stumbled. Tucker clutched the saddle horn as the horse fell and sank up to its chest in the mud. Tucker flew over the saddle, rolling, slipping. When he gathered his legs under him, the horse had righted itself and bolted away.

Tucker staggered down the hill, knowing he could not reach Lorna before Blue Boy did. Tucker's side screamed from lack of air, running, stumbling, fighting to reach her before Blue Boy plunged the knife into her to avenge the deaths of his warriors.

Tucker slowed, still sixty yards away. He drew his gun and looked for anything to rest his hand on. There was nothing, He spread his feet wide and grabbed the Remington with both hands while he picked up the front sight. He jerked the trigger; the shot burrowed into the gumbo off to Blue Boy's right. Tucker willed his breathing to slow, his heart to stop racing as he lined the sights on Blue Boy's broad back.

And pressed the trigger slowly.

The bullet kicked up mud between Blue Boy's feet but narrowly missed him. He stopped and turned, as if seeing Tucker for the first time, then disappeared over the bank toward Lorna.

Tucker holstered and ran as fast as his wounded leg and bursting chest would allow. When he reached the creek bank, he doubled over, his breaths coming in great gasps. His vision blurred as much from running as from the storm, and he rubbed water from his eyes. Blue Boy — now at the water's edge — dove into the creek; the only thing visible, his knife jutting out of the water. He gained his footing and splashed toward Lorna, now forty yards upstream from him.

Tucker drew the Remington. He knelt and rested his hand on a rock and fired his last shot. The slug hit Blue Boy in the shoulder, and he toppled into the water. When he came up, he still clutched the knife. He looked back at Tucker for only a brief moment before he stumbled toward Lorna, a man possessed with killing a woman for his own revenge.

Blue Boy was ten yards from Lorna when Tucker leapt into the water after him.

He saw Tucker splashing up behind him. Ignored him. Now within knife distance from her.

Tucker flung himself onto Blue Boy's back. He flicked Tucker away as if he were a sack of feed.

Tucker drew his Bowie and stumbled toward Blue Boy. He heard Tucker and turned just in time to avoid Tucker's slashing blade.

Blue Boy, a full head taller and sixty pounds heavier, faced Tucker. With a reach that put his knife at the end of those long, muscular arms, Blue Boy thrust his blade out. Tucker flung himself back into the water, catching the tip of the Indian's knife high on his collarbone, ripping muscle.

Tucker circled, his knife held high out of the torrent rushing down the creek bed. He fought his leg cramping, fought to remain standing in the swift water. A log rushing by just under the water line struck Tucker in the knee, and he stifled a scream. Blue Boy feinted right, then darted left. Tucker tried pivoting to meet the attack, but his leg buckled. Blue Boy's slice ripped a shallow gash just under Tucker's armpit.

Then Blue Boy hit him flush on the chin. Tucker fell into the water. The current carried him downstream. His arms flailed for a hold of anything, his knife lost to the flash flooding creek.

His hand brushed a submerged root, and he grabbed at it. He hauled himself erect and looked frantically for Blue Boy. He had reached Lorna. She fought to keep her nose above water, the water-soaked buckskins dragging her down, thrashing about, screaming as Blue Boy's knife plunged below the surface.

Tucker struggled toward Blue Boy and flung himself on the Indian's back. Tucker wrapped his arms around Blue Boy's thick neck and locked his hands together. Blue Boy clawed at him, and Tucker felt the skin on his neck ripped deep by sharp fingernails. He buried his face in Blue Boy's back, increasing the pressure on his neck, ignoring the shredded shoulder muscle ripped by Blue Boy's blade. His efforts grew less and less frantic, until the Lakota went limp in Tucker's arms. He let Blue Boy drop into the water and splashed toward Lorna.

Her leather thongs had been cut, and she had climbed atop the cottonwood. She coughed water from her lungs, her face as red as a fire from the effort. She threw her arms around Tucker's neck. He carried her, crying, to the weeping shore. They struggled up the slippery gumbo bank, and he gently laid her on the ground above the creek.

"He saved my life," Lorna sputtered when

she was able to speak. Tucker slapped her back, and water was expelled from her lungs.

"What?"

"Blue Boy. He saved my life." She held her hands so Tucker could see the freshly cut leather thong. She rubbed her wrists. "When the Indians left to find you, they tied me to that tree. The creek was dry then. They never thought about a storm. If Blue Boy hadn't come back, I would have drowned."

Tucker held Lorna close. "It's all right now."

"Not so, *wasicu.*"

Tucker turned around to face Blue Boy towering over him. His neck bore red marks from where Tucker had choked him unconscious, and blood seeped from the bullet wound in his shoulder. He held his knife low beside his leg. "She is my woman. For that I will kill you. And for killing my warriors."

Tucker pried Lorna's arms from around his neck. He used a boulder to help him stand. The wound in his leg had reopened, and the pelting rain slapped angrily against his trousers. He hobbled towards Blue Boy, keeping himself between the Lakota and Lorna, one arm dangling useless at his side.

"You can't have her." Tucker stared at Blue Boy's knife, aware that he faced an armed man half again as large as he. "She is mine. Lorna has always been mine."

Blue Boy looked past Tucker. "Is that true?"

Lorna nodded. She stood and stumbled to Tucker. "He is my man," she announced proudly. "And I'll have no other."

"And you, little man — you would fight me for her, knowing you have no chance of victory?"

"I would," Tucker answered, "fight you for her."

"You are in no shape to fight anyone. Especially me."

Tucker stepped away from Lorna and set himself for his last fight. "And any other warrior you send to kill me."

"Then you are a fool." Blue Boy wiped rain water from his eyes and motioned with his knife to Lorna. "For she will be mine."

Tucker stepped closer, preparing for the attack he knew he could not defend. "She's mine. Call it white man's honor."

"And if I kill you?"

"Then I'll die knowing I died as I've lived — with honor and dignity."

The rain cascaded down Blue Boy's face and streaked his war paint, his massive chest black with the pigment. He slipped his knife into his belt sheath and stepped closer to Tucker. "You are a worthy enemy. Where are you from? What is your name?"

"Tucker Ashley. From Pennsylvania way before the war."

Blue Boy nodded. "I have heard of you. A very worthy enemy. I will return and count coup on you. That is my assurance I give to you, white man. But I will do so honorably. When you heal sufficiently, I will visit you when you do not look for me. We will fight for the woman, you and me. But we will not fight this day." He motioned to Lorna. "This day it is sufficient that her life has been spared."

Blue Boy slowly backed away. He looked past Tucker one final time, and a faint smile creased the Lakota's face. He walked to his horse without looking back and swung a leg over the dun. He nudged the gelding's flanks. Soon he was lost in the storm, his fading hoofbeats a faint reminder that he was even here.

Tucker limped back to Lorna. She met him halfway and threw her arms around his neck. He winced and held her away from his bloody shoulder as she kissed him. Not deeply, just a brushing of the lips, for they were not married. And Tucker was an honorable man.

He held Lorna's hand, as much to prevent him from tripping in the mud as from her falling over into the wild water. They made their way toward Tucker's horse, which stood with his face to the rain, yards away. "Was that true?" he asked. "Are you mine?"

"You made the statement." She smiled. "And I'm going to hold you to it."

Tucker nodded. "Consider it held," he said as he helped her into the saddle. "Let's go find Jack and head for home."

"And find a preacher, too?" Lorna added.

"And find a preacher, too."

As they started up the hillside away from the creek, Tucker did an odd thing, for him. Since he was captured at Antietam, he told himself he would never look back on a battleground as he had that day. But today, he paused and looked back at where he had fought Blue Boy, the Indian's words echoing in Tucker's mind. Blue Boy promised he would find Tucker, and they would fight for Lorna when he had mended. Of that, Tucker was certain. He'd have to look over his shoulder until that day came.

But for this day, this time, this moment in his life, he would enjoy his time with her. This time next month, the creek would be dried up, hiding her secrets as it had today for the next hapless passerby to uncover. But Lorna would still be his.

Blue Boy's promise or not.

ABOUT THE AUTHOR

C. M. Wendelboe entered the law-enforcement profession when he was discharged from the marines as the Vietnam War was winding down.

He served in diverse roles during his career, yet he always felt most proud of "working the street." He retired after twenty-six years, when he pursued his true vocation as a fiction writer. He is the author of *Spirit Road Mysteries,* a Berkley Prime Crime series about law enforcement on Native American reservations of the contemporary West. He now calls Cheyenne, Wyoming, home.